Sonja Bigg lives in Ramsgate with numerous children, a mad husband and two dogs – one of which she regularly wants to murder, on account of his incessant squeaking.

Born into a highly abnormal family, she has followed an unusual career path, including jobs as a security guard, dancer, model, film extra, fruit picker and untalented makeup girl. She would have tried singing, but everybody begged her not to. Twenty years of being a Chartered Physiotherapist and managing Adult Therapy Services in a London Primary Care Trust came to an abrupt halt when she gave birth to a profoundly deaf daughter with cerebral palsy – and decided to use the fragments of time that she wasn't using to keep her daughter alive to pull on her weird and random selection of life experience and write a book.

This is the result.

OF VICARS AND TARTS

Sonja Bigg

OF VICARS AND TARTS

Vanguard Press

A CIP catalogue record for this title is
available from the British Library.

ISBN 978 1 84386 437 0

*Vanguard Press is an imprint of
Pegasus Elliot MacKenzie Publishers Ltd.*

www.pegasuspublishers.com

**First Published in 2009
Vanguard Press
Sheraton House Castle Park
Cambridge England**

Printed & Bound in Great Britain

Acknowlegements

Julian Bigg at Fresh Produce Design Consultancy for the cover design.

Tim Fennell, Author and Journalist for his help and advice.

Charming Baker for his beautiful painting.

Disclaimer

The author is a mad twit who believes that love conquers all.

All the fiction in this book is just that – fiction. It does not fully represent the Author's truest opinion regarding love, death, abuse, madness, religion and any other topic that arises in this book – but is more of an indication of her slightly warped and unusual mind.

All names, characters, phone numbers, events, and locales are inventions of the author, used fictitiously. Except for the mention of named celebrities and real places – to whom no offence was intended and with which artistic liberty was taken with all details for the sake of consistency, continuity, character development, and literary expression.

The fictional thoughts, opinions and dialogues in this work represent the fictional thoughts, opinions and dialogues of the fictional characters that are thinking and speaking. These are not to be taken as a representation of the views of the Author who does not necessarily agree in any way with any of the content, views or beliefs within the book.

The novel and author is not affiliated with, sponsored by, or endorsed in any way by any brand name mentioned in the book and has no bias towards or against any name or brand. She avoids brands in every-day life.

Please take proper precautions when reading this book. It may contain some foul and offensive language and tasteless ideas. There is some graphic and explicit content. There may be inaccurate content regarding newspapers, places, shops, clothes, the bible and eBay.

It is not suitable for children or pets. It may contain traces of nuts. It must not be read after its sell by date. An adult must be present when opening. Protracted use may damage your eyesight. Do not read while driving.

The Author cannot be held responsible for shock, disdain, information taken literally and deteriorating eyesight due to reading in a poor light, fury and frustration of partners due to neglect, or their acting upon suggestion that paying for escorts is desirable or acceptable. The author cannot take responsibility for disciplinary action at work due to lack of concentration, sleeping during meetings due to reading late into the night and illegal sick-leave taken in order to read. The author cannot be held responsible for children being ignored, homework unchecked and packed lunches not being made. Any DIY jobs unfinished, car engines melting due to lack of oil, bills unpaid, dental appointments missed and mascara worn for three days running is not the responsibility of the Author.

No animals were harmed in the writing of this book.

Dedication

To one beautiful, little, deaf, brain-damaged bugger of a daughter called Nessie, who has changed my life beyond all recognition by making me realize what is important and funny and that sad can mean happy. Without the carnage you brought into my life, I would never have learnt what mattered – or written a book. You are spectacular.

To Barney, Minty and Fin who taught me what amazing and generous and loving and hilarious really mean. I am so proud of you I am bursting.

To my bloody phenomenal husband (Mr Bigg, don't you know) who still makes me wet my pants with laughter every day. And is one sexy beast. Obviously.

To my amazing family who have put up with my personality all these years. And haven't left the country. Yet.

To the talented and generous Tim Fennell who ruthlessly hacked at this book for a bag of chips and a small sherry. You star.

To Charming Baker for the use of a beautiful painting. Ay up!

To all my lovely friends who I love with all my heart. I really do. Fancy a quick pint?

We miss you.
Mum. You'd have told me off for this book, wouldn't you! And then cackled like a witch.

David. One in a million.

Ken. Adventurer and lovely man.

Chapter 1

Sadie wasn't sure quite why all this had happened – to someone like her.

Why?

Or how a life that had seemed so fantastic and free and good and full of promise to start with, had ended up…ending.

Without warning.

Without deserving it.

She had been a good person – would have done anything for anybody; always tried to help others, always gave freely, unreservedly – had expected nothing in return, except a normal life. If life was ever normal.

Certainly there was no going back. And at this moment, forward looked a bit unpromising too.

Perhaps staying still and not moving for a bit might help.

Or drinking.

A nice fat line of Charlie.

A few cigarettes.

A momentary escape.

She'd read the book a thousand times now. Made the promises to herself. Bragged internally that she could do it – if she wanted. But she couldn't quite see it through. Her life had spiralled into such a quagmire, that there was no way of digging her way out, shedding the past.

Giving up was not a speciality of hers these days, although in former times it had been a way of life; something positive, valiant – something that added to the bigger picture, made things right in the world.

But now you are the master of a nice line in excess.

Excess filled a hole, made it all rosy for a bit; made the past disappear – until she could sometimes wonder if it had even ever existed. Thinking about it made waves of nausea and panic fill her heart; wash relentlessly into her mind, enveloping her brain – her stomach twisting and turning like a vast, angry sea.

Bugger. You are fucking hopeless.

She farted fairly loudly, unable to prevent it and felt embarrassed, even though alone. She laughed to herself, the sound soft and musical against the backdrop of urban life outside her windows.

You silly woman.

You have lost control of everything, even your bodily functions.

You are rotting from the inside out.

Outside, buses growled at the bus stop and a whole upper deck stared into her room, where she lay stark naked now, not caring, almost daring the buggers to look.

There really isn't much point in pretending to be coy after all these years.

Especially on a day like today.

Today is one of those first glimpses of summer that happens in April, when you've forgotten how happy it makes you for absolutely no reason, but suddenly it's there and warm and lovely and you're smiling and all's well with the world.

Well, all's hell with the world, actually. But for a welcome moment you can forget.

Only then a cloud appears, hiding the rays of sun and it all floods back.

You remember you're not living any more. Merely existing, just going through the motions, trying to get to the point when it will stop, the madness will all stop and then, hopefully, there'll be nothing.

No afterlife. No promise of heaven or hell. Simply a huge, unending nothingness, a vast relief – an end.

Until then, you're you – and you, my lovely, are absolutely buggered. And penniless, now you come to mention it.

The pub seemed by far the best way to block out the next few hours of grim reality until it was time to sleep.

A day over.

Day one of the next episode, or the final day of the previous episode; she wasn't quite sure. The days now all seemed the same; varying to some degree or other in their grimness.

She bounded out of bed – as much as an ageing hooker with a hip replacement and a knee shattered by a gunshot could muster up a bound – and pulled on a filthy, old pair of jeans that were spattered with paint and a liberal dose of ketchup on one front pocket. A tatty vest followed. She coiled her long, hoary hair expertly into a French pleat and looked critically in the mirror. *Not too bad. Could be a hell of a lot worse.*

He'd been jolly lucky to have you really. With his Mummy fetish and everything. And his liking for a good slapping with a ruler.

Not many people would have dished that out and, at the same time, managed to stifle laughter at the ridiculous sight of him begging (while tied to the radiator with an old pair of rainbow-striped, rave tights) as successfully as you did.

It was amazing what solace could be drawn from self-hatred so deep and vile, that doing this – for money – seemed like a diversion, a new reality, some kind of normality.

And a way of punishing men for their sins, whilst doing something positive for them. Something they wanted – but couldn't ask for, in normal circumstances.

Whilst at the same time, exorcising your hatred for those who were full of lies, secrets to be ashamed of.

Even providing this service for them, fuelled by your own hatred, wasn't enough for some of them.

They still had to take what they weren't offered, snatch it by force.

She felt a pang for his new girlfriend, a young slip of a thing, so they said, with a fresh mind and spirit for him to defile.

Perhaps you should tell the poor child what her superstud-sexy-monster-of-a-human is really like, underneath the costume of lies that he wears like a cheap suit.

She is so young. She is just starting on her journey. She deserves the chance of a future, ripe with promise.

But it is only a matter of time before he is at her feet begging for forgiveness for his cruelty. Meaning none of it. Trying to persuade her that he is human after all and it was a mistake, just a horrible mistake; that he won't repeat it.

And probably whilst wearing an outsized nappy.

She shuddered with horror, her toes recoiling in her shoes at the thought of him. And his disgusting soul.

She doubted that the fictitious rendition of his life that he'd undoubtedly fed her included various truths about his preferences in the bedroom department.

Or out of it.

How would he have described his job?

Banker? Butcher? Pilot? Surgeon?

He was certainly good with a knife, but his skills didn't extend into saving lives.

Changing them, certainly.

Life savings were things he took, not gave.

What an amazingly odd combination they must make. You can only hope their union doesn't give rise to offspring. A genetically disastrous mix of Julie Andrews and Jack The Ripper.

And if they were anything like their father, the whole lot of them would be in Pampers for eternity, a future family of horrors, sitting round the table at Sunday lunch tied to their chairs with stripy tights and slapping each other with rulers. While their mother, her life in tatters, looks on in horror to see what she has brought forth into the world: the progeny of a monster, out of her reach and out of her control, untouched by her guidance.

Because good is no match for evil, whatever it says in the bible.

Good does not always prevail.

Oh God.

She would have to find his new lover, warn her somehow, that young, un-ruined thing – before there was a chance for his evil to weave its way in. But as things were today, she was in no fit state to help anybody – she could barely help herself.

She resolved, yet again, that she would give all this up tomorrow. Face her demons. Change her life. Finally.

It was time.

But not now.

Now it's time for a pint.

Feet into socks, socks into shoes, line into nose, key into lock and out into the sun, squinting, eyes streaming.

The pub was three long minutes away.

Chapter 2

Quite how Judas' parents had named him this accurately was a mystery. Peter Cristian was a vicar in a downtrodden part of Camberwell, who had developed an avid love of the bible as a child – ever since he had discovered quite what his surname meant in Christian terms.

He was a good man and an avid Spurs supporter, who did stand-up comedy in a local pub. He was quite a celebrity in a low-key, local way and was loved by his congregation. He saw the bible as a good slice of history, with good lessons for mankind within its pages.

Didn't take all its nonsense as read.

Deciphered it well.

Genuinely cared about people.

Encouraged all into his church, preached without preaching.

There was a famous occasion when a local, notorious, gipsy family had rolled into the church at midnight mass one Christmas (bawdily singing filthy songs, clutching cans of Tennent's Extra) and he had stopped briefly, exclaimed "Jeeeeesus...saves!" and welcomed them in; much to the amusement, horror and indignation of his regulars.

He had continued the sermon without faltering, above loud snoring from the matriarch of the family who had passed out, instantly, on a pew at the back. At the end of the service, he had accepted a can of lager and had drained it with a flourish.

It was closing time after all.

He had left the church to a round of applause.

He was a tall, gangly, uncoordinated, runner bean of a man with unruly ginger hair and a face whose features were underlined and crowded out by freckles.

When his first and only son was due, he had asked his audience at the local stand-up what a vicar with a surname of Cristian should call a son.

The answer had been Judas.

He had laughed all the way home.

It had seemed fairly appropriate in a way; he and his wife had no children, despite years of fruitless, laborious trying.

The trying had indeed been very trying.

Enjoyable – but slowly the fun had been sucked out by the endless timetables of shagging, with ruthless, military precision according to dates. It had nearly – but not quite – put both of them off. They had carried on, regardless, with failing enthusiasm and introduced all sorts of exciting positions that would have had his congregation nudging and winking and sweating quietly, had they guessed.

He felt sure that most of them were not aware that vicars even had sex.

Ever.

Or only if forced.

And most certainly not doggy-style.

They were a committed, happy couple that shared everything. They were best friends and had been since early fumblings in the stationery cupboard at school: one of the few, shining examples of true partnership. Peter had suffered a testicular growth a year previously, finally ruling out any chance that he and Robyn had of conceiving; and consequently, the pair of them had been on a celebratory, second honeymoon. It was a weekend in Edinburgh (where they had first married in a quick ceremony on the cheap) – twenty years after the first. A celebration of a rare, but true love. A celebration that they were both still alive.

Judas was the result.

Against all the odds.

One devious and treacherous sperm, defying the wonders of the NHS.

Judas.

The name meant, "praise"; an acknowledgement of their small male miracle.

They shortened it to Jude soon after. Peter, despite a love of all rock music, found his congregation's constant referrals to Judas Priest too much for him to stomach. He couldn't imagine why the obvious joke hadn't occurred to him at the time. And then thought back to two of his friends at school – Pete and Andy (P. Ness and A. Ness) – and realised it could have been much, much worse.

Robyn had thought that the sudden tiredness and loss of menstruation was the menopause; and the pregnancy was unnoticed for four months, until she could no longer ignore the insistent kicking in the paunch she had been nurturing for the past few years. It obviously was not the result of too much lardy cake.

The test results had been met with a numb disbelief, a supreme joy, a feeling of completeness combined with utter fear.

Jude had been born early and had been a persistent pain in the arse ever since.

He hated his name, detested the life of a vicar's son and all it stood for, but adored his dad with every bone in his body, worshipped his mother. But their softness and leniency and suffocating understanding – combined with the peer pressure at a tough and rough school that rendered his holy upbringing a joke – meant that he had developed into generally the most dreadfully behaved child that most people had ever met.

He was revolting.

Literally.

So revolting that the locals would talk about it behind closed doors, sniggering at the Cristians' ineptness at child raising, laughing at the lad who seemed to prove all the preaching in the world about good and the truth to be a farce.

He sniffed fire extinguishers at lunch-break at school.

He took acid at eleven years old.

He shot a tomcat in the eye with an airgun at twelve.

At sixteen, he made a fifteen-year-old pregnant, behind some bins on the sort of housing estate that the police only went into in pairs and in daylight.

He stole cars.

He was rarely at school.

He was rarely at home.

He was rarely sober.

But he always adored them, however much his actions seemed to prove otherwise. He truly loved them with every atom of his flawed and troubled soul.

They were a gentle pair, used to only dealing with things with kindness and reasoning – ill-equipped to deal with the influence of Jude's peers on the Peckham housing estate which their parish served. Shocked by how hard bringing up a child was, so different to their expectation, so far removed from all they had thought.

Robyn was a loving woman.

She loved her son deeply, but she found him difficult to like.

She softly chastised him, gently tried to change him, tried to steer him on a better path. She had longed for a child for so long and yet his arrival had changed her life into one tainted by anguish, argument, and apology. She pleaded with Jude, time and time again, to see his actions were hurting those around him, to change. Each time, for a while, he seemed to listen. Each time, she believed his promises. And each time, he let them both down.

She spent years in fear and dread of the ring of the phone, bringing news of his latest misdemeanour. Her feelings of failure as a mother were intensified by the guilt she carried. Guilt for her feelings of resentment, for her own inadequacy. For sometimes wishing her own son had never been born.

She wanted to be proud of her son.

But she could not.

Peter was silent in his disbelief of his son's behaviour. Robyn interpreted his reticence as a lack of support and she found herself directing her frustration and fury at her husband.

She hated her husband's ability to cope, when she could not – be patient, when she could not. She hated her son's ability to drive a wedge between them. And she hated the fact that Jude could make her behave like the kind of woman she never wanted to be.

When Jude's daughter shot, screeching, into the world on his sixteenth birthday, he had run and run until his heart was tearing itself from his chest.

The mother was a girl at his school; petite, pretty, adoring in her own cold way. The girls all called her 'Strange Sam'. Jude had only shagged her because she had let him when he asked her to – had taken advantage of the fact she was desperate for a boyfriend like the others. Had let her think he was hers. It had been a bit of fun, a laugh, an experiment.

But she had not told him she was pregnant – not told anyone at all. The news of the birth had been delivered to him in the playground, during one lunchtime.

Panic-ridden, confused, his heart bursting with abomination and his face in a grimace of true agony, Jude had projectile vomited as soon as he realised it was not a bad joke.

He was not ready for this, no way; there was too much life to live for this, too much to be done.

Older looking than his years and with money stolen from his mother's purse, he went from pub to pub, alone in his misery, his life crumbling before him.

He had been woken the next day by a couple who had left the confines of their car to have a five o'clock in the morning shag, in the privacy of a bush. Neither could go home, as this was a strictly extra-curricular performance. Hadn't wanted to get caught on the job, in the car, by the pigs either. There were laws against it. Even if you were caught by a pig with a propensity for dogging.

They were already half-stripped and panting like two, overweight flabradors, with too many hormones and too little time, when Jude had opened his eyes and started adding to the puke – already half-dried from his excursion the previous night, covering his T-shirt and hands – with great gusto.

"Fuck me… someone's in here!"

Jude froze while the sound of frantic zipping up and struggling into trousers filled his ears. He hardly dared breathe.

"Hurry up, for Christ's sake!"– A man's voice this time.

Jude lay still, but was flattened as the courting couple fell out of the bushes, giggling, trampling all over him. They left footprints in his vomit.

He lay there, winded for a while, listening to the sound of the bin men's ribaldry getting progressively closer and breathing in the stench of rotting garbage.

Or was it his breath?

He huffed into his hand and decided it was most probably the latter. Licked his hand and sniffed it to double check.

Oh dear. Not good. Like the rotting innards of some roadkill that's been dead for a week.

Wondered how on God's clean earth he had got into the situation he was now in.

And then remembered.

A father. Him. Jude.

How was he going to tell his folks this latest gem?

How was he going to go home?

The Prodigal Son was about to be slaughtered instead of the fatted calf.

And by God did he deserve it.

Chapter 3

Cherry was a fine-looking peach of a girl. A beauty in her own way. Not the normal kind of good looks found in magazines, but certainly a real head-turner.

Her job in the Sloane Street Beauty Parlour was an attainment that her friends could only dream of. The vicious removal of excess hair from the parts of various stars that are only usually seen pixelated, afforded her a certain standing amongst her mates.

She was the willing recipient of more gossip and bitching than most people read in a lifetime in the tabloids.
She was discreet to the utmost degree with this information.
Playing by the unwritten rules of conduct of the salon.
Never divulging customers' secrets.
Well, never to more than one person anyway.
At a time.

She had grown up in a perfectly normal terrace in Scunthorpe, with a dinner lady mum and a hard-working, hard-drinking, hard-loving, long-suffering dad – sharing a room with three sisters, while her two brothers fought in the adjoining boxroom.

Since she was tiny, she had known she was special. *She would make it.*

By fifteen, she was obsessed with London. Every waking moment she dreamed of success, of making something of herself. She cut out pictures of the stars from magazines and made huge scrapbooks, carefully hidden from her family under the mattress. She pilfered her mother's makeup, smuggled clothes' changes out of the house and transformed herself in the bus shelter, before bunking school to smoke fags and talk of her dreams with Cath, her fat friend.

Every girl like Cherry had to have a Cath. Solid, chunky, dependable, adoring.

With a sweating-blushing-overheating-embarrassment type problem and thighs like two swollen pillows fighting their way out of stone-washed, denim jeans from the local pound shop. Bad perm. Acne. Snaggly teeth, with gigantic scaffolding masquerading as a brace. Unpopular enough to be desperate for her friendship. *Perfect.*

Cherry was the kind of girl who needed total, unrelenting adoration and understanding – and Cath fulfilled her role as worshipper and general dogsbody without blemish. Cath had spent her whole life trying to sound and act like Cherry – and even honing these skills in the privacy of her own bedroom. It was only her appearance that prevented her from being a clone.

They spent more time out of school than in.
Days were spent on the hill looming over a vast, industrial estate that overlooked not only the school from which they fled, but also the factory in which both of their fathers slaved. That way, they could be absolutely sure to make it to registration, school lunches – so that Cherry's mum could not tell they were absconding – and get to the factory in time to walk home with

their fathers, who knocked off at 3.30 p.m. after a five-in-the-morning start. The deception was complete.

Well nearly, anyway. Parents' evening always proved a bit of a trial.

At least once a week they were caught and Cath was walloped on her wobbling buttocks with a large and calloused hand until she was unable to sit, while Cherry was chastised lovingly and gently by the father whom she had wrapped around her little finger since she had first drawn breath.

But still the overwhelming desire that Cath had to actually *be* Cherry was enough to lure her once more into doing her bidding.

And the threat of the ferocious sulking that would ensue for days at a time should she fail her friend, was enough to convince her that sticking razor blades dipped in bleach under her eyelids and then rubbing them with chilli juice would be less painful than enduring the wrath of Cherry.

Selfish as she was, Cherry also served as Cath's protector in school and out; and many times had flattened anyone who had dared be foul to her chubby, sweaty, needy mate. Which was daily.

It was the perfect, symbiotic relationship.

Beauty and the Beast.

In fact, it was whilst discussing the perfect relationship between rats and fleas, in a particularly mind-numbing, biology ordeal, at the hands of Busty Lusty, the moronic science teacher (with the metallic, maroon, 6-inch talons that she tapped, revoltingly on the wooden lab-top and used to pick her scalp through her bad wig) that the girls decided to finally make a run for it. And – each unable to survive without the other, at the ripe old age of sixteen (approximately twenty-eight, long minutes after receiving a combined total of three, grade E, C.S.E.s) – that is precisely what they did.

They arrived in London a few hours later, having raided Cherry's Dad's Christmas-savings pot (she knew he'd forgive her when he realised it was to better herself) and landed on the doorstep of Cath's second cousin twice removed's ex-wife's son by another marriage.

Simon lived in a large squat in Kilburn, with a few squalid, but charming friends and looked a bit like Elvis. Not 'The King' variety, but certainly the Costello. He was quite heart-stoppingly gorgeous and glamorous to the pair of them and proceeded to deflower both of them over the coming fortnight.

Not at the same time.

But with an ungentlemanly amount of time between the two events.

But they were both overcome with passion for him and neither cared that the other was also being inexpertly shagged by the figure of their joint affections. They convinced each other that it was fine, as it was a 'London Thing'.

Within three weeks of their departure from home, Cherry had secured her place sweeping up toenail and pubic clippings from a beauty salon floor, while inexplicably – and resulting from a web of lies that a politician would be proud of – Cath had landed a job, as a runner for a film company.

Chapter 4

So your husband is dead. Your son is in prison. They are, were, always will be your life, your love, your joy, your pain, the very guts of your soul. You are mourning, twice. You are filled with a deep loathing, horror and hatred of one, whilst adoring every atom of his fault-filled body, the body that you created and grew and nurtured and tried to teach to love like you. And you are missing the other, more than life itself.

You failed, failed, failed.

You are a filthy, wretched, wreck.

You don't deserve to be a mother. It is all your fault. If you'd been a better parent – seen the evil for what it was, not painted it with bright, warm colours and forgiveness, given more, taught the right things, been firmer, been softer, been more loving, been less loving, believed more in God, believed less in God – things would all be different.

Your husband, soul-twin, partner, friend, would still be here, wrapping you up in his warmth, so close there is no separation in your bodies, your very breath shared, your hopes, future, life, knitted together. His 'Hello, my love', his passion, his kind words, his pride in you and yours would be real: not a distant memory. Your son would not be the warped, twisted weapon that had ended the life of the father who loved him with all his heart, given him his all.

You have lost both. The mourning for one cannot begin without forgiveness for the other.

But you cannot forgive.
You are gnarled with disgust, anger.
You despise.
You cannot move on.

You are an empty, soulless vessel filling with poison.
Ordure is seeping out of every pore. You are plague-filled,
rotting like an apple left decaying in an orchard, feasted upon by
maggots and vermin.

It's all your fault. You want to die. But death would be too
easy for you, too quick. You don't deserve to be able to not feel
this way. You deserve to feel like this. You need to pay. You need
to suffer like your loved ones suffered, because you have failed
both of them. Failed yourself. And this is your penance.

Robyn stared at herself in the long mirror. The mirror that
for years she had sat in front of, in the evening, talking into its
depths. Talking to the husband who ran a nightly bath behind
her. A bath for her, run with warmth, love to soothe her aching
bones, a candle, tenderly lit. Her cheek softly stroked by his kind
hand, with a 'Hello, you' as she disrobed and was naked before
him. Talking and laughing about daily events, as she sat before
the mirror, with its cracked, aged corners, brushing the tangles
from long, dark hair carefully unwound from an ordered, tight
bun and released into tangled waves of chaos.

There was nobody behind her as she sat on her bed today.
The bathroom was deserted in the reflection, cold. She was alone
and lonely. He was gone, unreachable, lost. She too was lost;
lost, desperate and alone. She unwound her hair. She wound her
thin fingers into its depths and clung to it as if it was rope, the
rope stopping her from falling into an abyss. She pulled and tore
into it. She seized a letter opener and attacked those same locks,
watching them fall to the floor, matted and tangled, lock-by-lock
until her scalp resembled that of a prisoner of war. And she dug

the same tool into her arm, dragging it across her flesh, feeling no pain, feeling her sins released, feeling some of her self-hatred fall with the drops of bright, red blood to the floor, soaking the hair that lay there, matted and unwanted.

She looked around her, at the boxes of her belongings, all packed neatly. There was nothing much. Certainly nothing that held any meaning for her now. She wanted none of it; remnants of a life past, full of pride and valour and hope; now gone, now broken into tiny, irrelevant pieces.

Her home was her home no longer. It had gone with the job. She was a vicar's wife no more. A wife no more. A mother no more. All, for her, was lost and shattered and destroyed. Her soul was crushed and fears that she had never had the imagination to think of, even in her nightmares, she now realised in glorious, repeating, Technicolor.

Not a soul that lived and loved her would be able to reach into the vast, gaping hole she was in, digging further down with each breath she took, each lid she blinked. Those that she had trusted and loved all these years could not touch her. Her friendships were rendered non-existent by her sense of hopelessness. She had to run and keep running from the pain and the fear that stretched before her, further than the horizon, to a place where nobody knew her, knew her shame. Where she could not taste the pity, catch the whispering as she passed, feel the endless eyes upon her wretched frame.

Her whisky bottle lay; empty, on the bed beside her as she sat. She had no money for further liquid relief. So she smashed the bottle on the dressing table. She picked up the broken glass, piece by piece, licking the inside for even a taste of the contents, but finding only the scent.

The final piece of glass she used coldly and calmly to cut a message into her flesh.

'igneus in abyssus'.

Chapter 5

Cherry stretched her weary bones towards the heavens.

Completely knackered.

This beauty salon malarkey was not all it was cracked up to be. She was supposed to be having a wild life of glamour. Not living alone, in a fetid bed-sit on Kilburn Lane. Not having to put up with a lecherous, boss-eyed, wanker of a landlord, who she was sure was somehow watching her, naked in the bath. Although she'd had the light fitting down many times, looking for secret filming devices like in detective books and found nothing but decomposing bluebottles.

Stuffing her head under her partly disembowelled pillow, she tried, in vain, to block out the rhythmic clattering of the faux-brass bedstead of her neighbour, Fiona – who made a handsome living out of screwing an array of squalid men in the next-door room. At two hundred quid a pop just for a bit of oral-with-no-extras, Fiona was making more in a good afternoon than Cherry could earn in a week.

Fiona didn't even have to put a smile on her face.

She accepted clients of every age, creed, colour and state of cleanliness.

She was the epitome of equal opportunities.

Cherry on the other hand, had her work-face set in the permanent grimace of a perpetual smile, wheeling out clockwork lines of affected interest in her clients' stories – tales that bored her to the point of suicide. She plucked, waxed, and waxed lyrical, nodded keenly, swept and listened. Listened all day to the whining of bored housewives, with too much money and too much time on their hands; excitable city girls having affairs with their bosses, preparing for illicit evenings with excuses of fictitious meetings; haughty, indifferent, would-be models bragging about their jobs, both real and fictitious.

And then listened some more at home, by night, to Fiona's bedroom Olympics, intermingled with the steady hum of buses warming up in Queen's Park bus station, opposite.

It was no good...clanging of brass – and brass beds – was one thing; but Roy the Screamer was in the depths of enjoying anal delight with Fiona, who was now howling like a dog and shouting,

"Finish, you tosser, you're over by five minutes and costing me money! There's a queue outside!"

And a fracas had started between two bus drivers; and an old bag, walking along the middle of the road opposite, was shouting inanely at the cars, whilst throwing bottles out of a huge stash in a carrier bag at the drivers.

It was Monday after all.

Cherry hauled herself out of her sagging bed, nearly breaking her foot on the baseball bat that she kept just under it, in case of any room mix-up with Fiona's clients in the dead of night. There were better ways of being woken after all.

She removed the complicated arrangement of elastic and gaffer tape holding her fridge door almost shut and purveyed the scenery within.

It was not a pretty sight.

37

Rotting potatoes, bread with a fine film of green fur. She picked up the milk, took a swig and spat immediately into the sink that was half a pace away, her foot slipping on the grease on her kitchen floor. The milk was clotted and beyond even passing for yoghurt. It was fizzy.

She shut the fridge door again. The thought of cleaning it out made her feel dizzy with disgust.

She went over to her ancient sofa and picked up the phone, wiping the mouthpiece out of habit, although no-one else used it.

She withheld her own number, dialled half of Cath's number, put the phone down again. Picked it up once more, redialled, waited for the ring and then chickened out as soon as it was answered. Cath was only one person in the world she wanted to speak to. The one person who would understand her despair and loneliness.

But that one person was no longer in her life.

And she regretted it.

And wished it was different.

But could never quite bring herself to change it.

Cherry pulled on a pair of outsized, boyfriend jeans over her pyjamas, stuffed her feet into a pair of enormous, furry-dog-head-slippers and walked out into the night of Queen's Park, with a regretful shiver.

All she could think about was a bacon and egg sandwich big enough to blot out her pathetic life with its grease.

And Cath.

Bugger.

Three rain-soaked minutes later, she was in the late night café, having run there with a lumbering, bear-like gait; her slippers like gigantic, sodden, troll's feet, soaking up puddles by the litre.

"Hi, gorgeous, " said George, the shiny, red-faced owner of her favourite Sunday morning haunt, wisps of hair carefully arranged over his shiny pate with what must have been superglue, his cheeks a motorway map of drinker's broken, purple veins. "I think your clock is wrong. And your calendar for that matter. It's night-time you know. And Monday! And your pulling attire is not going to work, love. Where's the glamorous woman who's obviously just had her body nicked and ruined by someone else?"

"Treble bacon and egg with ketchup. And mustard. And a bucket of tea. Of the builders' variety. You cheeky sod."

"Boyfriend trouble?"

"That well ran dry so long ago I daren't count. Haven't got enough fingers," she said, sardonically and sat down with a stained copy of *The Sun* from three days ago. "Bloody nerve," she mumbled to herself, irked.

She sat, munching, enthralled by the enormous pair of fake-bake-hued-cantilever-suspended-torpedo-breasts before her on Charley, 19, from Enfield.

They'd be swinging round her knees before she was thirty. By sixty, she'd need a roller skate under each one just to stop the friction burns from the pavement. By ninety, they'd be like a pair of flesh-coloured tights, dragging along the floor behind her, with a misshapen tennis ball in the end of each foot. Nice.

The tea was orange, thick with milk and tasted more like the coating of filth on loose change than anything drinkable. But it was perfect. Around her, clusters of long distance lorry drivers sat hunched and bemoaning 'her indoors' and the latest rise in the price of diesel. A couple of fantastic, fresh-out-of-a-nightclub, drunken lovers sat bickering in hushed snarls at each other. Her ears pricked up.

A row. Goody. Always much more interesting than the paper.

She tried to lean slightly closer to hear the ranting they were attempting to muffle from prying ears and they glanced round at her, suddenly silent. She turned a shade of vermillion – and bending to rearrange her slipper by way of a diversion, cracked her head on the table with such force that her eyes began to water. Her tea leapt from her mug, spilling onto the back of her head.

And she realised for the first time what a state she looked.

Please God that none of her salon clients would inadvertently stumble in and catch sight of her.

She found her fags and fumbled in a sweet-wrapper-filled pocket to find a light.

Nothing.

It was pissing with rain outside and even if she did manage to light the bugger it would be out after three puffs. Oh, the desperation of nicotine addiction.

She looked around the café for a good candidate for the loan of a lighter and met the gaze of the bloke by the door, whose foot she had smothered with one monstrous slipper as she had entered.

My God, he was gorgeous.

She looked down rapidly and then glanced up again for another peek, to see if he really was as lovely as on first reckoning.

Fuck, he was still looking at her.

Inadvertent eye contact, for the second time.

Bad enough the first time.

She sat straighter and coyly wound a lock of un-brushed hair between her fingers.

That was rule one in the book of looking alluring, as far as she could remember.

She composed her face into the disinterested, but sexy half-smile she had practised a million times in the mirror and looked down at her paper; wishing she was reading a book that would make her appear intelligent and enigmatic, instead of *The Sun*.

She ran her hand over her lips, in what all the best women's magazines said was a suggestive and irresistible manner and looked up again.

He had gone.

Then she noticed the huge blob of ketchup that had decanted from her sandwich down the front of her Mickey Mouse PJ top and her tongue found an enormous wedge of soggy bread, nestling between her front teeth.

Chuckling to herself, she lurched to the counter with a hand full of loose change and piled it onto the chipped, Formica top, on top of the words "dogging is cool", written with an illiterate hand in Biro. She said her thank-yous and walked out into the cold night.

As she got to her front door, fumbling for her keys – with her eyes screwed into tight slits to avoid the smoke from the fag held between her teeth, as she fought to have a breath without dragging on it – she paused in faint alarm. There, fluttering damply in the wind, penned in ink fast smudging in the horizontal rain, was a yellow post-it note.

"CHERRY. DATE SAME PLACE TOMORROW AT 9PM?"

Chapter 6

Jude had entered the hospital ward where his new child lay, after loitering outside the door for what seemed an eternity, terrified out of his wits.

His parents had taken the news well, considering.

His mother had cried. Had paced the kitchen floor – where all family meetings relating to Jude's latest misdemeanours took place – wringing her hands. His father had remained still, saying nothing, cheek muscles twitching in internal turmoil.

Jude had not been in a position to argue. And underneath it all, he knew that their unfailing support of him, whatever his crime, was a mark of their undying affection for him. All cast out to sea as he felt, he knew he was not really alone, that help was there for him, come what may.

He could have not returned home, not faced the music, disappeared without trace. But he was suddenly faced with being a man, for the first time in his life; and the determination he had always had to swim against the tide, to do the unexpected, was thrown into overdrive.

He would do the decent thing.
For once in his life.
He would finally not let them down.

And as he gawped at the tiny scrap of humanity that lay before him screaming bawdily – pale, frizzy hair standing atop the wrinkled head, fists clenched and purple, eyes like small currants in a crumpled, purple-tinged bun – he was filled with a fascination deeper than anything he had ever felt.

This was his tiny thing, his flesh and blood, 7 days and six hours old.

"Hi, Sam," he said feebly.

Sam began to cry. Jude stood, shuffling from foot to foot. "Are you OK?"

Sam said nothing at first. She was looking down, holding the baby dispassionately. A silvery glacier formed between her nose and top lip.

"They've kicked me out," she said, eventually.

"Who?"

"Who do you think?" She looked at Jude, her face drained, empty, defeated, and hostile. "That's why I'm still in here."

She put the screaming baby down on the bedclothes and held her head in her hands.

"Sorry, Sam." Jude didn't know what else to say.

The baby was caterwauling now, abandoned, hungry, needing love.

"Why is she crying like that?" asked Jude, feeling anxious, the sound strangely piercing his heart. *She was so tiny and helpless.*

"How do I bloody know?" Sam rounded on him, tired and angry.

"Do you think she's hungry, or something?"

"I TOLD YOU, I DON'T KNOW! SHE DOES IT ALL DAY AND ALL NIGHT!

Jude reached out towards the baby and picked her up, clumsily, the tiny head lolling backwards over his forearm.

"Support her head...look; hand underneath, like this. You'll do her a mischief like that!" – A nurse had bustled in with water in a baby bath. "Come on, Mummy...time to bath baby."

Sam didn't look up.

"Is this Daddy?"

Jude nodded.

"Well, you'd better give me a hand, then. I think, by the looks of it, Mummy needs a little break."

The nurse looked into his face, serious, eyebrows raised. "Come on love, we're rushed off our feet, here."

Jude stayed all afternoon.

He stayed until he was kicked out. He couldn't bear to leave her.

He couldn't believe it.

He was blindly, completely, happily, unexpectedly in love – and finally understood just what that word meant.

And he realised at that moment he would happily give his life for this minute piece of himself.

A week later, Sam brought the baby home to Peter and Robyn's house. There had been no choice. There was nowhere else for them to go.

Jude called her Connie. She had waited long enough for a name. Sam didn't complain.

Jude watched Connie grow, with a wonderment that changed into a bond greater than anything he could have ever imagined. Armed with the realisation that the continued support of his parents now hung precariously in the balance, he knew he had to change, to start afresh. And he needed them now, more than ever.

His mother had made it abundantly clear that she could tolerate no more – she had taken in not only his child, but also the mother of his child who was barely out of nappies herself.

She could no longer disguise the resentment she felt towards her son.

Connie's arrival seemed to have firmly removed Jude from his mother's heart.

She could barely look at him.

Yet she went through the motions of looking after him and his new family without complaint: washing, cooking, cleaning, feeding, and bathing. She helped Jude every night when the habitual crying woke all of them – the crying of a baby, usually followed by the wailing of a girl too young to cope with being a mother.

And as he witnessed Robyn's tired eyes, pale skin and her diminishing frame – hunched with weariness as each morning spelt the end of the previous night's ordeal – Jude realised his mother was at breaking point.

He got a job: working in a local betting shop, to the dismay of his parents.

But worked he did – supporting this tiny being, caring for her, sweeping her into his arms on his return home each day, tickling her until she screamed with laughter and farted uncontrollably into her fat, soaked nappy.

He bathed her, read to her, dressed her with care, cut her hair as it grew into a mass of unruly knots, smothered her with kisses, played 'this little piggy went to market', shared soldiers and egg. He wiped her face, smeared with putty-like food, as her fat arms pushed him away, clenched fists caked with broccoli bake, kissing him back with pursed, wet, baby lips and a 'mwah'.

He loved her.

Oh my God, he loved her.
Loved her madly.

As he gradually lifted the burden of care, piece by piece, from his mother's shoulders – taking responsibility, earning her trust, gently showing his love – her smile began to return.

And his parents exchanged looks full of slowly growing pride.

Chapter 7

"Your eleven o'clock's here!"

Guffaws of smothered laughter followed; the rest of the staff were hiding behind the till counter with ill-disguised glee, pissing themselves.

The hair on the vision that had entered the salon for Cherry's 11a.m. slot resembled an enormous, tangerine puff of candyfloss, which would not have been out of place in 'Dangerous Liaisons'. Peach powder lay clogged in the folds of her jowly face. Her false eyelashes were several millimetres removed from her own upper eyelashes, in the grotesque manner of a bad showroom dummy.

At least one was.

The other was at half-cock and only hanging on at one corner, while the other end dangled tantalisingly close to her rheumy eyeball. In fact, it looked as if she had thrown the decaying contents of an antique cosmetics purse, complete with fluff, onto her dressing table and rolled her face from side to side on the resulting chaos; until it had adhered to the lard, liberally applied to the parchment masquerading as skin.

The old baggage trotted, leaning forwards, at top speed towards a swivel chair, which was parked before the banks of super-clean, stark mirrors. She clutched the back of it for stability – hoping, in vain, to aid her deceleration into a faltering halt.

The chair swivelled.

She fell towards the neighbouring customer who was at a crucial point in the waxing of her eyebrows – which could have proved disastrous, not to mention hilarious, had a collision occurred. Cherry caught her arm and only just averted disaster; but then had a great problem getting the old lady to bend in the middle to sit in the chair. She rather fell backwards like a board and lay stiffly across the back of her chair, as if she'd been embalmed after death and thrown at it.

"Make me beautiful, daahling," she purred, in a voice that had seen many super-king-extra-strong-bargain-bucket-tabs. "I am going on a date this lunchtime and as you can see, my Parkinson's does not allow me the pleasure of doing it myself. I want to look like Catherine Deneuve – or possibly Mae West. But not Barbara Cartland, which is the effect I seem to have created this morning."

Cherry immediately felt a wave of remorse and guilt – an unfamiliar feeling to her. This was not a freak, but an old lady with a debilitating disease and an enormous amount of pride and courage. And Cherry was suddenly ashamed about being a judgemental bitch.

OK, she was a pretty freaky, old piece of crumble.
But let's face it, Cherry – that'll be you one day.
And, what's more, she has a bloody date.

There was awkward silence.

"Don't worry, dear. I know I'm unusual. Don't be frightened of the old lady!"

Cherry laughed and stuttered, "It's not that…I was wondering how you've managed to get a date, when I've been in the biggest drought of all time, for at least a year." Another awkward silence ensued. "Please don't take that the wrong way," she added hastily. "There's no reason why you shouldn't have a date, it's just…"

"I'm too old to take things the wrong way, my dear. All men are scoundrels of the first degree, in my experience. But I love them still. In fact, I'm paying for this one."

Another pregnant pause followed as Cherry wished she had kept her big mouth shut. She decided that it was best to not pursue the last comment and to just get on with her job. And it was likely to be a tricky job at that. The woman looked like a disaster.

Cherry ran her fingers through the old woman's hair. Which then came off in her hands – to reveal an unkempt, mad, steely-grey, Brillo pad of hair that hadn't seen the benefit of a cut or wash for years; the back of which was matted into a texture closer to wool and stuck straight up, like a cockatoo. She stifled a scream as she tried to free the matted wig from her ring, where it had snagged itself – and then dropped it on the floor, out of shock. It landed over the old lady's orthopaedic shoe. She half expected it to start crawling away on its own and make a bid for freedom through the salon door.

Cherry was now puce with embarrassment. She retrieved the 'syrup' and placed it, with unhidden revulsion, in the lady's handbag; using her fingers like the pincers of a crab, so as to avoid any more contact with her own skin than was humanly possible – and trying not to gag.

"I hope you don't mind me getting rid of that thing! You have lovely hair of your own. Well, you have some hair of your own. And I'll try and make it lovely."

"You may do as you wish, dear. As long as I don't look ordinary. I may be old, but I do not wish to look like any of those poor, old dears out there who have given up the ghost and retired from life. The ones who sit all day, wetting their pants in front of the television and then drying them off in front of the three-bar heater when they're expecting company. And talking to the characters on Coronation Street as if they're actually part of it. Life is a precious gift that should not be wasted for a second. And you're wasting some of it standing there with your mouth agape like a lunatic. Did you know that 'lunaticus' gains its stem from the Latin term 'luna'? I don't suppose they teach you anything these days. Anyway, get on with it, dear. Time stands still for no man. And neither do I!"

She winked.

And stroked her creped cheek with a surprisingly elegant hand. "The name is Mabel De'Ath," she said. "And don't forget the apostrophe next time you book me in."

Cherry gently tipped the old lady's head as far back over the basin as she could – about two inches of movement before it ground to an arthritic halt – and started to soak it, kneading her scalp with tenderness and care, respecting the years it had lived through, massaging the tension out of her scalp, paying more attention than she normally did when bored by flippant, tedious, run-of-the-mill clients.

She sensed something overwhelmingly different about this one: something worth time and reverence.

As she silently worked, doing her best, cutting and tending as if it were a garden, her client purred: cat-like, gracious, and grateful.

"Thank you for making such an effort with an old lady," she said in her raspy, phlegmatic voice.

Cherry wondered quite how many cigarettes she managed to get through in one day. And whether she smoked them two at a time, lighting one from another in a continual stream of yellow-stained fug.

As she worked some Cherry magic on the proud, old lady's hair, they began to talk. For once, Cherry was spellbound.

****

Mabel had lived through World War Two.

In the first year of fighting, she had lost both her parents.

In the last year, she had lost her husband of three years; the news brought apologetically by two army officers, shortly after all the action had stopped. She had been eagerly awaiting the return of her love; he had written only two weeks before, promising his homecoming. She had been making bunting out of old parachutes to celebrate his return. Her hair had been freshly set into tight curls; a new suit, fashioned from two woollen blankets and a shirt, cunningly hewn from another old parachute – stitched lovingly to hug her neat curves – lay nearly perfected on their bed.

She was only 23, her skin glowing with youth and promise, but her hands gnarled too soon by hard toil in the factory where she made grenades. She was proudly wearing his ring – the one he had sold his beloved motorbike to buy, the one he had presented her with as an engagement and wedding ring as he could not afford both.

He had been a kind, loving man; true to his word, writing as often as was humanly possible, always with humour so as not to worry her as she lay alone at night, longing to hold him, giggle with him under the sheets.

She received many of his letters after she had been told of his death and re-lived her loss again and again.

The pain never did go. Search as she might over the years, she never managed to find anybody who had matched up to him, nobody worth the ground he walked on.

There were many others, of course. And a fine, tight circle of strong, bawdy, loyal female friends; some sharing her experience, some sharing their lives with husbands who survived – all sharing a loyalty and humour that grew with the years, as good friendships were carefully kept and bad ones were not.

She had taken her firm, young, graceful body and trained it as a dancer; in local productions she was quite well known. But over the years, the work had slowly dried up; her body had withered like an apple as it lies on the orchard grass. She had then worked as an artist's model, holding her aching bones in complicated shapes for hours at a time; her legs still elegant though the skin was puckered like an old paper bag, her breasts drooping like a pair of deflated wind-socks – but her poise remaining.

****

As Cherry cut and massaged, removed Mabel's fake face, peeled the mask back to basics, stripping her disguise with the absolute promise of improvement; a fresh, though old, glorious and glowing Mabel emerged.

"I do love men, you know," she said, beaming, as though Cherry had asked her a silent question. "Rotten through and through, most of them. But don't you just love that little thrill they give you when they're new, dear. Nothing like it in the world!"

She let out a wheezy sigh as she rummaged through her voluminous handbag, its cracked, patent leather flaking like reptilian skin, shedding its contents of old tissues as she fumbled.

"Want a mint? Must have fresh breath, you know. It's very difficult to get close to a man, otherwise."

Her ancient, fluff-covered mint imperial clattered on her false teeth, setting off her hearing aid into a fine whistle, as she tossed it around her mouth with her tortoise-like tongue.

"I've given up on finding men by the normal means. I advertise these days. For a price you can get quite a catch. And I always did like to cause a bit of a stir among the other old dears. So I pay for quite young ones so I can see the jealous, disbelieving faces as I walk into places for lunch. Makes them think I'm quite a goer! Tremendous fun. The chaps can be quite keen, you know – and will do very interesting things for a bit of extra cash. Oh yes – you may look shocked my girl; but us old ducks do have needs too, you know! There's plenty of life in the old girl yet. Takes them a bit of time in the trouser department though, until they realise that all I want is a damn good look and a little rummage. Everything has its price in this life. That you'll learn, one day. How old are you, 16? 17?" – a wink, a twinkle, a smile revealing still present and rather beautiful, ageing dimples in her crumpled-autumn-leaf-like cheeks.

"I'm 26 actually, but you've made my day!" said Cherry.

"In fact, I made a few saucy films in my day too, young lady...but don't tell a soul." Mabel whispered, conspiratorially. Cherry, in shock, dropped the scissors onto her own flip-flop-clad foot, blades down like daggers, impaling her big toe and drawing blood.

"Not the kind of saucy films you youngsters are used to though. A bit classier we were, in our day. The tease of a boot unlaced, a glimpse of a corset, an air of mystery. Not like the utter filth they show youngsters now. No wonder they're all in therapy or whatever it is and taking up with rock stars and smoking pot. Although that's quite fun too and has quite a calming effect on my shakes, you know."

Mabel stopped to ponder her new, improved image in the mirror.

"I can't quite see what you've done to me, dear, but it looks terribly grey. I want to maintain some sort of faded glamour, you know. Don't go too far, or I might have to give you a lashing of the tongue and you won't like that."

Mabel was transformed.

Her hair was pure salt and pepper, but trimmed, straightened and twisted into a low bun. Devoid of ten tons of slap, she looked a good decade younger, despite her worry.

"It's looking lovely, Mabel," said Cherry, through lips that were welded to a pair of scissors to free her hands, simultaneously dribbling and trying unsuccessfully to suck the string of abseiling ectoplasm back in before it went past chin level and her customer noticed.

While Cherry turned her attention to the old lady's face, Mabel probed her for information about herself.

"Tell me about yourself, dear. I'm fed up with hearing about me. I know the story already."

Cherry found herself telling Mabel all about her drought in the man department, her falling out with Cath over the last one, her misery without her pal...it had been years now and she missed her like hell.

As she finally took the robe off Mabel, the old lady looked in the mirror curiously. She was transformed. Elegant, mature, still a little racy with her rather daring fitted suit, face glowing and natural – until you reached the lips.

Bright, blood-red, film star lips.

Red enough to punch you in the face.

Red enough to shock on the face of an old lady.

Red, red, red.

"Perfect!" she cried, clapping her shaking hands together with genuine glee. "I look like a very naughty school marm! A little slutty even! And rather extraordinary! Perfect! Perfect!"

"Except the shoes, Mabel."

They both looked down.

Only her vast, stomping, orthopaedic-type ankle boots let her down now. Ruined the entire effect. Like wearing an exotic, crocheted 70's bikini with a pair of clown's shoes.

The old lady grabbed Cherry's face between her old hands, kissed her full on the lips staining Cherry's mouth with lipstick and grabbed her fiercely by the hand.

"We'll have to rectify that!" she exclaimed, dragging her out of the salon while the rest of the staff fell about laughing.

They spent Cherry's lunch hour in shoe shop heaven; finally settling on a pair of forties wedge heels to complete the outfit.

Mabel couldn't walk in them at all, of course. Cherry had to take Mabel's arm, dragging her to her destination for her lunch date. She heaved her clumsily towards her table as she tottered appallingly; and, like in the salon, was forced to bend her brutally in the middle before she sat, holding the chair up at the same time.

"One last thing, dear. Never lose your friends. Far more important than men, my darling. Arguing with them makes life miserable. And they're for life if you look after them properly. A bit like shoes. You'll realise, when you're my age!"

She winked.

Chapter 8

Jude awoke abruptly, with a wildly beating heart, from an unusually long sleep, unbroken that morning by Connie's usual noise and giggling. She habitually rebounded on him like a trampolinist, waking him forcefully, way before his body was ready; her arms laden with rolls of fat as if bound by rows of elastic bands, her legs as muscled as a Russian gymnast. She would thump at his shoulders, tug at the hairs on his chest, peel back his eyelids viciously to arouse him from his slumber; grinning all the time, with tiny front teeth exposed like a row of tic-tacs in a mile of wet gums, soggy with sweet-smelling spit.

Longing for his attention.

Where was she today?

Every bone in his body was rigid with fear – some kind of sense of dread.

His tiredness was gone instantly.

Instinctively he knew something was terribly wrong. *But why?*

The house was silent. *Too silent.*

No childish clatter, no voices, no music. He glanced at his wristwatch.

11.13. God, he was late for work. Why had no-one woken him?

The silence was broken only by the hum of traffic.

In his mind spun the strange dreams he had been unable to wake from until this moment. He tried to grasp onto the noise and thoughts that had filled his sleeping head, but they slipped rapidly away, leaving him feeling uneasy.

Barefoot, he padded down the stairs, the fraying carpet beneath his feet muffling his steps. He walked apprehensively from room to room, his heart rate slowly returning to normal as he saw all was well.

The shabby sitting room was empty, the television on in a haze of poor transmission, the sound on mute.

The dining room lay silent, displaying only the remnants of breakfast: crusts of toast on faded china, milk filmy in a jug, tea gone cold.

He turned into the kitchen, also deserted and began to feel relief. No sign of life: his beloved child and her foul mother not in evidence. He began to think that his imagination had played tricks on him. He rang the betting shop in apology, saying he was ill all night and had slept through by mistake. *He was sorry. He wouldn't let them down again.*

He could have a few minutes of peace before Sam and Connie's return – and before the familiar sense of dread that always accompanied Sam's arrival was stirred by the sound of her approaching voice.

His mum must be doing the shopping. It was the day for it.

He made his way towards the sink, crumbs irritating his feet on the quarry-tiled floor. He tipped his head, sideways under the tap and drank its contents, greedily. The water was cold, London-tasting, rejuvenating.

As his head tilted to taste the contents of the tap, he noticed the cellar door open, the light on.

His mum would have a fit if she came home and found that open.

It was a cold, damp house; their poverty as a clergy family allowed for the bare minimum of heating. The cellar greedily sucked the heat from the kitchen with its stale, musty, damp iciness, draining the life from the warmth of the hub of their home. He finished drinking and moved towards the cellar door to snap off the light.

What the hell was that?

On the cobbled floor was a dark dampness, spreading towards the foot of the stairs leading down into its depths.

Jude walked towards it, curious and tiptoed down the stairs, expecting to find one of the vast tins of his mother's cash-and-carry cooking oil turned on its side, oozing its guts.

Instead, he saw his father, back against the wall, legs stretched out straight; in the way that a child sits.

He stared straight at Jude, glassy-eyed, his face blank, with an accepting horror in his wide, pale eyes.

His lips mouthed the word, "Jude."

Jude ran down the steps two at a time, stumbling, his toes hitting cold stone, any pain drowned out by the feeling of foreboding.

"Oh Christ!"

His own voice sounded like that of another as he screamed, screamed, screamed, "NO! NO! NO! NO! NO! NO!"

Screamed again as he squatted by his father, his hands clutching his own face, nails digging into his skin, taking in the horror as he realised he now stood in the thick, dark ooze of his father's blood: his feet sliding in it, warm underfoot, sticky like treacle, smelling of fresh kill.

"WHO, DAD? ARE THEY STILL HERE?" He started to look wildly around him; suddenly realising they might not be alone. "WHO?"

His father shook his head, mouthing words Jude could not understand. He sounded with each breath as if he was about to drown. He pulled back his suit jacket and gestured toward his chest.

Jude reeled with shock when he saw. Bile rose into his mouth.

He reached towards the chipped, red handle of his father's favourite chisel. The blade was deep in his father's ribs. *Right up to the handle. My God, so deep – right in, right into his soul.*

Their eyes met in shared horror.

He pulled his hand away. He could not touch it. He could not bear to feel his father's very guts on the instrument that was causing his death, right now, right in front of him.

"WHAT DO I DO?" he screamed at him; at his father, the man he always relied on for the answers, the man he needed to help him now. "Tell me what to do! OH my GOD OH my GOD OH my GOD!"

Jude's father's hand was on his now, his eyes looking deep into his, his skin paling – as a child now, as a frightened child, *a child needing his help, help he couldn't give.*

Jude turned to run for the phone; *help, he needed help, would somebody, somebody please help. Please. Please. Please. Please. Please.*

"Don't leave me," – a whisper, the arms reaching out to him, the strong arms that were always supposed to be there to protect him. *The arms that still hugged him every day. The arms he loved like no other.*

"What do I do? Dad! Please! Don't die! Help me. God help me. Please...God...What do I do? WHAT DO I DO? PLEASE,

PLEASE, PLEEEEASE!" Jude was wailing, helpless, screaming at the top of his voice. "PLEASE DAD, DON'T DIE, DON'T LEAVE ME...OH GOD, WHAT DO I DO?"

His father's hands, always so soft and warm and welcoming, now damp with blood, held onto his own now, not letting him go, gripping him, clinging on for dear life, crushing his bones.

They were growing cold now, so cold.

"Take it out."– Another whisper.

"No, Dad...I can't, I can't, I can't...I can't hurt you, I can't...no no no no no."

Jude held the handle. He could feel the fast rhythm of his father's ebbing life on its handle. He could not pull. His dad's very heart lay touched by the end of it. He was abhorred, desperate.

He needed him, he loved him, he couldn't go, he couldn't leave him now. *Dad, I need you. Dad, don't go. Dad, please stay.* Sobbing now, loudly, unable to say anything to this wonderful, dying man although he wanted to say everything in the entire world, to have another day, another minute, something, *anything.*

"Love you, Jude. Love you, Jude. Love my Jude." He was blowing bubbles. The words were inaudible. But the nightly mantra, chanted by a father to a son, every bedtime since Jude was born, was instantly understandable.

"Don't go, Dad," whispered Jude, recognising goodbye.

The hug. Covered in blood now, covered all over, his chest on top of his father's, the handle digging into his ribs too, coating his hands, on his lips where he kissed his father's chest, on his eyes and cheeks as he smeared the rivers of tears away so he could still see his father's beautiful face; so he could remember his every pore, every lash, his nose, his eyes, his freckles, his lips. Trying to hold onto him, let him know he adored him, stop him slipping away from him, this man he loved so much, this father, husband, brother, son: this good, good man.

"Love you. Love Mum. Tell her."

"DAD!"

"Look after Mum."

There were no more words.

Jude would never forget the sound of his mother's scream as she had found them: her husband glazed, an empty body where his soul had once been, her son anointed with his blood, his bloodied hands on his father's head as his eyes turned to look into hers as she stared down the stairs, open mouth covered with her hands as she screamed and screamed and screamed and screamed.

The police had come then. He had tried to explain, tried to tell his mother. He screamed at her hysterically, "WHY WON'T YOU LISTEN TO ME?"

But she would not speak: just stared at him, believing him, not believing him, as he was led away, cuffed, crying – crying out to his mother, crying out for his father – dragged by police officers, neighbours agog and excited, watching.

The crowd had parted as Sam arrived with Connie. Sam looked blank, gazing dispassionately at the scene unfolding before her, emotionless. Jude's eyes turned towards his beloved baby. His tortured mind began to spin.

"CONNIE!" he shouted to his child, arms outstretched, imploring, expecting her to run to him. But she stayed still, not looking at him as he was thrown into the back of the police car.

Chapter 9

She hadn't meant to do this.

This was not supposed to be like this.
This was not the ending she was looking for.
She had meant the old man no harm.

She had needed the money. He hadn't understood that she needed the money – or how much she needed it; the door to her next fix and her escape from her life, the life she hadn't ever wanted. She needed it so much it was a fire, burning deep in her heart.

It was his fault. He shouldn't have tried to stop her, been so kind, frightened her so much as he reached out to her kindly. Should have recognised his charity was no match for her desperation.

She hadn't meant for her child to see this, quiet and staring at the top of the stairs as she looked up to make her escape. She hadn't wanted to take Connie with her as she fled to her future, fled from the responsibilities she wore like handcuffs, fled from the husband of so few months who repulsed her with his cloying love, fled leaving him his suffocating child and prying, stifling family, fled to the life that she should have had.

Now it was all ruined.
It was all his fault.

Shaking, she tore up the stairs, snatching car keys from the table, dragging the child under her arm, shutting out the horror behind her as she shut the front door. She waved, happily, to her next-door neighbour as he left his house at the same time as her; waved again as she started the car parked next to his. She was barely able to concentrate on the key in the ignition: tearing at the key with her shaking hands, barely able to concentrate on where to put her feet. But she carried on; knowing only that to save her life now, she had to appear normal, not give the game away.

There had been so much blood.

It had started to pour from his chest as he sat, slowly, on the floor against the wall. But it had not been immediate.

There was only a small amount on her sleeve and hand; it did not show on the dark wool or on her dirty, denim jeans, where she had wiped it in horror. It had started to pump out, pulsing rhythmically and repulsively as she watched him sink. She had expected him to get up again, be OK, forgive her immediately in the nauseating way that he always did.

But he had just sat, staring at her, saying, "Please," – dreadful as he emptied.

He had wet his trousers as he sat.

She parked calmly at a meter. She walked with the child into the shopping centre. She rang a friend, chatted about the night before, paraded in front of CCTV, said she needed to get home as she'd been out for long enough, should get back to the family now, could not meet up now, but what about tomorrow?

The heroin would have to wait for now.

She would have to be careful.

Her daughter walked with her, in silence, no sign of emotion on her grubby, beautiful face, speaking not a word, not driving her mother mad with her inane, kiddie drivel as she normally did as she tried, unsuccessfully, to communicate with her seventeen learnt words.

****

The stealing had started out small. She knew they were being good to her. Kind to take her in after her own parents had kicked her out – parents horrified that she, their little daughter, had had sex, known a male body, defiled herself with his smell and his semen and his bad ways: their 'perfect' daughter, who was now making them look foolish to their friends, the friends her mother needed so much to impress.

She had only started using to numb her brain from the monotony of motherhood: something she hadn't wanted, something that had taken away her life, freedom, future and landed her in a time and place she loathed and despised to her very core.

It had been too late for an abortion. She had been too frightened to even tell them of the small life growing inside her. Tried to ignore it, thought she was mistaken, thought it would go away.

It didn't really show. It couldn't be there, that small growing life.

It had been five months. She had not been sick. She was no fatter really. Her school jumper more than hid the evidence. She was still able to do sport.

It must just be one of those things, you know, when your periods stopped of their own accord. If you were stressed.

And stressed she was. She had really liked Jude. Well, as much as she ever liked anybody. She always felt numb about other people, somehow. But he was a very bad boy. Part of his appeal. Was good for her standing in the school. Made her cool.

Made her hot too, inside her, feeling her warm depths, breathing into her neck, panting like that, first his fingers, then his thing, so hard, hurting her gently, making her feel important, like a woman. Handsome too, and popular.

Yes, she had really liked him.

****

Having a baby had been unexpected. Even when, during her second GCSE, she was crippled with a strange, deep pain – a feeling of being open down there: something strange and unfamiliar happening, her insides unfolding, turning inside out – she had not believed it. Even when she had locked herself in the toilets, gushing blood and water, trying to stifle any sound from the next-door cubicle with a jumper sleeve in her mouth, she had not believed it. And when she had brought forth a ball of blue, hard, ugly, human life into her hands, she had still not believed it. *They were supposed to be pink, soft, crying. Not joined still to you by a veined rope, face screwed up, unyielding, mouth open in a silent cry, kicking. With genitals. A hole, like hers, hers now torn open.*

It had started to cry, louder and louder.

It was going to give her away.

She had heard people outside.

"Shut up," she had whispered, jaws locked together. She was shaking. Huge shakes: her legs had taken on a life of their own – she could not control it – her whole body shook like she stood amidst an earthquake. "Shut up!" she had said.

There was banging on the door. Adult voices, hushed, outside, only inches away, guessing her secret; shadows of feet under the door, right in front of her, separated from her only by a thin barrier of wood.

65

It had started to cry more urgently, its eyes shut, slippery body fighting against her, blood blisters all over its face from the force of the birth, hair on its shoulders and the top of its ears.

A face had appeared under the door.

"It's not mine," she had said, pants sodden round her ankles, the cord still connecting it to her very guts, school shoes and socks covered with gore.

She had needed the heroin. She was disowned, cut loose, sailing in a strong wind that took her helplessly towards an unwanted horizon as she tried, desperately, to swim back to shore.

Only a little hit, every now and then. She didn't need to buy it. *He gave it to her freely, because he liked her, could see the situation she was in, was just being kind. And he gave her a little attention. She deserved it. Everyone had to have a little happiness in life, if life is what you called it. He knew she had no money. All she had to do was suck his cock once in a while. Nothing else.* And the bitter taste of him and his now familiar smell faded within seconds. Leaving her able to go back to this thing, this baby.

Connie they had called it.

Jude seemed to ignore her now.

So caught up with his baby.

Couldn't see she was just as important.

Pushed her away as she fumbled with the zip on his trousers, as she tried to put her lips on his, push her tongue in, envelop him with her heat.

Just because it was crying.

He held it all day, smothered it with the love and affection and kisses that should have been hers, changed it, bathed it, and fed it tenderly.

She hated both of them.

His mother hadn't helped. Had just said to Jude that he should marry her, make her feel loved, secure, that that would help stop her constant physical and mental attacks on him.

The more Jude tried to help her, tried to understand, the less she wanted to be understood – the more she wanted to hurt him, destroy him; the more she loathed his weakness towards her, lashed out at him, biting, punching.

She needed more heroin now: to block out the reality of what her life had become, block out the loss of the parents she had loved, block out their rejection of her, block out her hatred of her own actions – of the thing that she was becoming.

It was like a beast within her, a growing rage.

The more it was unleashed, the more she was forgiven, the more reckless she became with this demon inside. She could almost watch herself, detached, from afar, as she spat hatred at the very people who had taken her in, rained venom on them, knowing they always seemed to be able to forgive her. Apologising only if it seemed, momentarily, that she had pushed it too far – but then attacking again as soon as she had been absolved of her sins by their forgiveness, secure in the knowledge that people like these could never desert her.

They were too soft.

She was too important to them.

She knew Jude adored her, the mother of his child. She was protected by his love. He would always forgive her. And his god-fearing parents risked sure and certain hell, she was positive of that, if they did not forgive her too.

****

It was only a Toby jug to start with. A few bits of jewellery. Nothing much.

They'd believed she'd broken the jug, when she'd said so.

She'd only lost it when his mother had started going through the bin to look for the pieces to glue together.

Why be so precious about something that old and ugly? Not exactly the height in taste.

She had shouted and screamed abuse at them all – *how could they not believe her, how dare they accuse her, how dare Jude not stand up for her if he expected her to love him?*

Until Jude had broken down and begged them to stop, taken her in his arms. Defended her, told them they were wrong, mistaken; she wouldn't have lied.

They'd not said anything after that.

So she'd got away with it.

It was never mentioned again.

And that night, when her veins were filling with liquid pleasure, she knew all the aggravation had been worth it.

****

They married when Connie was eighteen months old.

Something to help her feel really a part of the family.

Because that was what the problem was, wasn't it? She was just insecure.

A small, family affair.

They were all watching as she signed the remains of her life away, with stupid, happy looks on their faces as she signed her death warrant, made promises she couldn't bear to keep, became a wife.

Wife.

What was that? A prison. Another door shutting.

She hadn't liked him that much.

They were all watching as she searched desperately for a moment to snatch, to blot it all out with a quick injection. She had felt the familiar wave of fear and panic wash over her as time ticked on and the opportunity didn't present itself; desperation filling her very bones.

But then there was a slot, a brief gap when relief could be hers. The family were gathered, chatting excitedly, no longer noticing her as they waited for taxis to go to the reception – a small affair, in a local pub.

She slipped to the toilet in the church, hauling her demure, antique, white lace dress over her slender thighs, undid the wrap of foil tucked into her garter and slipped the needle into her groin.

It hit faster there.

And nobody could see any telltale black marks.

Except Jude, who said nothing, but tried to ignore, thinking he, in time, could mend her.

She emerged into the sun and the gaze of her new family; calm, serene, sweating slightly – but once again warm inside, cosseted, life feeling fine, a smile on her face, her eyes slits in the brightness.

"You see. She looks happier already!" said Robyn to her husband and son as they walked slowly on the gravel path, arms entwined.

Jude looked away.

Chapter 10

It was failed theft, the police said.

His prints were all over the handle of the chisel. So there was no point in trying to get away with it.

And he had been drenched with his father's blood, every piece of him.

Patricide. Always a nasty, little crime.

The chisel that had been used to kill his father had been, minutes before the kill, used to try to prise open the locked lid of a wooden box: the wooden box where Jude's dad kept his savings. The savings that were a secret from all his family, even his wife.

Saving for the past six years.

Savings that were gathered to take his loving wife, his precious son, beloved granddaughter and daughter-in-law – treasured despite her failings – on the holiday that he had promised for his entire life, but never been able to afford.

In a box, away from the bank where his wife would have seen it in their joint account, so as not to spoil the surprise.

He had never been able to afford a house of their own on his wages.

Vicars didn't earn much.

Should have kept it in the bank, the police said.
To avoid temptation.

The money was spent on giving Peter Cristian the funeral he deserved.

It was an open and shut case, the police said.
They were alone in the house together.
The two wives were both out shopping. Perhaps it wouldn't have happened if they'd been around.
And he'd seemed like such a changed, loving boy.
You never could tell.

The court took ten minutes only to reach the verdict.
Guilty.
Unanimous decision.
Custody for life.
No bail.

He was 6 months past his eighteenth birthday.

Chapter 11

Cherry spent the entire afternoon getting ready.

There was a lot to do.

She realised what a serious state of disrepair had been going on under her winter wardrobe. Inch-long leg hairs, leg dandruff, chipped nails, armpits that would have kept a family of bears warm in winter and as for her bikini line…well, considering her day was spent making already glamorous, beautiful people even more so, it was all rather a shock.

The hair removal itself took most of the afternoon.

Waxing oneself was more difficult by far than doing it to someone else. She had been too ashamed to let any of her colleagues loose on her nether regions. It would have been the sole topic of conversation for weeks and she'd have had to change jobs afterwards to preserve any form of dignity, such was her disarray.

She sat on the floorboards, one leg waving awkwardly in the air, attempting to reach the fleece of wool that grew around her arse. Swapping legs, she shifted her weight onto the other buttock to find that she was stuck to the floorboards with a residual clump of wax.

She attempted to get up.

Jesus, really stuck to the floorboards.

She took a deep, preparatory breath, winced in advance, ripped herself from the wood and bent down, head between her knees, to survey the damage in the mirror from behind.

Rather a large chunk of raw skin winked at her, swelling before her eyes. And a fetching puff of hair remained round her arse, when all else was bare. Twat topiary. She resembled a badly-parloured Poodle.

She turned round. The landing strip at the front was lopsided in a rakish fashion.

The whole effect was fairly petrifying.

Pubes were there for a purpose, obviously.

And it had all had a most unwelcome effect on the size of her thighs: shifted the balance, somehow.

Thank God for clothes.

She stood straight again, blood rushing from her head towards her feet – and nearly passed out.

Her entire armoire was now empty, clothes strewn all over the floorboards.

What remained was not a wardrobe, but a floor-drobe.

Her flat looked as if it had been totally ransacked.

At least she wouldn't be tempted to invite him back.

If he turned up.

Whoever he was.

She hoped that it wasn't one of the many freaks that walked past the salon – especially as this one obviously knew where she lived.

She made a mental register of every nutter who shuffled past the window each day. There were plenty of them. She conjured up a vision of one in particular who always leered at her through the window and often loitered outside. Hump. Killer's eyes. Meths bottle.

Oh deep joy.

There were a good few handsome sods too, usually meeting beauties, as they emerged from her tender hands in the salon, while she waved them off and shuffled back into the darkness like the Grinch.

So probably not one of them.

At approximately two hours before time, she was ready – each outfit on and off at least eleven times until she settled on the final one.

It was a cracker. Vivienne Westwood at its finest.

Well, a good rip-off that had escaped the eagle-eyed attention of eBay's counterfeit goods department, anyway.

She knew she looked good. She was still able to pull the cat out of the bag, when pushed.

She got to the café fashionably late.

About 6 minutes late…not wanting to appear too keen.

She had chain-smoked at least half a pack of fags outside in a state of anxious trepidation.

She ordered tea.

"Looking a bit better today, love. Definitely on the pull," a voice said from behind the counter. She looked at the sweating countenance and visibly balked.

Surely not.

She imagined their offspring.

And shuddered.

"Definitely not. I've just come back from a date," she lied, unconvincingly and scuttled off to a table in the corner, from where she was unable to see the door.

The sight of the entrance would have made her even more nervous.

She would be twitching like a maniac by the time he arrived, whoever he was.

She realised she was stranded, with no reading matter to hand, looking suspicious and out of place in her bondage suit and platforms.

The place was empty.

She had drained her tea instantly. She was starving, but dared not eat in case she was caught with a face full of bacon butty.

Men came and left – for what seemed like an eternity.

Nobody came over.

They glanced approvingly, several monstrosities of men. But she did stick out – *like the Pope in a betting shop.*

And she found herself getting progressively more terrified. Her palms were running with sweat, there was a moustache of moisture on her top lip oozing nicely into her carefully applied lipstick and a pond of perspiration forming above her eyebrows.

Her armpits would soon be far from being charmpits.

She was beginning to feel angry.

She finally rose to her feet and turned to leave, brows furrowed.

And there he was, sitting at a table three behind her, by the door, smiling.

Mr Gorgeous from the other night.

Oh God, she felt stupid now.

Obviously not her date, however much she'd hoped.

But sitting there, watching her being very publicly and obviously humiliated, waiting for someone who was obviously not going to turn up. *Because he'd had a better offer. Or seen her in daylight. Or something.*

She started to walk past towards the door, hurriedly, trying to preserve her dignity, head down, avoiding his gaze.

As she passed, he caught her arm.

"The car is waiting outside," he said.

"What?"

"The table is booked."

His arrogance was amazing. She was overcome with fury.

"Was it you who left the note?" she said.

He nodded. "I'm sorry. But you're stunning. I just wanted to spend a little time taking in the view."

"I'm not coming."

She was now absolutely seething.

She marched out, cheeks ablaze.

Not the finest start.

She hated him already.

He chased her out, grabbed her arm. "Like I said, your car is waiting."

He gestured over to a stunning, vintage, Mercedes convertible. She thought about it for a moment and – not being materialistic or anything – she got in.

They arrived at The Ivy.

"I quite like it here," he said, in unimpressed tones.

"So do I, from time to time," she lied, having never been there in her life. "Where are the toilets?"

Two bottles of wine and a suitably neat and conservative amount of delicious food later, Cherry was well-oiled. She was now a bleary, flirty, hair-twirling-finger-sucking-eye-batting nightmare.

"Sho. What do you do?" she slurred.

"10 guesses."

He had very nice shoes.

"A banker."

"Nope."

"A doctor."

"Nope."

"A dustman." *God, she hoped that one was wrong.* "What happens if I don't guess?"

"Then you are compelled to invite me back to your place and let me fuck you."

A statement; bold, brash, verging on obnoxious, but compelling all the same. And she could do with a bit of nookie.

She paused for a moment. In her alcoholic haze she remembered her sore nether regions, her catastrophe of a flat and her promise to herself to never, ever do this on a first date as it gave people the wrong impression, *she being a classy kind of girl and all that.*

"What number are we on?"

"Four."

"Do I get a clue?"

"It pays well."

Obviously.

She'd been in the car.

He hadn't divulged any news with that particular comment.

He was very, very sexy.

Perhaps in those circumstances getting it wrong would be a distinct advantage. She couldn't guarantee he would want to see her after this anyway. Perhaps she'd be able to sway him into dating her again if she ravished him. But it had been so long that she was distinctly out of practice. And Fiona would be bashing away in the bed of steel on the other side of the wall – and maybe sashaying alluringly down the hall in silken, swishy things which would make Cherry look like a troll in comparison.

"Butcher? No, no, scrap that one."

"Five."

"Not fair. I scrapped that one."

Perhaps he was a bit flash. Nice suit, well tailored. Hair a little too trendy, in that trying-to-look-effortless-but-so-overworked-it-probably-wouldn't-move-in-a-high-wind type of way. Hairdresser? Surely not.

"Gambler?"

"Six."

"I need clues, proper ones. Solicitor."

"Seven."

"Surgeon? Historian? Writer?"

"Eight, nine, ten, get your coat."

"But I retracted one…"

It was no use: she was defeated on a technicality.

And it had been a very nice meal.

Chapter 12

Sam was sitting, bleary-eyed and ruffled on the other side of the glass, as Jude was led into the visiting room. Connie was sitting on her knee; limpid, wide eyes staring at him, her face frightened. She tried to struggle free from her mother's lap, move towards the glass, towards her father as he drew close.

"SIT DOWN," her mother snarled at her in her habitual low, controlling voice.

Connie sat still, frozen, waiting.

"Hello," Jude said, "Hello Connie, honey. How are…"

"DON'T talk to her."

Jude looked up, momentarily taken aback. "Why? I didn't do it, Sam. I haven't done anything."

Sam reached into her bag, her hair falling forwards, and stray strands of it sticking across her face. She was perspiring. Her hands shook as she rummaged.

"Here," she said, "We've come to give you something."

A small, filthy piece of paper was pushed under the glass. The prison officer who was chaperoning watched intently.

Jude unravelled it. Inside was a small, plain gold band.

"I won't be needing this. You can keep it."

"Sam! I've done nothing! It wasn't me!"

"Murderer. Say bye to Daddy, Connie. You won't be seeing him any more."

Connie's face was crumpling, her lips quivering and twisting into a bawl.

"SHUT UP!" Sam hissed.

Connie sucked her tears back in, swallowing repeatedly and heavily, too frightened to let herself cry, her gaze still fixed on Jude, eyes blinking a silent plea.

"Stop it, Sam! Mummy doesn't mean that Connie."

"Oh Mummy does mean it." Sam was impersonating Jude's calm voice with spiteful sarcasm. "Mummy means every fucking word!"

Connie had begun to rub at her usual worry-patch – a spot of red skin below her left eye – with her tiny fingers as she became more agitated.

"Sam, STOP. She's terrified!"

"Terrified of YOU!"

Connie still locked eyes with Jude, her tiny hands white-knuckled as she held a filthy teddy bear tight. Jude realised it was the one he had given her, the one he was not allowed to wash, because it "smells of Daddy."

Tears welled in his eyes, squeezing their way to the surface as he tried to blink them back, tried not to upset his child.

"You're not scared of Daddy, are you baby?"

The guard was pacing a few feet away now, trying to give them some privacy.

Sam had risen to her feet, sliding Connie off her knees to the floor. She leaned in towards his face, her breath a grey mist on the glass, coming and going with her softly spoken words.

"You won't be seeing her again. She doesn't want to see you, do you Connie?"

Connie shook her head in a 'no', eyes still on his, not meaning it.

Jude began to sob. "Please, Sam," he said, "Please don't do this!" His shoulders were shaking now. "I've got to see her! You can't do this!"

"I can do what I want," she said, bitterly. "Say goodbye to your daughter."

"YOU CAN'T DO THIS! I'LL GET A COURT ORDER!" He was shouting now, the guard had turned and was watching again.

"If you try to see her I'll kill *you*."

"WHAT?" Jude was incredulous.

He looked, horrified, at his daughter, as Connie's head turned abruptly towards her mother and a look of sheer terror crossed her tiny face. She had lifted her bear over her mouth and had started to cry loudly. As Sam reached to grab her arm, Connie flinched and looked back at her father, face wild, begging.

"DADDY!"

Sam dragged her away.

And Jude knew.

And his brain spun. And he remembered Connie's face as he was thrown into the police car.

Had she seen? Had this innocent, little being borne witness to the killing of his father, unable to speak, unable to understand? Did she know, still clinging to her mother as Jude was dragged away? Still clinging to the mother who stood: stood with her face a picture of feigned confusion, knowing Jude had done nothing? The wife saying nothing as he was blamed; the wife of only a few months, saying nothing, trying to read the carnage around her, sweating with fear, clutching bags of shopping as an alibi and squeezing out a few, cold tears as he was dragged away? Had his beautiful baby seen?

Jude called his lawyer.

Chapter 13

Cath opened her eyes as sunlight streamed into the hotel room, blinding her. She blinked into the light and craned her neck backwards, towards the window behind the headboard of the old French bed. Not wanting to wake, she moved to turn onto her side.

But he was sleeping on her hair, as it lay stretched out on the pillow, so she was pinned where she was.

She dug him in the ribs with a bony elbow.

"What the hell…?"

"Sorry," she whispered, smiling and then tried to accost him due to the impressive quality of his early morning erection.

He was having none of it.

"Moody bastard," she muttered to herself, immediately unsure as to whether she had said it in her head, or out loud – and starting to worry.

He was not as light-hearted these days.

****

Cath had started at the bottom in the small, Soho film company. She had been a runner for three years – then a production assistant.

Finally – having produced a great catalogue of ads and short films, getting on with everybody like a house on fire, working from dawn till dusk and keeping her nose to the grindstone and her arse out of the pub – she had been given directing experience.

It had been a long, nine-year grind.

It was a role in which she flourished.

She adored it – excited to get out of bed each day, working tirelessly.

She was amazingly creative, had great vision and talent and an unfailing smile on her face, however tough things got.

She deserved her success.

She had also blossomed over the last few years. Cropped, black hair was replaced by a long mane of gloss, her fat arse whittled to no more than a pair of brussel sprouts and her wobbly thighs trimmed to neat, but muscular pins that an athlete would have been proud of.

A mixture of several years of starvation by virtue of her supreme-skintness-inducing mortgage – and a penthouse flat at the top of a mansion block in Elephant, where the lift never worked – had honed her body to its present state of finery. She was indeed a transformation of her former, lardy self. Her acne had long since gone and an outrageous amount of dental work had transformed her gnashers from crossed and buck, to straight and Hollywood. Her confidence had also improved in bounds. She was quite a catch.

****

You should never start an affair with your boss.
Everyone knew that.

John was an attractive, salt-and-pepper-haired, stylish man. Most of the women in the company had the hots for him and there was an underlying aroma of competition amongst them.

Not in a friendly way.

He had arrived as the new MD of the company a few months previously. He was a quiet (kept himself to himself, never divulging any personal information) but ruthless businessman, who was not to be messed with and inspired a certain kind of awe.

He had bombarded Cath with indifference since day one. She had never known quite what she did to annoy him that much, as all the others were treated with the same quiet authority and respect. He would criticise her work, frankly, in front of the others, until she squirmed in meetings – her toes curling in her trainers under the table, as she was once more taken politely to task about the quality of her work.

And yet no-one was harder working, more conscientious, more keen to do well than she. It was a mystery to all in the company; but he inspired too much fear – and there was far too much brown-nosing – for anybody to defend her.

One afternoon, he had summoned her to a lunchtime meeting to discuss her future in the company.

They walked, stony-faced, through the office as the 'hard at work' spectators mouthed, "Good luck" to Cath as she passed them, flushed and shaking with trepidation.

This was it; her job was obviously on the line.

They went to a local pub, where he had already booked a table in the restaurant section.

She sat, silent, waiting for the axe to drop.

"I'm sure you know why you are here," he had started.

She said nothing, her fists clenched deep in her long jumper sleeves, her face fixed to not let her fear show to him, feeling weeks of unfair treatment at his hand burning a hole in the pit of her stomach.

"I have been looking closely at your work," he announced.

Here goes...prepare yourself, girl. Her crippling mortgage of only six months started to flash before her eyes.

"It's very good, Cath. In fact, quite honestly at the moment I think you're wasted in your job."

She was visibly shocked and picked up her goldfish bowl of a wine glass – draining half of it at once – with a shaking hand still enveloped in sleeve. *Perhaps he was trying to sack her kindly. Perhaps this was the one and only time he was going to be nice to her – while he was tying the noose and preparing to kick away the trap door.*

"I thought..." she said, before fizzling out, all lucid thoughts gone.

"I know what you thought...mean bastard, always criticising, la la la la la. Sometimes the only way to get the best out of someone, really test them, is to push the fuck out of them; sink or swim. You swam. I'd like to make a new position for you, where you are one of our chief directors. I think you are absolutely right for the job."

He smiled. *Warm, friendly, great teeth.*

Suddenly she saw him in a totally different light, no longer the enemy. *Thank the fucking lord. Her mortgage was safe. She could stop eating her own tongue. Had she really heard this right?*

She had left the meal in a haze of drunken confusion. She barely dared face the rest of them, back at work. This was almost worse than getting sacked. She knew what their reaction would be.

****

It was difficult, her change of position.

It was a tough, competitive company with its fair share of bitches and bastards, all trampling remorselessly on each other's heads as they clawed their way to the top.

The news had been met with bitter resentment from several of the men who had thought themselves far better placed to do the job. *Fucking stupid bitch. What was John thinking? Bloody arsehole. Only just arrived himself and now right royally fucking them over. Arrogant tosser.*

And by endless digs and bitching from female counterparts.

One morning, Cath went in, head down as usual these days, to find John waiting for her at the doorway.

"Walk through with me." It was early, too early for anyone else to be in.

On every desk was a saucer of milk.

"What the hell?" She was intrigued.

"Wait in my office."

One by one, over the next hour the rest of the team came in and sat down as normal as he watched in silence.

There was giggling, a few puzzled glances and a sense of unease.

Eventually, John addressed them all.

"The milk," he said, "is for the cats. The catty, pathetic people with the catty, pathetic remarks. Cath's desk is now in my office. And any comments about this should be directed at me. Not Cath. I want this to end now. Along with the long lunch hours, the skiving, the time-wasting and the fucking huge expense sheets. I am not fucking stupid. And if you value your fucking jobs, you'll fucking absorb this information. There are a million people out there who would be glad of your jobs. And not one of you – not one – is good enough to not think that their fucking job is on the line. This ends now."

And it did.

A few weeks later, they had gone to Barbados to shoot an advert.

It was on the last night that John and Cath had been at a bar, with the others. One by one, the others had all peeled off to bed leaving them together planning the next job.

Throughout the trip, Cath had realised that she felt more towards him than was decently allowed in a working relationship – partly due to the fact that suddenly, in a glamorous location on a beautiful beach, she had become aware that she was, in fact, bothered by the fact that he was surrounded by beautiful models.

Long legs, oiled, glistening in the sun, impossibly beautiful faces. They looked almost normal on TV, or in magazines. One could almost be critical about their appearance, picking holes in any feature deemed not quite perfect.

But in the flesh, nobody could have picked holes in any of them.

Unless, of course, personality counted.

But, quite frankly, who needed a personality if they looked like that? Most of them hadn't had to go to the trouble of even developing one.

She had observed him, going about his daily work, completely unfazed by them and felt relief at his lack of interest. It hadn't occurred to her that she had any chance of him noticing her, in her outsized combats and a sweat-dripping T-shirt, with the skinny body of a prepubescent.

She was purely grateful that no-one else had grabbed his interest.

Which she knew was not how she should feel at all.

So, when he had grabbed her face and kissed her sweetly for just a bit too long, she had nearly died of shock. Her stomach had turned itself into a large, bubbling cauldron and she was quite literally shaking as they fell into his bed and he tore at her clothes, hands soft, all over her, mouth never leaving hers, while she shook and fumbled and made a mess of even trying to extract him from his trousers: quite clearly out of practice and inexperienced into the bargain.

She should have enjoyed it, but was so convulsed with every emotion imaginable from fear to adulation, that she was glad when it was over and he'd gone to sleep, cradling her tenderly. *What the fuck would they all say about this? 'Oh, so that's why she got the job. What a slag.' She'd have to get back to her own room before anyone noticed.*

She was in a dreadfully uncomfortable position, but dared not move in case she got comfortable enough to sleep. *That would be a bloody disaster. They'd make her life misery if they saw her emerging from his hotel room in the morning. But she wasn't ready to get out just yet. She wanted to look at him some more. He was fucking beautiful.* She had not grabbed a second of sleep: she'd been too busy reliving the kiss, time and time again in her mind so that she couldn't lose the memory, feeling butterflies every time.

And she was sore.

My God, she was sore.

Even her hips felt bruised.

It hadn't been an altogether unpleasant experience. He was obviously a very accomplished lover – expert even.

It was just the fact that she was so riddled with nerves and lust and disbelief and rampant fear that had somehow ruined the whole thing. And yet it had been truly fantastic and unbelievable and embarrassing *and she'd have to talk to him in the morning and try to seem unfazed and face him at breakfast and in the office and they'd all know what they'd been up to immediately*

because of her blushing problem and they'd hate her even more.
Oh fuck, yes really, oh fuck.

Oh sleep.

She needed some.

She drifted off again, uncomfortably.

It had been such a long time since the terrible, teenage fiasco with Elvis and she had not really been near anyone since.

A friendship had died as a result of that stupid twat and it had completely put her off men.

And John had been the first since then.

****

This morning, lying in bed with him in a very fine hotel, preparing to wake and go into the office as usual, she had a vast, unwavering smile on her face. It was months since that first, nervous shag.

She was truly head over heels.

She had overcome her sexual nervousness and had since enjoyed endless, mind-numbingly good sex.

He had been surly recently, but that seemed to be his wont – something he swung in and out of at a whim, with no warning, no reason. Just a moody bastard, when all was said and done – but she adored him, warts and all. It was worth all the long silences, the times he had retreated firmly into his man-cave, the shrugging off of her affections, the gaps without call or text. All worth it for the glorious times that he was all hers: loving, passionate, funny, attentive.

Hers.

He eventually awoke, stretching like a cat, arms in fists over his head as he lay, blinking the sleep from his eyes.

He rolled from the messed-up sheets and marched into the shower without a word. She took the opportunity to quickly pick some encrusted snot from her blocked nostril and to remove the previous night's smudged mascara. The sound of his habitual and furious scrubbing drowned the radio, as she strained to hear a politician arguing ferociously with a rather up-her-own-arse presenter.

As she lay on his side of the bed, enjoying his smell, the bedside table became alive with vibration as his mobile rang. It was 6 a.m.

He had always made a rule that they both turned off their phones as soon as they left work, to avoid the endless stream of calls – from the office, from clients or from shoots – that would always come his way, morning, noon and night. Such was the life of an important man. But today was a crucial day of early starts and late finishes…a huge amount to do.

She answered.

It was an unfamiliar female voice.

"John?"

"Hi… he's in the shower. Can I take a message?"

After a pause that lasted an eternity, the phone went dead.

Suddenly, Cath knew something was very wrong.

She said nothing as he dried himself off.

She said nothing as they ate breakfast.

After a perfunctory kiss, he left the hotel, went on his way to work.

No, you should never start an affair with your boss.

Cath sat on the side of the bed feeling shaky and nauseous. *It was probably nothing, the sick feeling – just a strange reaction to such an abrupt ending of a phone call.*

Every bone in her body was drenched with the fear that he had gone off her – had found someone else more attractive, funnier, more what he deserved. Someone who didn't know he was with Cath and had rung to speak to him. *He was going to leave her for someone new and fresh and exciting. Someone with big boobs.*

She couldn't face going in to work. She rang in, informed them that she was working from home and spent the morning working from her flat, doing a treatment for an advert; her mind in a scramble, unable to gather any relevant thoughts, unable to function at all. She paced around the flat endlessly, wanting to call him, wanting to call anybody. But there was no-one to call. She felt panic, horror; her heart rate had doubled, her breaths came harsh and rapid, uncontrolled. She didn't know what was wrong with her except an instinctive certainty that something was wrong. Nothing was truly tangible. Except her feeling of doom.

She finished her work and went into the office at lunchtime ready to embark on a busy afternoon.

She was hit by a commotion of gossip and chat.

A woman had appeared at the office, before open of business that morning, with three children.

A woman wanting to see her husband.

A husband who had never once confessed to those he worked with that he was married.

There had been heated words.

He had taken his children from the woman shortly afterwards – leaving her in the office he shared with Cath – and escorted them to school.

He had not returned.

The woman was still in his office as Cath walked in.

The woman had sat there, calmly, for four-and-a-half hours.

The woman stood by Cath's desk, radiating cold calm and ethereal, redheaded beauty. *Cath's desk was packed into boxes.*

The woman was easily recognisable from the last film that she had appeared in and was sitting on Cath's desk, waiting for her: waiting for Cath, spelling out her doom, the end of her job, her humiliation.

It was a humiliation they both shared, however.

The woman was devoid of make-up, her skin like porcelain: flawless except for a fine spattering of freckles, which only added to her utter gorgeousness.

"You're not the first, you know," she said coldly, "And you probably won't be the last. But be under no illusion. He may be a bastard, but he's my bastard."

Cath took her belongings and walked from her desk; through the silence so tangible she could have held it in her hands, down the stairs and into the street below.

Everything she had worked for, everything she held dear was ruined, poisoned, gone.

As she walked home, unable to face public transport, uncaring of the faces of passers-by looking into her tear-sodden face, she felt broken, alone, failed, ridiculous and stupid.

Oh so fucking stupid. Betrayed.

Lost.

She climbed the stairs to her flat. All concept of time had vanished. Time spread before her and behind her like a huge, gaping void – *full of nothing worth having, empty of everything worth anything.*

She was no longer crying.

She was in agony, recoiling from her very self, feeling so alone she wanted the world to swallow her up into nothingness.

Chapter 14

It had been nine lonely years.

Nine years of wasted life – a life now smashed at the bottom of an abyss.

Nine years of confusion, injustice. And of pain; pain for his father and mother and daughter.

And for himself.

Jude had kept his nose clean. Spoken to few. Chosen whom to trust carefully.

Always watching, observing, judging, avoiding. Always hoping that the mistake would be noticed, they would realise their error and his life would be returned.

His daughter would be 11 now. Would have just started secondary school. His angel would hate him, her brain filled with lies, un-remembering of his face, his warmth, the arms that had enclosed her lovingly every day, protecting her from the mother whose indifference and ineptitude hurt her on a daily basis.

He remembered Connie's small, fat arms, the way they clutched at Sam, the small face searching for a mother's smile, some small hint of solace, some sign that she was loved by her.

Love was something the little girl had been given in abundance by the father who adored her, now incarcerated...

and the grandparents both destroyed in one sad morning. *What would she know of love now?*

Jude ached with it, unresting, pacing, seconds turning into hours into days into months into years.

He had had no visitors for the past few years and had slipped into silence.

He was skeletal, food a necessity and not a joy – and often something his state of mind did not allow him to face. His back teeth were ground down, his jaw muscles twitched in a lock that prevented any reaction, at any time, to the hell that he watched around him.

****

His mother had visited twice.

On the first visit she sat, distanced by glass, her fingers touching his through the screen. Tears had rolled down the pale cheeks, the mouth he adored mouthed, "Why?" in a secret torment, her once handsome head of hair lay unbrushed and uncared for, further ripping him apart.

"Not me! Not me! Not me!" he had said. "I loved him, you know I did. Mum! It was Sam. It was Sam. I KNOW it was her. Please help me, Mum."

He knew she believed him, knew her faith stayed strong. *Please God that she knew.*

"My daughter. My Connie," he whispered. "Where is my daughter? You've got to look after her."

It had been the end of their time then, an hour gone in a second, with no resolution, no ending to this; she was gone, led out away from him, as he too was pulled away from her, their eyes still linked, both streaming with tears.

Chapter 15

At first Robyn had wanted to believe, had *made* herself believe. Even when everyone around shouted her down. The weight of evidence crushed her spirit and her own verdict swung like a pendulum.

There was no way it was anyone else. There had been no forced entry, no evidence of an intruder. There was evidence of Sam and Connie being in a shopping centre at the time of his death.

And she had seen.

My God, she had seen it.

It was burned into her memory, finding them like that, her son's face, turning towards her, covered in her husband's innards, looking wildly at her, caught in the act.

How could it possibly be any other way?

But there had to be an explanation. She couldn't give up hope. There had to be something.

She had wanted with all her heart to believe her son. She had been to see him, incarcerated, waiting for his trial, surrounded by killers, thieves, rapists, evil. She had wanted so much to believe that he was innocent, that a huge mistake had been made, that the son she had loved and nurtured and forgiven all these years, taught the lessons of life carefully, was not the person that she had feared. That despite all his past faults, the goodness she had always known was deep inside him had been real, not imagined, not just a vain hope. She reminded herself again and again of how hard he had tried these past two years since his daughter had been born; what a loving father he was, how he had changed. She filled her head with how much his father had adored him, how much he would have wanted her to stand by her son, as he always had when she had been too weak.

She had looked at him, suffering, in the pain that she too felt and had tried to touch him through the glass, offer him some kind of solace, tell him she knew it was all untrue.

Even after the conviction, she had been in a state of suspension, disbelief. She had been at the police station time after time, pleading, telling them that they were wrong, that they had to have faith, like her, that there had been no reason, refusing to leave.

Finally she had been taken into a waiting room, given hot, sweet, warming tea in a plastic cup, been hugged by a female officer who had sat holding her hand while all the evidence was gone through a final time with her; photos shown, fingerprints revisited, CCTV evidence of Sam and Connie's whereabouts demonstrated. There were copies of Sam's mobile phone bill calling her friend, there was evidence given by the friend of the details of their conversation. Sam had sounded fine. Certainly not like someone who had committed a murder.

And there was the shirt. The shirt worn by Jude. It was on the table in front of her, sealed in its plastic envelope, dated, labelled with Jude's initials, marked 'evidence'. It was plastered in a man's blood, now black. *She could smell it. Blood. Her husband's blood. Her husband's guts displayed before her.* The sight of it hit her in the face like a punch from an iron fist. *Her husband. Her dead husband.*

There was no mistake.

All she had thought she had known was an illusion – nothing was real. All lay smashed and wasted.

She had left. Slowly walking. Trying to hold her head high as they watched her.

Afterwards, she had returned to her home – the home that was the last remnant of her past. *The home that was to be snatched from her.*

She went from room to room, absorbing, hearing voices from happy times in her head: so loud, so real, so vivid that she thought she was possessed by demons, had entered another universe, gone back in time.

Her nails bit into her palms, carving slices from her flesh.

She could not go into her kitchen, once so warm, with its mess; the signs of life that no longer existed.

She climbed the stairs into her bedroom – their bedroom – and went to the mirror.

And she began to cut.

She had gone to the prison for a final time then, plethoric with repulsion. She hated him for what he had done. She hated herself for believing his innocence. And she hated herself for failing as a mother.

She needed to say goodbye.

Chapter 16

On the second visit, Jude's mother had been cold, distant.

She had shorn off all her hair.

She had cut words into the flesh of her arms. Words of hatred.

She looked ruined.

He knew then all was lost. *There was no going back.* He was sick to the pit of his stomach.

She had shaken her head at him, her face gaunt, the blood drained from it, almost green, transparent, ghostly; her eyes black and soulless and empty. She had looked at him without emotion. No hatred, no love, no compassion.

Nothing.

"Connie? Have you found Connie?" he had said. "Where is Connie?"

"Gone." *Wanting to hurt him now, as she was hurt – wanting to kill him, her flesh, this man she had borne. There was no doubt now in the evidence. No small chance that her son had not committed this evil. He was the devil. She despised him. She no longer wanted to remember any detail of him, no matter how small.*

This visit was to remind herself how much she loathed his every molecule and cast his face from her mind.

And to make this known to him without any doubt.

He had known then that this was her last visit; and that he was now totally alone, with nothing that he held dear in the world remaining to him.

After grieving relentlessly for seven days, his mind slowly became awash with an anger deeper than any emotion he had ever felt; seeping in to his mind like an oil-spill into the ocean, squeezing his brain in its confined space, the pain of it making his body shake, until his cell was ringing with the horrific sounds of a man's screaming; screaming that tore his vocal cords, cut his throat, echoed in the corridors, remained unchecked by shouting guards.

He was led away to solitary confinement and drugged.

Chapter 17

Robyn had left the house that afternoon. She had taken a small case with fresh underwear and a change of clothes, some spare shoes, her face cream and toothpaste. Her handbag contained all the essentials.

The new vicar was due, with his huge tribe of kids, in one week. They could no longer remain in temporary accommodation.

The church had been very kind; although they could not let her stay any longer in the house…it had been months now. She had been given every opportunity to find a new home. But she had been unable to bring herself to even seek one. They had sent the appropriate help, with forms to fill, questions to ask, things to consider; but she had refused to agree to anything. In desperation, they had found her a nice room in a women's refuge.

Friends had offered her a roof over her head. They had meant well. But the grief that gripped her soul, the depth of her loss, was tearing Robyn apart. Grief twisted her thoughts, distorting them, bending and mangling the truth.

She became too ashamed to see her friends. She imagined their derogatory comments behind closed doors, the hushed gossiping about her failings as a mother, their critical judgements of her. She could not accept their charity. She could not face the friendship offered, or believe that it was genuinely meant. The punishment she wanted and needed to inflict on herself for her own guilt was solitude. Her heart was so heavy with sadness that she no longer cared what became of her. She hated herself too much.

She had tried to see her daughter-in-law. Tried to see Connie.

They had run to their "friend's" house not far away.

Robyn had knocked on the front door, chipped and faded, many times; standing forlornly on the step like a nervous schoolgirl, peering through the letter box into the rancid hall, smelling of piss, that lay behind it.

The filthy net curtains had twitched on a few occasions. On one, Connie was clearly visible at the window, her pale, wide grey eyes peering down at her, only then to disappear quickly, as if pulled by force.

Robyn was frantic with worry. She wanted to hold her, her beautiful granddaughter, the only piece of flesh and blood that she had left. She wanted to tell her that she was still there though her life had changed out of all recognition, irreversible in its madness. She wanted to feel the heat of her beloved granddaughter in her arms, hug her until she could barely catch her breath, bury her face in the wild, curly, fresh-smelling hair, lie to her, persuade her nothing was real, it would all return to normal, it was all going to be fine.

On her final visit, the door had opened.

Sam had stood in the hall, blocking the door with her foot, preventing her entrance, only part of her angry face revealed in the darkness within.

"Murderer's mother," she had said, her voice sharp and harsh. "Don't come here again. Ever. I'll call the police. You're not coming near her."

The door had slammed shut. From inside, came the high-pitched wail of a child screaming.

And then silence, sudden and ominous; followed by the slam of a door.

Robyn had stood still, for what seemed like an eternity and then resumed her knocking, unrelenting, needing to see the only thing that she had left.

There was no answer, nothing at all.

People were gathering on the street, gawping at the spectacle, whispering, nudging, giggling at the sight of the middle-aged woman, hair butchered, in clumps, like a victim of cancer; clothes still neat, with her suitcase.

She had dropped her head in pain and despair and left, pushing through the gathered onlookers – some looking away in embarrassment, some openly staring at her as if she was insane. She had hurried away, down the busy street, her face damp with tears.

All she now had left in the world was in her bag.

She had gone to the refuge where she would now live.

Chapter 18

Fuck fuck fuck fuck fuck fuck fuck.

It had all gone horribly, terribly, dreadfully wrong.

Cath was no longer eating and had shrunk even further into a tiny scrap of a thing. She had huge circles under her eyes, her hair was unwashed and unbrushed.

She smelt.

Bad.

She was still gorged with every feeling: toe-curling embarrassment, anger, emptiness, sadness, fear, loss.

She longed for the old days of fat Cath, when she knew her place and her purpose and had Cherry to lead her astray, abuse her, protect her and make her laugh. Missed their shared humour, their sisterly love. All she had accomplished in the years since that time, so long ago now, felt empty and pointless. All the effort, the skills she had gained, the fat she had lost, the career, the apartment, all seemed worthless. None of it had made her happy. She had achieved all this out of a drive and will to shed the old Cath, the underdog and to come out on top: to show the world she was really something. And now it was all spoilt. The bits that remained seemed devoid of any remote appeal.

News travelled fast in the world of advertising.

John and his wife had tried to wreck her reputation in the industry – rumour-mongering about her childish infatuation with him, her 'having to go' as she was 'stalking him'. But they had fooled nobody except themselves – and it was they who were being laughed at more than Cath.

In an industry crammed to the gills with bastards like John – messed-up, hung-over, in-demand, demanding bastards with families awaiting them at home, while they humped the latest piece of young skirt over the desk in the office after hours – John had shown himself to be the usual, tedious cliché. He'd got caught and was squirming like a maggot as his reputation nose-dived and his true identity as a right royal turd emerged publicly, like a butterfly from its pupa.

In the cutthroat world of advertising, there were a million young, hopeful film-hyenas picking the bones of this latest scandal, revelling in his stupidity, gathering it as ammunition to bring him down. *His card was marked. The wanker.* They hadn't forgiven him for his treatment of them after Cath's promotion. *The shit.* And now he had embarked on the long and slippery black run that would be the next stage of his career. And they were all happy to bend over backwards in support of Cath, to help push him over the brow of the hill.

Not that Cath realised any of this.

She knew some of the kind words to her were said with a smirk. She knew they were laughing at her – *yet another in a long line of young, gullible hopefuls who had fucked their own careers by following their hormones instead of their brains.* She knew how it worked.

Once a slag, always a slag in the film industry. She could not face the gossip, the bitching, the environment. Or the expectation that she might 'put out'.

And her inner dread and deep humiliation prevented her from being able to face turning up somewhere – on day one of some new job – in the knowledge that they'd have already all had a great time discussing her indiscretions. And probably her knockers.

She was simply not strong enough.

She was excruciatingly lonely.

She had many friends in the industry, but nobody close; nobody she could really bare her soul to, who understood her implicitly. She didn't know whom to trust.

She longed for the days of 'fat Cath' and 'funny Cherry' – partners in crime, close as sisters, thick as thieves.

She longed for Cherry.

Oh, how she regretted Elvis.

She had never even liked him that much.

Chapter 19

Initially, when Cath and Cherry had both started their simultaneous – but never together – shagfest with "Elvis", swapping horror stories of his personal hygiene and his small gnarled penis, it had all been a teenage laugh.

"Have you seen the end? It looks like it's been chewed by a dog!"

"No! It looks like the end of a sausage roll that's exploded in the oven!"

"Do ya wannit? Do ya wannit all? Huff puff!"

"No! I don't wannit all! Just the end!"

"Just the end with the pubes and not the other end! Eeuurrgghh! Who would actually say do you want it all?"

"Only him, I think. And Freddy Mercury."

They were in the bedroom they shared, in huge, out-of-shape T-shirts and vast, woolly slipper-socks; lying on their backs on the bed, bums wedged up against the wall, feet up in the air, heels resting on the peeling wallpaper.

"Does he squeeze your boobs like he's moulding plasticine?"

"He can't find mine! He hasn't even bothered looking! Mind you, I'm still waiting to grow some."

"Horrible, wet, slobbery lips too. He dribbles. It's like kissing defrosted liver. Or a St. Bernard with a saliva problem."

"And have you seen his face when he, you know…"

"Comes?"

"Yes, his cum-face… Eurgh! Eurgh! Eurgh!"

They both started pretend-running, still lying on their backs, soles of feet pounding into the wall, legs still in the air, squealing with the thought of it.

Cath's eyes were screwed shut in horror, her hands slapped over her mouth, filled with a prudish repulsion of the thought of his bodily fluids exploding inside her, dribbling out of her, pungent smell filling the air when he had finished with a grunt.

The pair of them were talking in not-so-hushed whispers, words magnified in volume by their shared bursts of laughter, not so subtle in their communal living space. They could still hear him clattering around in the filthy, squalid kitchen – *checking to find the last dirty cup to put his third-hand tea bag in, probably. Dirty sod.*

"Has he ever come all over your face so it's dripped into your eyes as you're trying to get away? Has he? Has he? Has he grunted and got you right in the ear as he spurts?"

Cath was screaming now, really screaming, top volume with repulsion, she had clamped her hands over her ears to block out Cherry's stream of filth.

"OH GOD. YOU. ARE. DIS. GUS. TING. La la la la la can't hear you!"

"COME… IN… YOUR… EYES!" Cherry was on top of her now, jumping up and down on top of her, astride her stomach; dry-humping her, being Elvis.

"D'ya wannit awl, bitch? Phwaugh, phwaugh, I'm coming! Aargh! Aargh! Ta love! Snore."

Cath was squirming, squealing, trying to wriggle away, writhing underneath Cherry as her friend pinned her down; knees now on her forearms, flattening them to the bed as she viciously rubbed Cherry's breasts with her palms in a circular motion, as if she was swimming on them, or performing in the intro of 'It Ain't Half Hot Mum'.

"Cor babe, noice balloons!" Cherry shrieked into her ears in a gruff, dumb male impersonation. " Open yer legs and let me in!"

"AAAAARRRRRGGGGGHHHHHH!"

"Cam on, jast a quick won before the footie, you slag!"

Cherry now was face to face with Cath; directly on top of her, pelvis on hers, hands encircling her wrists in an iron grip, licking and slobbering all over her face, all over her shut eyes, like a randy Labrador, humping away at her at a million miles an hour, roaring like a bear in her ears.

"Can I join you, ladies?" The words broke through their laughter.

Cherry rolled off, immediately, in shock and they lay sniggering and red with mortification, trying to feign innocence, which slowly turned into disbelief, as they simultaneously took in the spectacle before them.

It was Elvis!

****

To Elvis, the situation in the squat was a dream come true.
Two young girls.
He had them both to himself.
Never at the same time, sadly.

But sex on a plate when he wanted it, with two schoolgirls, ripe with innocence and inexperience, loving it, *loving his cock in them.*

Not one for foreplay was he. He liked to get in there straight away. No point in fine detail.

He was a coming machine. And they loved it. The filthy, little slappers.

He loved fantasising about Monica, the top bird from the café round the corner with the great barnet, while he was inside them. She'd given him so many knock-backs, the bitch. Always coming on to him, letting him buy her drinks and then not putting out.

God, how he fancied her.

Nice ripe arse, great juddering breasts, too much lipstick.

Lipstick that just belonged all over the end of his cock. She was all woman that one, not like these two.

But they were good for his credibility amongst his mates. Wanted to hear about them endlessly they did. And he'd only embellished a little bit. About their multiple orgasms and everything. He didn't think that either of them had had one in reality...*(how could you tell?)* but it didn't bother him; as long as they were happy with the arrangement, it was good for him.

It had only been the night before, in the local – stale with ageing halitosis combined with the subtle hint of b.o. (*bring back smoking, all is forgiven*) and enough to make your eyes water as soon as you walked in – that he'd been telling a group of them about 'having the pair of them at once'. *All over him like a rash, one sitting on his face with her young, fresh cunt, juicy above him, sweet smelling, plump thighs wobbling above his eyes, while the other was sucking him as hard as a new-born lamb.*

It had only been a small lie – and his penis had risen uncontrollably hard in his Peacocks' chinos while he was describing it, obvious to all as he told them every detail, picturing it in his mind as he spoke, desperate for sex as he walked home.

He had found a bargain-bucket prostitute on the way home, needing to shag something new – unable to wait as he had got himself into such a frenzy. Twenty quid's worth of expert attention in an alley. With a snaggle-toothed hag who must have been seventy, with thighs that were a catastrophe of deep, dark purple stretch marks hanging in folds out of her tight, pink PVC pelmet.

She'd been grateful of the money, of course, grinning at him expectantly afterwards, with a hand like a bunch of bananas outstretched for the cash.

It almost looked like a man's hand. Surely not!

He trembled, paid and shuffled off as quickly as he could.

****

That night, as he lay in bed with the girls only a few feet away from him, in their room, doing their 'chatting thing' before sleeping, the thoughts of the prostitute returned. He shuddered. He walked into the kitchen for a much-needed drink, delving into the sink full of dirty crockery for a cup almost hygienic enough to drink out of.

And as he rummaged quietly through the bin for a cigarette butt long enough to smoke, he heard the girls clearly. *They were laughing and making schoolgirl sounds of sex!*

He couldn't believe his ears.

Creeping to outside their door, he was almost certain they were taking the piss out of him. His fury rising, he opened the door a crack to hear more, silent in his eavesdropping.

They had been drinking Blue Nun all evening and were too pissed to be successfully quiet.

To his surprise and abject joy, one was on top of the other, writhing, grinding, pinning her down, licking, and laughing. He knew it was in mockery, but maybe they'd been fantasising about him screwing both of them – of them screwing each other – as he had.

He had shed his trousers outside the door and entered, watching them.

****

When the girls had finally noticed him, he had lost all control. He was standing over them, his penis soft as a marshmallow in his hand – still in his D.Ms and socks and white vest – and was trying strenuously to force some life back into it. Eyes glazed, he was a disgusting sight.

"Can I join you, ladies?"

For the first time, they had in reality really turned him on, really done it for him... he'd have done anything at that moment to be able to join in. *But what had happened to his willy? One too many, obviously. Shit! What a wasted opportunity. He couldn't let this chance go.* He carried on thrashing away, rabidly, with gathering speed.

"Carry on as you were, girls," he said.

They looked at the sight before them, grotesque in his desperation and then turned to each other open-mouthed, agog with repulsion.

At least Cherry was agog with repulsion. Cath, who had never known attention of any form – with any man – before Elvis, was just agog.

Any form of normality for Cath had long since been skewed by the activities that Cherry had decreed acceptable over the last few years. Cath no longer had any idea of her own morals – any idea of what she really felt about anything. But she was prepared to go along with anything, purely to remain desirable to both Cherry (as her friend, on whom she relied to even sustain any form of personality, so far removed was she from herself) and also Elvis; the one man who had ever showed her any desire, who had been attracted to her rotund, giggling, desperate frame when all else had treated her with ridicule.

Cherry's eyes widened as she heard the words, "I only need a minute. Try sucking it."

And her friend – far from recoiling and mocking Elvis as she had expected – lay back on the bed, legs akimbo and welcomed his pathetic, wilting, blue penis with her hands outstretched, reaching for him. *After all they'd just been saying about him.*

Cherry moved back on the bed, sitting with her bum on her hands, knees around her ears, clutching them for security as Elvis attempted to enter Cath without apology, humping away on top of her like a demented jackrabbit. She was too shocked at the appalling vision to speak. He started to pump a bit harder, for variety, in the vain hope that a change in pace would stimulate his spongy knob into some form of rigidity.

Cath was shrieking, "Yes, yes, yes!" as if to pretend she was in some kind of ecstasy, although it was obvious that even a chance of entry was out of the question.

Cherry tried to make a sound, to say *no*, to say *stop*, to shout *Cath! Don't do it! Not with me here. Not at all!*

But nothing came forth from her lips.

She turned her eyes away at the sound of Elvis grunting, shouting, "Fuck. Fuck. Fuck," in rhythm as he pounded at her friend – her friend whose legs lay open in gratitude to this monster. She heard the vile, wet sounds of her friend having greedy, needy, animal sex; seeing it in her mind even though she now faced the wall. *It had obviously got harder after all that effort. He was obviously in. Euurgghh.*

"STOP IT, CATH! STOP!" she finally heard herself shout.

She felt sick.

Warm saliva was flooding into her mouth without relent; she was swallowing harder and harder. *Oh God, she was going to puke any second.*

And then, Cath grabbed Cherry by the wrist. And pulled Cherry forcefully towards them. And then lifted her head towards Cherry's face, mouth open, tongue reaching for hers, her fingers refusing to slacken their grip as Cherry tried to escape from her grasp.

In all their exploits, this was a step too far for Cherry.
An amusing situation, prior to this.
And now – pure horror.
It had been a laugh.
But this...this was far from a laugh. This was abhorrent.

Cherry now saw Elvis for what he was – all the fun gone in an instant, overtaken by pure, unadulterated loathing and disgust. And as for Cath...

For Cherry, something fundamental in their friendship had changed; a switch in her brain had been flicked.

There was no going back.

She felt a horror that overwhelmed her.

She needed to erase from her mind the full, foul glory of that night forever.

When Elvis had finally finished with a resounding snort and rolled off, shining with perspiration, both he and Cath looked around at her.

Cherry was turned away from them, rocking backwards and forwards like a mental patient.

She got up silently, unable to even look at either of them.

"You're a fucking animal," she whispered, to neither of them in particular. "And you..." She turned to Cath. "You can keep your dirty hands off me and never come near me again. We were supposed to be friends."

That night, with Cath begging and crying, not understanding, pitiful in her despair, Cherry left the flat with her few belongings, never to return.

It was the last time that she saw either of them.

Cath felt as if her world had ended.

She could not understand what had happened.

Why was she being punished?

What had she done that had been so bad? She loved Cherry, would have done anything for her.

How was it any worse than what had gone on before?

She stayed with Elvis for several more months, clinging on to him, needing his sex as a mark that she was still wanted by somebody – anybody. Her world had exploded without warning.

She cried and cried; tried to contact Cherry in the salon in which she worked, tried to make any form of sense of things for herself. But there was nothing back, no glimmer of hope, just a huge, heavy darkness all around her.

The more she clung to Elvis, the more he despised her, pushed her away, made her know how little he cared for her. He stopped coming back to the flat.

On the rare occasions that he did return, she tried to cook for him, talk to him, woo him – sick as he made her now feel. She accepted his body gratefully, smelling muskily of the scent of other women; not daring to turn him away as that would leave her with nothing, no-one. Hating him, loving him in self-torture, crawling away into a black hole of self-pity in her own brain that threatened to devour her whole; not eating, caring, not caring.

Work was her only refuge.

And work she did; day and night without reprieve, using toil as a way to block out life, tiredness as a way to deaden all thought.

****

And now, nine years on, having built up her life from the moment she had finally left him – made good, made friends, made a new Cath – it was all in tatters once more.

And because of a man.

Again.

She suddenly missed Cherry like never before. Cherry had left a gaping, deep hole in her soul, impossible to fill. She had been like her sister for sixteen years – and had vanished without so much as a single call since those days.

Nine years without her suddenly seemed like a lifetime.

She knew then that she had to find her.

Chapter 20

Mabel was waiting.

Cherry glanced at her in terror, her own face set in the expression of a rabbit glued to the road with concrete boots on. She was tugging madly at the wild, Afro hair of her previous client; a not-quite-so-young-model, who had come in for a loose, relaxed, natural-looking perm and now seemed to resemble a maniac with a licked finger deep inside a dodgy socket.

"It will settle in a few washes," Cherry said. "It has to be this tight to start with so that it lasts."

Saffron was due to go to Paris fashion week later that day.

Botoxed to Jackie Stallone weirdness, teeth bleached to infinity, brows plucked off and tattooed back on, skin the colour of gravy, she had been attempting to hold back the years to match the fictitious date of birth she had been boasting for ever – and the "naturally" wavy hair that was her trademark was, in fact, as straight as the proverbial poker.

Cherry had been perming it in top secret for years, joining the ranks of various surgeons who all conspired in the upholding of her natural, untouched good looks.

This was nothing short of career disaster; a calamity of epic proportions.

For both of them.

Saffron rose from her chair with fists clenched, spitting huge blobs of drug-fuelled saliva into Cherry's face at a single millimetre's range, as she hissed, "You haven't heard the last of this, you stupid, little bitch. No-one makes me look stupid…"

Cherry tried to apologise, face as red as a radish, cheeks boiling hot with a blush that had risen from somewhere by her belly button and emerged, mottled up her neck, finishing just below her eyes. She put out her hand to take the very non-glamorous, black, nylon cape that swathed the model's shoulders. But it was slapped out of the way with a two-tone-talon'd-never-washed-a-dish-in-its-life hand.

Saffron attempted to make her exit, picking her Gucci freebie bag from the floor; but the strap was caught on the underside of the revolving chair wheels, spinning it around at top speed, until it freed itself before she was expecting it. She lost her footing on the marble floor, heels sparking and slithering, her handbag expelling its contents across the salon.

A chemist's counter of pills and potions rolled around over the tiles, along with loose change, moth-eaten, old make-up and a couple of ageing Tampax that had half made it out of their wrappers, ends inflated and grey with grime.

And a large bag of white powder, Clingfilm wrapped.

A vast bag, in fact.

The kind of quantity that would have put someone away for many years for dealing.

A silence fell across the salon.

It had been closed for the morning to allow privacy for Saffron, who always demanded it and was accustomed to getting her own way, about everything, always. Mabel, as Cherry's lunch-date, was the only member of the public – except the staff

– who was an allowed exception, as Cherry had lied that she was her mother.

Mabel had been happily sucking on Ginger Nuts, false teeth in a handkerchief in her lap, a cup of tea vibrating in her shaky hand.

Saffron was on her hands and knees, as were the rest of the staff, foraging on the floor like refugees after a drop of food parcels.

But all eyes were on the package...except Saffron's.

She had not yet noticed and was still swearing obscenities, top volume, like a fishwife; her usual mid-Atlantic drawl replaced by her natural Liverpudlian. Some of the abuse was an education in new insult techniques and was being noted for future use by some of the younger hairdressers.

As she crawled on the floor, all eyes upon her, she came across the package and stopped screaming, instantly silent.

She looked up, met with nine pairs of eyes and stopped herself from picking it up, hand stuck midair; time and space for her having now stopped. Hair was all over her face, stuck in her lip-gloss, a false eyelash had peeled off and was now stuck firmly to her top lip, like a highly-trimmed moustache.

Her skirt had shuffled itself upwards until she was virtually wearing it around her neck – and her lack of underwear shone like a beacon, disturbing to all.

"Did you forget something this morning, dear? Were you in a rush?" – an old voice from the other end of the salon. Mabel had been disturbed by the commotion and torn herself away from *Good Housekeeping*, reinserting her teeth for clarity, to be met with an unflattering front-end view of Saffron's nether regions.

"Just as well you're in here and not outside, my dear. That's an offence." She popped her gnashers out again, covered in half-chewed biscuit and resumed her Ginger Nut conquest. *You didn't get a view like that in Good Housekeeping. Youngsters, these days. You could tell they hadn't been through a war.*

Saffron – on a probationary period with her agency (having being found in the coat cupboard at The Ivy, whilst at a post-show meal with important clients, face down in a bag of coke) was about to have a coronary. Any thoughts of her disastrous new hair catastrophe had now flown out of her head, replaced by the horror of her current predicament. The horrible realisation was upon her that in front of many people (and probably on the salon CCTV) her well-publicised drug problem had been proved once more – and was probably captured forever for posterity on film.

Not only that, but only the night before she had been on *The Jonathon Ross Show* declaring herself clean and ready to once again take the modelling world by storm.

Mabel's comment had inadvertently sounded like a threat.

Cherry helped Saffron to her feet.

A cup of coffee and a fag were put silently into her shaking hand and she was dusted off, sat down forcibly and handed back her belongings.

All of them.

"As I said," continued Cherry, never missing a beat, "The waves will drop in a matter of days to be much more natural. And you'll find that this look is actually very cutting edge. You'll be leading the way, yet again. You just see."

"Yes. If that's the case, we shall keep this just between us. Yes?"

The strange drawl of universal model-speak had returned, the panic in the voice tangible, the eyes imploring.

"Yes." Cherry knew that her own neck had just been prised from the chopping block. "Just between us."

Seconds later – the salon rapidly emptied of the model – Cherry hauled a startled Mabel from her chair and danced round the room with her, toes being trampled, holding the old lady up as she lurched unsteadily to the applause of the others.

"I should be so lucky, lucky nearly fucky, I should be so lucky in love!" she sang: her career obviously just saved by some divine intervention.

"Come on, Mabel, lunch is on me!"

Half an hour later they were both tucking into a vast plate of Luigi's Special Lunch Deal Spaghetti Bolognese in a tiny Italian restaurant behind Harrods, having spent that entire time convulsed with laughter at the morning's events.

Mabel and Cherry had by now struck up a strange, but fantastic friendship and met at least once a week for a roundup of events. They had one main area of interest in common and that was dating.

****

Cherry had now met up with her new boyfriend on many occasions and it was getting serious. Well, serious for Cherry. At least, she thought it was. He was wildly unpredictable and ranged from seeming adoration to raging indifference. It was part of his charm.

He was a rogue – in the true meaning of the word – that she could work out.

But he seemed mostly to adore her and she certainly felt as if she was falling for him.

In a big way.

He had eventually confessed to being an airline pilot for British Airways – not quite as glamorous as she'd hoped from first impressions. But at least it had a uniform, wads of money and the added bonus of him disappearing regularly. This meant that she could retreat once more into a comfortable squalor in front of the TV, whilst eating Pot Noodle and cold spaghetti hoops straight from the can – instead of transforming herself rapidly after work into a vision of unadulterated (in a certain light) beauty, in order to stun him with her gorgeousness and keep him keen. Which was always a time-consuming and effort-filled process and one that she could only maintain for limited periods of time before feeling suicidal.

She had kept Mabel up to date with the entire dating saga, information which Mabel hoovered up greedily; advising her, humouring her, goading her, whilst simultaneously reliving her own gracefully disgraceful past.

Mabel, on the other hand, was slowly making her way through an entire catalogue of lonely men (who had joined a dating agency for eligible people of a certain age) one by one.

She only ever had one date with each.

When she had no responses to her adverts, she would instead pay for the services of surprised, male escorts; who were always grateful that she let them out of her clutches – sex free – at the end of the date, to escape back to a land of younger ladies in need.

Occasionally, however, she would offer one lucky gent such a tremendous, financial bonus (and a night in a 5-star hotel room, should they really take her fancy) that they would have been mad to turn her down. And she would have a night of pretending to herself that she was young and beautiful – and making them do anything she desired.

Which was Karma Sutra with knobs on.

Providing that she had remembered to take her medication, of course, and her body wasn't so shaky and rigid that only a quick servicing was the order of the day.

All the gory details would in turn be relayed to an open-mouthed Cherry, who would sit in silence, leaning across the table of wherever they were lunching, in an effort to urge Mabel to speak quietly about her exploits.

This was always tricky as Mabel – her hearing not quite up to scratch (and also used to speaking to folks of her vintage, with the same deficiency) would follow Cherry's lead and lean in herself. She would then turn the volume up several notches instead of down, as she took it as a sign that Cherry was not able to hear her. Invariably, the entire restaurant would fall into a hush, as all diners strained to hear Mabel's tales of debauchery; while Mabel's hearing aid would pick up the sounds of her false teeth as they fell down from the top gums – exposing two layers of teeth on top of one another at the bottom and naked, shrunken gums at the top – and whistle eerily as she whispered at the top of her voice.

****

This meal, they were still discussing the downfall of Saffron.

"So what is the problem with white powder?" Mabel asked. "Every presentable, young lady should travel with a means of washing her smalls. You never know when you are going to be caught short. Perhaps she had a small bladder problem that she wished to remain discreet about. Hence the need to remove her soiled underpants prior to her arrival at the Salon."

"Have you not heard of cocaine, Mabel?" Cherry was now screeching with muffled laughter. "NOT washing powder!"

"Oh. I see. How silly of me. Uppers and downers in my day, dear. I've done both. And smoked pot. And opium... now that was an interesting experience. Only pot these days, mind – for pain relief don't you know."

"Cocaine is all over the place these days, Mabel; half of London seems to be doing it. Not me though... two glasses of wine and I'm anybody's."

"One sniff of a barmaid's apron and I am! Did I tell you about this week's young man? I did rather like him. Nervous fellow, very clean and well turned out, though. From a small ad in the back of *Horse and Hound*. We started off in here, funnily enough. And then I kidnapped him by way of a taxicab and took him to a lovely little bed and breakfast around the corner from here. He wasn't the sort to have appreciated the finery of an hotel and my accountant is a little suspicious of me at the moment. I didn't want him to think I'm misappropriating my own funds. He goes to church, poor man. Anyway, when we got inside, instead of being discreet when I asked to have a room, he said I was his mother! The proprietor looked very dubious, I must say. When I finally got my corset off and requested that he made a start in the proceedings, he started to cry. It transpires that I was his first date as a male escort and he'd chosen me carefully as he thought he was – how do I put it – 'safe' with me. He was doing it to earn enough money for an engagement ring. Strange, weedy little fellow. So I let him off with a spanking only. No rumpy-pumpy at all. But afterwards, he was very chipper and asked if he could see me again! What in God's name do you make of that?"

"Was it the spanking? Perhaps you've educated him in ways he'd never even thought of. Maybe his girlfriend has a big smile on her face following that!"

"Definitely not. She was a born-again Christian type who would only entertain the act of copulation if he married her. I think I may have been the start of their downfall as a betrothed couple. I feel terribly guilty."

"You've probably saved him from a life of boredom, Mabe. Think of it as a favour. Are you going to see him again?"

"Certainly not. I've a new one lined up for this week that looks like an absolute darling. He's my age."

"Oh my God. Have you gone mad? No nice, nubile, young flesh to grapple with? You're obviously losing your touch! Someone of your age might well die on the job... oh, I'm sorry..."

"Anyway, my dear, enough of me. What about you and your chappie? Is he around at the moment or flying above us as we speak? I'd love to meet him."

"That you will. I wanted to ask you over to mine next week so you can give me your honest opinion. It's going well. A bit weird – he has constant phone conversations on his mobile, arranging to meet people left, right and centre whenever we are together. And a bit evasive – as men seem to be. But a great snogger. And I think I'm about to finally make it back to his beautiful Docklands flat. So far, I've seen photos of it, but can't engineer going there. But he's said we could spend the weekend there, next weekend. Don't suppose we'll come up for air! And it saves me having to muck out my flat with a pitchfork in preparation for a romantic evening. All this tidying is making me sick."

Mabel's shaky hand deposited a vast forkful of spaghetti onto the pristine, white tablecloth.

Spaghetti was by far her favourite meal, in part due to her stubbornness.

She had never been one to give up – and as her disease steadily progressed, had been forced to give up soup of all kinds, anything slippery and most puddings… it was impossible to get them into her mouth. Spaghetti at least was windable around the fork, so gave her a small chance of reaching her face before she lost it.

She looked upon meals like this in the same way as she looked upon her stairs: something to continue with until the bitter end, something to keep her limbs in training. She lived in fear that giving up any of her daily events would be the start of the final slide into oblivion and a wheelchair. She was far too proud and mule-like to give in to the demands of her disintegrating, old body.

She stabbed the escapee pasta with the fork, on top of the tablecloth, twisted once more using both hands and scraped it into her mouth, which was suspended barely two inches from the table. It really was like dining at the chimps' tea party eating with the old lady. Cherry never knew what would happen next, but was always guaranteed to have superb fun. *It was always just a question of ignoring gawping onlookers and trying to pretend that the conversation was remotely normal – in both content and volume.*

Lunch over, and feeling a bit tipsy following half a bottle of cheap, Italian plonk, Cherry bundled back to work hoping that her afternoon's celebrity waxing was not as eventful as her morning.

Chapter 21

Loneliness ground at Robyn's soul relentlessly. All her tears had been shed. She was run dry, numb; all feelings pushed to the back of her brain, banished. If she let any thought in, even for a second, she knew that she would lose control and never regain it, *be lost forever.*

Her day had become a strange pattern of unnecessary routine. She would wake from a restless sleep in an uncomfortable, unfamiliar bed and rise. She would wash, scrubbing brutally at her skin for over an hour before breakfast. She was red-raw, her skin now so thin and over-cleaned that it was cracking: weeping at the elbows, knuckles, behind the knees. She would then disinfect the squalid bathroom with the bleach provided, cleaning the plug chain with a spare toothbrush, cleansing every millimetre of cold, hard enamel, oblivious to the irate shouting of those waiting, queuing outside.

Dressed in the same sombre clothes as the day before and the weeks before that, she would walk – head down, not speaking – to the dining area where food was provided for all; and sit alone if she was able, not responding to any human contact, to any communication.

Then back to her minimal, possession-free cabin of a room where she would sit in prayer, eyes shut, the whole world blocked out, reciting passages from the bible, remembering its teachings, chanting as if it were a mantra – anything to pass the day without thought, reach night time and the welcome relief of another day being over.

The hostel was, in its way, a prison to her.
Outside was too terrifying to contemplate.
This prison seemed freer than the outside; where nothing was true, everything was a lie. Here felt like a place of relative safety, an escape from hell.
She was rooted inside by fear of life, of loss, although she had nothing left to lose.
The people who ran it were pleasant and caring, tried to reach out to this sad and lonely woman; to reach in and pull out what was now hidden deep inside.

The hostel was mainly used as a refuge for those who were homeless, or in danger, or who could merely not cope with life.
Some came running from violent husbands, seeking a vestige of safety, often with sad-eyed children with them. They would not stay long; they would be found new accommodation where their violent counterparts could no longer track them down, where the threat of pain or death was no longer to be their life, and they could start afresh.
Others were there for longer, being rehabilitated, helped to cope, find work, be able to breathe and live, find hope.
Some, only very few, were there because there was no hope, no escape. Not insane, not criminal, but terminally lost, unable to cope with the outside world at all. People had gone through amazing ordeals, unbelievable trials and survived with all but their souls intact. Others had unbreakable spirit, despite unimaginable misery in their lives. All were damaged in some way.

Mary ran it.

****

Mary had been held hostage in a room, in a flat above a shop in Lewisham, for over four years.

Her husband had kept her prisoner there.

A violent and possessive man, he had once seen her talking in the street to a neighbour, shortly after they had moved to the area. He had become convinced, totally without reason that his wife, whom he had adored, was going to embark on an affair with this man.

That week – having driven himself into psychosis with his insane jealousy and after many brutal rows – he confined Mary to the flat, belting her wrists to the radiator where they burnt to the bone, slowly.

After complaints from the shop below of the shouting and banging on the radiator, he returned from work in a fury. Having made apologies for his wife's "agoraphobia and mental problems" he had gone upstairs; anger a fire consuming every atom of his body.

"You're trying to get away – to be with him, aren't you?" Cold rage made his voice quiet.

Her pleas and begging made no difference. His love had turned into hatred. Such was his insane state of mind.

That night, he had blinded Mary in both eyes with a cigarette lighter.

Nobody had responded to the screams.

It was an area dense with shops with flats above. The shops were empty at night. Nobody ever stuck their nose into anyone else's business; it wasn't worth the repercussions. They were all used to the sounds of rowing and screaming. Everybody was allowed to just "get on with it" without being interfered with.

He had told his neighbours that his wife had left him, told his work colleagues the same.

Nobody ever came to look for Mary... his jealousy had kept her friendless for years. He had not allowed her contact with her family back in Ireland.

Nobody knew that she was gone.

The windows of the flat were nailed down so that they opened only a fraction to allow the stench of Mary's excrement to escape. She was kept on a rope, where she could reach the bucket that was her toilet and her jug of water, but not the window... he'd found her screaming for help at the window on the one occasion he had not tied her – he couldn't have that. The door was locked. There was no escape.

He fed and washed her. In his own way, he still loved her. But love to him meant control, obedience.

After four years, Mary no longer knew what month, what year it was. But she never lost her faith. She was not quite broken. She still trusted in God.

One day, he went to work as normal, but had forgotten to tie her.

She was too frightened to shout and break the window in case she was not rescued – again, he would know and she would pay the consequences with her flesh.

So she had groped her way to the drawers and found paper and a pen. She knew that the window could open an inch before the nails prevented further movement, as she could feel the breeze on her face. She did not know if the pen worked. But it had been worth a try.

She wrote, "HELP ME" and the number of the flat, shakily on bits of torn paper and posted them out of the window.

For the whole day, she stood at the window, unseeing, listening for footsteps – so that she could post the notes out of the small gap, hopefully, to the pavement below as someone passed, praying they would look up and see her, help her.

Praying that it wouldn't be him, back early.

He would surely kill her for her actions.

After lunch, one of the shop owners, having passed twice to see crumpled fragments of paper dropped from the window, picked one up and read it.

That afternoon, Mary had been rescued. Taken to Lewisham Hospital where she remained under police guard for many weeks, she was finally free of him.

She was eventually taken to the hostel.

Following her long and gradual recovery, she worked there as a volunteer.

These days, she ran the place.

Better than any other living person could have done, with the knowledge and compassion coming only from bitter experience, the school of life, not from schools of learning.

****

Mary was worried about this poor woman, this vicar's wife who had lost everything. She had called the doctor and antidepressants had been prescribed, but not taken.

She had tried talking, but to no avail. Most of her residents gave in eventually to Mary's kindness, her huge Irish heart, and her warmth.

But this lady was different; proud, a huge wall of silence and privacy around her, almost a hostility that nobody could break through.

Mary, finally, after three months of laborious effort, broke her personal rule.

She sat her down and explained her own story, something that she had only done once before.

At first, there had been no response. But after three or four minutes of uncomfortable silence, the crying started.

It was an eerie, animalistic sound from the pits of the soul, relentless and alarming.

Mary had finally broken through.

Robyn had finally broken.

But it was positive. Robyn started taking her tablets, the welcome numbness making her feel a little better, able to get through each day a little easier. She started to speak to the other residents, to occasionally smile.

It seemed that she was taking the first small steps to coping, to recovery.

Chapter 22

Cherry was hung-over.

The devil in her head was going at it like hammer and tongs with a small, red-hot and extremely sharp pickaxe.

If she stooped, there was some small relief.

If she stood tall, the immense pain rang loud like a clock-tower bell, deep within the sockets of her bloodshot pig-eyes, sending kaleidoscopic patterns onto the inside of her lids if she tried to close them.

She felt the warm bitterness of saliva rise and raced to the toilet where she jack-knifed over the bowl like a lorry on ice, spewing hot torrents of bile and identifiable chunks of food, some from meals she had no recollection of even eating. Some of the frothing brew hit the seat. The rest trickled south, clinging to the outside of the bowl, depositing small peaks of solid gunk at intervals on its travel. There appeared to be sweetcorn on the floor. *How interesting. She hardly ever ate sweetcorn.*

They'd had a great night.

He'd told her that he loved her.

Actually, she remembered, perhaps it had been the other way around.

They had met in a small, basement pub by Charing Cross station, where the wine was good, the olives succulent and the bread stale.

But it hadn't mattered.

They had been seeing each other for weeks now and Cherry had fallen hard. Still wary, still nervous of him, slightly overawed by his confident nature and left-of-centre remarks, but loving him in a lustful way, anyway.

After drinking way too much, they had travelled to a beautiful, wharf-side restaurant and attempted to eat steak. Cherry's head was already spinning. He was intense, looked into her eyes a little too much, his hand lingering between her legs as the waitress took their order. Pressing her thighs together to prevent his entry only made him delve deeper as Cherry tried to remain composed, tried to explain to the waitress – who was pitifully aware of what was going on beneath the tablecloth – how she would like her steak.

He had remained, expressionless, fingers deep, talking to the waitress about the wine list for far too long. The waitress had blushed as his eyes met hers, without looking away, as his hands worked Cherry.

"Anyone would think that you were trying to shock her. Or pull her."

The waitress had gone.

Cherry was flushed with horror.

It was typical of him.

His behaviour was always on the wrong side of decency, always pushing the boundaries.

"Don't you like being watched, Cherry my love?" he said simply. "I do. I would like us to be watched together. I think we do something very special together. Something worth seeing. Don't you?"

She was silent. Did he really mean that? And if so, the special bit – or the voyeuristic bit? Perhaps she was just a little prudish.

Maybe it was real love.

Maybe real love meant no boundaries, no fear, and no regret.

Maybe he was just a weirdo.

But he was gorgeous. He seemed to be obsessed by her. Texts a score a day. Calls, loud and dirty, always when she was at work, or waking her in the early hours, or when she was on the bus; telling her exactly what he was going to do with her, what a filthy girl she was. She would be flushed and panicking, her stomach twisting its strange, little dance; trying to maintain normality while maintaining strange, fictitious conversation on her end of the phone, in order to not hint to anyone in earshot at the lewd nature of the conversation.

His flat was beautiful.

An urban space with clean sharp lines, views all over the city, a lift climbing into its very heart and spilling cruelly onto his living space's concrete floor.

It was a far cry from the hovel that Cherry called home.

He had told her that he was a pilot. He was also an art connoisseur. He took her to galleries and waxed lyrical about the meanings behind each work. Any opinion she might have tried to muster he shot down in flames. *Maybe he was a fighter pilot?*

He was an unmitigated snob. His hobby was putting people down. He would make Cherry feel small for an entire evening, subtly but surely – and then, when she was quite chastened, tell her how much he felt about her.

How special she was.

How unlike any other.

That the two of them were perfect together.

That there was so much that he was going to share with her.

Teach her, show her.

She'd never met his friends and was, so far, too embarrassed to let him meet hers in case he despised them, put them down, caused a chasm between herself and her confidantes.

But she couldn't give him up.

She was hooked.

He was her drug.

She spent all her life between the times with him, waiting for his calls, waiting for more time with him, anything he could spare.

****

The meal had arrived, but Cherry was in such a state by then that she could barely eat. Her first mouthful, hardly chewed in her state of nervousness, had been an enormous chunk – more the size of your average Chihuahua. As it was in her mouth already, she had attempted to gnaw the moist flesh into two manageable lumps.

She had swallowed, reaching for her water. But the descending section (which was by now fighting its way down her tubes) had still been joined to the half that remained in her mouth by a tough cord of gristle. It was a rump steak bungee jump. Except down didn't seem to be an option. Death had seemed more likely.

Before she had known it, her eyes popped out of her head like organ stops as she gagged at the table, plunging fingers deep into her mouth, trying to break the length of sinew that was causing an internal wrestling match with no referee. She was retching loudly.

People were looking.

One was leaving.

But in the internal tussle between the two parts there was no clear winner as yet.

And the loser may well be Cherry.

He had watched coldly, until she had conquered prematurely meeting her maker by somehow swallowing the entire ball of meat whole. It inched down her gullet with painful lethargy.

"Have you quite finished?" he said, coldly. "Sometimes I think that the local kebab house is where I should take you. You seem to have a problem going to anywhere with class."

And that coming from somebody who had just had his fingers in her pants.

She was too humiliated to reply.

She was still wondering if she had given herself some kind of rupture. But would have rather died quietly in the corner than requested an ambulance.

He had disappeared shortly afterwards, to make his usual round of calls out of her earshot and returned in an entirely different mood some few minutes later, with a glass of port for them both.

Cherry, in the meantime, had sobered up after her starter of embarrassment, followed by a main of torture, shortly chased by a pudding of humiliation – and was outside the window with a healing fag in hand. She had been waiting for his return with a nervousness that had risen from her shoes and was now hovering in her chest. He had been cold and distant and she was certain that he would return to deliver the news that their whole relationship was over, on account of her dreadful ineptitude at the simple task of eating.

She was looking nervously through the window trying to gauge his body language as he swaggered towards the table – on a scale of 1 to 10 on the Status Horrificus measure.

He was, however, smiling – seemed a little excited... and suddenly all was well with the world.

"My flight for tomorrow morning has been cancelled," he said, simply. "Let's celebrate."

She hated port, but let the thick, strong taste wash over her tongue in relief. She listened to him bombinating on about yet another artist whom she had never heard of and yet more places that she'd never been to. The room was spinning strangely now – and he seemed very far away, his voice in the distance.

The port was obviously reviving the contents of her wine-filled belly.

He was droning on and on and on and on. In his usual repetitive, monotonous way. Oh my God, he was now onto cars or something.

Her eyes seemed to be flicking, her vision blurring a little, her thoughts erratic as she struggled to keep her mind focussed, to listen to him. He played with her hair, as she felt hot and then shivered.

He had been talking without pausing for breath for hours.

"I need to go to the ladies. Now." – Her voice, but she wasn't sure that she had said it.

Her head was spinning now. Her brain was someone else's. Perhaps she was having a haemorrhage.

He was by now in full flight on the topic of politics in the USA and how they could improve the running of the country if the President just listened to his simple, ten step plan. First....

Oh God he was still going on about something – **need water now** *– she should understand but she was too thick to know what he was –* **need to lie down** *– on about and where was she anyway? Oh food, food she was in –* **need to go home** *– a restaurant and there was music and she was feeling funny maybe nobody would realise and it would be OK but he –* **need my mum** *– was still talking to her and she was laughing but the sound that came out sounded like someone else and –* **need the bathroom** *– a bit witch-like perhaps she was in a horror film –* **Oh God, she needed to get out of here now.**

Cherry walked an urgent and winding path towards the LADIES sign, which wobbled in and out of focus – her head taken over by a mission to reach the panelled door. It took what seemed an eternity to reach it. She pushed her way in, feeling better to be there, a relief… and sat on the deep, red, velvet sofa, in front of the mirrors spanning the whole wall.

She gazed at her reflection, expecting a vision of hell and being quite taken aback to look strangely beautiful this evening. The panic in her brain was starting to subside, now she was on her own. The respite from his incessant chatter seemed to have released a kind of pressure valve in her brain and the world was gradually slotting itself into its normal position. The noise had died down. She still felt weird.

But she really was looking quite gorgeous.

Something about her eyes.

She couldn't stop looking. She pouted at herself and pulled her best model faces, the ones she practised when home alone, just in case she was ever talent-spotted. As she washed her face with clear, cool water, feeling it flow, cold and strange, beneath her fingers, her vision flickered once more and she struggled to see herself at all in the mirror.

What the fuck was going on?

In the back of her mind, she knew he was out there waiting, knew she had been some time, couldn't tell if it was seconds or hours, but no longer cared. If she just sat for another minute, she would feel all right, she was sure.

She felt strangely peaceful.

She could have been in there for a month.

The concept of time felt suddenly elusive.

The door opened.

It was him.

As he walked towards her and bent slowly to kiss her, she no longer cared if anybody walked in. He pulled her towards the door and pressed her into it, so that it would no longer open. Fingers now deep in her mouth as he bit her nipples, he lifted her skirt. Kissing her softly and sweetly he pushed himself into her, pants pulled to the side, with one deep push and then stayed still, no movement, just kissing her until she was desperate for him to move.

Her eyes were flickering sideways faster now. She didn't feel right, but it felt good. *Or did it? She could no longer tell.* She was aware of the cameras in the corners of the ceiling, observing, tried to think how much they could see, but felt powerless to stop, didn't want to stop, wanted to carry on. And then she didn't want to carry on. Her brain had allowed her a few seconds of clarity. She tried to shift position to make him release her, but he would not.

There was a knock at the door.

"Just coming," he said, sliding out of her, pulling down her skirt, pushing her back over the basin, roughly forcing her head over the sink, holding up her hair as if preventing her from soiling it with vomit. He pulled the door open.

"So sorry," he said. "My sister has had too much to drink. I am trying to get her out of here."

He pulled her, tenderly, out of the lavatory and led her through the few remaining diners to the doors.

The bill had already been paid.

The cab was already waiting.

Inside the cab, Cherry was aware of the blur of lights of London sights. Passing cars left streamers of colour in their wake and the sounds of urban night were amplified and eerie. She felt sexy and good but her brain was not her own.

He talked calmly to the driver as he stroked her through clothes, roughly enough for her to want him to stop; then stopped until she was desperate for him to continue, pushing her off as she tried to touch him, holding her wrists prisoner with one hand.

Cherry was aware of the cab driver's eyes, in the rear view mirror, looking, but did not feel able to do anything about it. She was faintly aware that this should not be occurring, but was also not quite sure that it even was.

They climbed out of the car – Cherry's skirt around her waist, but unable to get it together to sort herself out – and he walked her to the lift, up, up into his apartment.

****

She woke in the morning – with a brain that felt as if it was moving too fast but enveloped in cellophane; tightly bound. Her wrists had the welts of bondage around them and she was sore, still felt open, and was confused and anxious and spinning. Minute flashes of the night before were resurfacing in Cherry's mind at intervals, but she was unsure whether they were imaginary or had actually taken place.

And far too embarrassed to ask him.

If they had, she had been to places that she had never before wished to go. She didn't think she was unhappy about it... just didn't want him to think ill of her, to have let herself down, to have put him off.

She had limped to work, late, red and puffing like an old geezer; full of confusion and smelling decidedly suspect, despite a shower with half a bottle of shower gel. Her skin seemed to have aged ten years overnight and she was finding it incredibly hard to engage in any form of conversation, with anybody.

Even the driver on the bus had thrown her into confusion when he asked her for her destination.

Hell?

Not sure.

"To my work," she had said. Which hadn't helped him much.

Her mind was wandering so rapidly from topic to topic she hardly dared speak, in case the ramblings of a confirmed lunatic poured forth from her lips.

God, she hoped that there was no evidence on her black shirt. Or some telltale trail on the back of her skirt.

Or that the bus was not full of mind readers, flicking through the treble-x-porn-flick that had now overtaken her mind.

She had clearly lost her marbles. Perhaps this was what the onslaught of Alzheimer's was like. You could identify the fact that you were going mad, but could do nothing about it.

Flu perhaps.

She couldn't wait for bed.

But she'd only just got out of one.

She got through her first five clients in what seemed like three minutes flat, worrying about the conversations she'd had – or not had – with them, conversations that she was totally unable to remember. She knew she was behaving bizarrely. She could read it in their faces. But she felt removed from herself, as if she was watching from a place just out of reach.

Lunchtime left her unable to eat.

But able to poo a lot.

Oh my God.

What else had happened?

She fought to catch fragments of memory as they flew past, too quickly to grasp.

Surely not.

She felt sick.

He must feel pretty sick too, once he'd realised he'd lost his way in the dark.

Best not to say anything in case he hadn't noticed.

She hoped to God she hadn't shat on his sheets.

The afternoon was a 'dragger', only relieved by the arrival of one of her favourite customers.

Tracey was in at least once a week and extremely funny and articulate. Could talk about anything. Found the humour in everything. She was some kind of high-flying businesswoman.

Suited.

Stilettoed.

Briefcased.

Immaculate.

She was waxed to oblivion, facial-peeled to excess, manicured, coiffed, tanned, and stiff with Botox. She looked fabulous in an utterly unbelievable, unnatural way, with a glamour and the disposition of a woman that you didn't mess with.

Like Joan Rivers on speed with a heavy Mancunian accent.

She adored Cherry, who was outspoken enough to frequently offend – but never pissed her off. She liked Cherry's honesty.

"So what is it to be today? Brazilian? Pink-dyed love heart? Topiary chicken?"

"Today, Cherry my sweet, I want a leopard-dyed landing strip. A wide one."

"Joking?"

"Serious."

Cherry got to work, still sweating and slightly shaky and not – as was her usual way – talking nineteen-to-the-dozen. Tracey was flat on her back; long, hair-free limbs aloft, wearing beige, organic, unbleached paper knickers, as she was waxed viciously and then tweezed.

"Ow. Fuck!"

Cherry had grasped a lump of flesh, having lunged for a stray hair with the tweezers and missed, head still reeling. There was blood on the paper, roll-out plinth cover.

"Fuck. Sorry," she said, looking up and meeting the gaze of her surprised customer. "Double fuck. Really sorry. Bad night. Or good night, I don't know which. Are you going to sue me for ruination of private parts?"

"It's going to sting when you bleach the bugger. I may slap you, but I won't sue. As long as you don't damage business."

Cherry looked up.

"Why do you do this to your pubes? Is it like a quirky way of rebelling against your seniority? Like wearing preposterous underwear, while telling a bunch of suits how best to do their business. Do you thump the table?"

Loud and raucous laughter followed.

"What is it you think I do?"

"Big important business. Or are you just very rich? You always have a briefcase."

"Do you want to see inside it?"

Cherry nodded.

"By the way. I do deal with a lot of suits. I do tell them how best to go about their business. I do thump the table. But not in the way you are thinking. And if you tell a soul, not only will I never come back here, but I will also tell all and sundry that you are the worst beautician ever in the history of mankind. Publicly. In the newspaper. I am an escort."

Silence.

For a possible 27 seconds.

The briefcase clicked open. In it, was an array of torture equipment.

"And yes, my speciality is hurting the pitiful, little fuckers. But it does *not* mean that I ever – and I repeat EVER, have to even touch their foul, little cocks with any part of my anatomy. Only with these." A pink neon, feather-embellished pair of rubber gloves emerged.

"Oh my God."

"I do hope that this will not affect our purely professional, working relationship. You being my wax genius. But you look like an open-minded girl. Who indulged rather too much yourself last night, from the looks of you." She cackled. "Now get on with it, for fuck's sake. I have a 3 o'clock with the managing director of a recruitment company, who likes a bloody good whipping in a suite in the Dorchester, followed by afternoon tea, before he goes home to his wife. I've not let him down in thirteen years and I'm not about to start now, just because you quite clearly don't know what you are doing this afternoon."

"What do mean?"

"You are so obviously on a drugs comedown, love. Nothing passes me by after all this time."

"I am not!"

Indignant silence, followed by furious plucking, bleaching and dyeing.

Cherry brewed for a few minutes before speaking. "I really am not. I don't touch them. I just feel bloody awful – I don't understand why. I'm not sure even what happened last night – I just went out for dinner and it all went horribly wrong. Or right. I really don't know. I feel like such a twat. And you've blown all my dream images of getting out of here and learning some big business skills and taking over the world. I thought you were like superwoman."

"Oh I am. And a large number of London businessmen think so too. And I couldn't imagine being told what to do by anybody. And I love my work. Total freedom. Lots of cash. Absolute discretion. Best table everywhere I go. Accounts in the best shops that I do not ever have to foot the bill for. And BUPA. Now tell me about last night. I am interested."

A confused account of events followed.

"At least, I think that's what happened..."

"That's reprehensible, Cherry. In fact it's a statutory offence."

Cherry's heart missed a beat. "What are you talking about?"

"Non-consensual drugs. Non-consensual sex."

"No, that's not how it was. I was all for it."

"You're not 'all for' anything if you're off your face, Cherry. Have you looked in the mirror today?" She paused, looking at Cherry sharply. "Watch him. What does he do for a living? Who is he?"

"Pilot. Rich. Handsome. Non-rapist. The kind your mum would like and absolutely NOT someone who would ever lay a finger on me unless I was gagging for it. Which I was."

"Unconscious, more like. You'll learn," sighed Tracey "Now book me in for next week. I need to be bald. There is a member of Royalty coming to visit me who doesn't do hair. He likes to beg to look at it and beg to touch it, but to be refused. He calls me auntie. Bloody disturbing if you ask me, but it pays for the new extension."

As she watched Tracey leave, Cherry's mind was whirling. What was it with these prostitutes? She lived with one and now it appeared that a woman she had known for years was also in that trade.

And they all seemed to be having more luck than she was.

And then her mind turned to him, to the events of the previous night. Unease made her pulse quicken.

There was just a tiny bit of doubt in her mind.

Chapter 23

Fiona's line in prostitution was entirely different.

They queued.

It was usually over in minutes.

With any luck.

****

When Cherry had moved into the bed-sit she called home – and been shown the kitchen and bathroom she was to share with the other bed-sit, on the first floor of the crumbling Victorian building – she had not been forewarned that the room adjacent to hers was inhabited by a prostitute.

The landlord, a huge, sweating, bald, cockney twat in a stained, string vest had seized her deposit in his greasy clutches with glee and vanished quicker than the speed of light.

Cherry had been so relieved to actually find somewhere that she could afford and that she did not have to share with the standard family of rats, she had signed the lease for a year. Especially as the landlord had made it very clear that she could decorate just as she wanted. Even strip the floorboards.

It was carpeted with a swirling and sculpted nightmare, with a supplementary layer of brown, sticky slime that had nearly removed one of her shoes as she had tiptoed across her new room. *It would have to go.* But the wallpaper was a stunning, vintage flock. Peeling at the edges where damp had loosened it, it had been there since the seventies – and had obviously been a vastly different shade when it first went up. Ghost-like scars of un-faded and beautiful pattern, preserved by years of previously hung pictures adorned the walls, like crooked teeth.

The room had obviously been used as some kind of gambling den in the past and had a fashionably ironic, white, padded bar on one side, complete with dusty-with-disuse optics and time-fogged, mirrored shelving on the wall.

There was a shared kitchen, minimally furnished and not updated since the fifties, but immaculately clean and fresh. Cherry smiled as she saw the chipped vase of fresh blooms on the pressed tablecloth, the notes and postcards stuck to the fridge, the neatly stacked crockery: small insights into whoever was already living there.

The bathroom lay beyond; a roll-top bath with ornate feet, ancient taps dripping their yellowing track onto the clean enamel, an immense sink on a rickety stand upon the faded linoleum, a rubber duck wearing sunglasses.

It had potential.

Cherry saw a quirky charm in the place and its anonymous inhabitant that enticed her.

That first weekend, gardening gloves on and a scarf over her nose and mouth, she had ripped up the carpet, finding to her dismay a layer of lino underneath. It crumbled as she prised it from the boards, thick dust rising into the air. She screwed up her eyes and tried not to inhale. Original, wide boards began to grin through as she worked, humming to the tune of her radio as it echoed around the room, no furniture to absorb the sound. In the middle of the room, a large, suspicious stain revealed itself, marring the beauty of the wood. She hoped it wasn't the residue of a previous, deceased occupant and rapidly wiped the thought from her mind.

She had hired a sander from the ToolHire Company and watched as it was loaded into the back of the bashed, old, ex-Post Office van that she had hired for her move, which spewed vile clouds of grey smoke as it backfired down the road, enveloping passers-by with its fumes.

She parked, inexpertly, outside the flat and struggled with the unfamiliar key in the warped, front door. Door open, she returned to the van and untied the string that was holding the back doors together, to unleash the sanding beast. It was the size of an industrial lawnmower. She grabbed the body of it and attempted to lift it. And realised immediately that she was unable to move it more than a couple of inches.

Half a hernia later, hot tears of humiliation had started to well in her eyes and passers-by were sniggering, but not offering any help.

Bollocks.

She was going to come back in the next life as a man.

Or as a girl with a boyfriend.

She didn't see her other friends attempting this shit on their own.

She felt singularly sorry for herself.

And very alone.

She lit a fag and tried to control her escalating feelings of panic.

The curtains upstairs on the landing of her flat had been twitching. As Cherry sat on the bumper of the van, arms trembling with the huge adrenalin rush that is physical effort mixed with failure and a liberal dose of fear thrown in for good measure, the street door opened and a very beautiful, mixed race

149

girl appeared with a cup of tea, which was held out to Cherry sweetly.

"Hi. I'm Fiona. I live here."

"Hi. Thanks. I'm Cherry."

Cherry felt another flush of humiliation.

Fiona perched on the pavement at her feet, reached out for Cherry's fag and drew on it heavily.

"I've just given up," she said, smiling. She nodded towards the back of the van. "You look like you need a hand."

The girl was about five foot nothing, with the build of a featherweight ballerina.

"I do. I'm having a bloody nightmare. But I think this thing may take another six of us. The blokes at the shop asked me if I would be able to get it out at the other end and I scoffed at them and did the 'of-course-I-can' thing. They must have pissed themselves laughing when I drove off."

"Wait a minute. I'll be right back."

A couple of minutes later, two enormous, gold-toothed Rastas appeared around the corner and marched towards Cherry. One of them reached past her, lifted the sander with the easy grace of a well-trained athlete and tossed it over his shoulder.

"Where d'ya wannit, lady?"

"Up here darlin'," – Fiona's soft voice.

Holding open the door.

Letting him into the flat.

Fiona and her two friends had then sat, idly, in the hallway outside Cherry's room, watching her plug in and start up.

The sander had leapt into action with a grinding roar that would have woken the dead. It dragged Cherry along, brutally chomping like Godzilla at everything in its path, until she managed to hit the 'off' button with a shaking toe and the grinding decelerated slowly to a final, gurgling standstill.

She had purveyed her work.

A deep trough eaten into the floorboards, a mangled radiator oozing rusty water from its now decimated feed-pipe and a crater in the wall: her stunning achievement for the day.

She had started to cry.

At that moment, she had felt a skinny arm slip round her waist and had been led to the stool, which was her only item of furniture in the room so far. She had been sat firmly down on it.

The Rastas took control of the sander, while Cherry and Fiona watched the paint-splattered boards become denuded of their filth and the tawny warmth of the mellow, mature wood reveal itself. Even the stain – which had only needed a white, police line around it to confirm Cherry's suspicions – had gone.

Cherry had then been forced to smoke an alarming amount of weed, not totally against her will, whilst the rest of her van was unloaded and arranged in her new home.

She and Fiona had been friends ever since.

And she had now renewed her tenancy, year after year.

It was on day three of their friendship, however, that Cherry had realised her new flatmate's mode of earning money

****

Fiona was quite cold and calculated about it. She wasn't fussy, except for being religiously hygienic and a safe sex fanatic.

It was for the money, pure and simple.

She had long-term goals and a life plan.

No-one else was involved in her business. No-one took any of her money. She had a boyfriend – who adored her and simply tolerated what she did because he had no choice in the matter – and a large lump of cash in an ISA account, which was growing daily.

Fiona was going to buy property.

In a good area.

With the smallest mortgage she could possibly manage.

And when she'd done that, she was going to stop.

Simple.

She had started as a student; finding it impossible to make ends meet, she had been forced to take a year out of her course to earn the cash with which to complete it. Following a short interlude working as a stripper in a well-known London strip club (and for the first time earning well), she had quickly progressed to joining couples in anonymous threesomes.

The first of these had paid her a cool three thousand pounds.

They had been an incredibly wealthy, smart and funny couple. They had offered her a thousand pounds to dance for them and then join them at a table for dinner.

When she was offered another two thousand pounds to go back and sleep with them, she had jumped at the chance. It was the man's fortieth birthday present and they had been watching Fiona dance for weeks until they finally approached her.

It was more than she would have earned in a month as an office junior.

Fiona was an intelligent girl and her determination to do well in life meant that she was able to switch off mentally and think of her actions as a long-term investment.

Not all nights earned as well, obviously. But she always went home with at least two hundred pounds, often a thousand – and with "extras" could make a hell of a lot more.

Within a year, working, living frugally and never spending any money that she didn't have to, she had earned in excess of eighty thousand, tax-free pounds.

She had had her fair share of terrifying moments, but had learnt along the way to only sleep with regulars.

Sometimes at hotels, never in their homes, but often in hers. No emotion, no perversion, always a condom.

It was clinical, simple and lucrative.

Many of the other girls did the same; in fact only a few of the strippers did not offer anything else. But even they did well.

Many of the clients were rich, city boys, looking for harmless fun with someone that would not look at them twice in the real world. Some were old widowers, with cash to spend and a lonely life. Some were vile perverts – but word usually got around and they would have to move on to another club, where they were not recognised.

The girls all looked after each other, in a backstabbing and competitive way. And the club prided itself on its safety. No extras were supposed to be provided by the girls...and they would be sacked if they were found out to be proffering them.

But there was always the underlying understanding that it went on.

As time had gone on, Fiona had built up a selection of regulars that would meet her at her flat.

No weirdos.
No funny stuff.
No drugs.
Strictly cold, calculated business.

****

Fiona was forced to explain to Cherry what was going on when Cherry had started banging on the wall of her bedroom, at three in the morning, for the third night running – and witnessed yet another unfamiliar, male face leaving Fiona's room.

Cherry had looked appalled for a few seconds after hearing Fiona's explanation and had then sat down and started to laugh.

"So... what do you think of me now?"

Cherry hurriedly gathered her thoughts, not wanting to get it wrong, to offend Fiona with her response. "After the initial shock, I don't really see how it is any different from the flash, young girls who decide on a footballer – whoever they can get – just for the cash. Or twenty-year-olds that marry ninety-year-old men, hoping they'll pop their clogs any minute. At least you're not fooling anyone into thinking you like them!"

"Oh, yes I do; they all think I like them. I do like some of them, have a soft spot, you know. But not like that."

"Ever actually fancied one?"

"Yes, actually. But his wife had terminal M.S. He felt better about seeing me than having a relationship with someone. Less like he was being unfaithful. Made me feel pretty shit though."

"Will you be doing it until you're 90?"

"God, no. I have only a few thousand more to go before I will be able to afford to buy a flat and go back to Uni."

"Uni? What are you studying?"

"Criminal law."

Chapter 24

Robyn was doing better.

Not well, but she had shed a minute grain of the dark, lonely torture that had gripped her soul for the last year or so and replaced it with numbness.

Enveloped in some sort of cotton wool, she could get through each day without thinking. Her life had taken on new meaning.

Daytime television was her new world.

Doctors came and went.

She had been sent to a counsellor, whom she had sat in front of, week after week.

The whole point was that you were supposed to find your own answers.

By talking things through.

But Robyn did not want to 'talk things through' with this silly woman, who seemed far too well-presented to have ever experienced anything even resembling a problem of her own; who sat there in Prada, with her shiny shoes and a new handbag each time. *Staring into her soul.* Waiting for Robyn to be struck with some sudden, deep, inner revelation that would suddenly mean that everything made sense. Or delving into her past and childhood, for an explanation of why she was feeling like this today.

She knew why she felt like this today.

The stupid woman had told her that she needed to stop feeling like a victim.

But couldn't she see? She WAS a victim.

And sadly, that was just life. Her life. And she didn't want to think about it, talk about it, acknowledge it – or live it.

Oprah helped.

So did Jerry Springer.

In the fine company of a carefully selected audience of freaks, such as they had, she felt run-of-the-mill. Normal, even.

The pills took the shards of glass out of everyday life, but not the thorns. And recently, the thorns were getting sharper. She had asked her G.P. for a higher dose, but she was already on the maximum. Any more was simply not prescribable.

So she had told a few little, white lies.

She had lost some.

Some had been stolen.

That sort of thing.

But the Doctor had caught on. He was not going to give her more than she should have. Her tales of tablet loss no longer rang true with him. He had seen it all before.

For the last few months, Robyn had struck up a curious friendship with the young addict in the room opposite hers. Reminding her of her son, with his mixed-up, but ultimately sweet nature, Sid was a surrogate, something she could nurture. He was out all day, leaving her to the mercies of T.V. and the dubious pleasures of the communal sitting room. But by the evening, she had become accustomed to his tentative knock, his young, worn face at her door.

She told him of her problem with the G.P.

She really needed the pills. It got her through, made each day bearable.

He had a friend, he said, who could maybe get her some extra.

Cheap and maybe not quite the same, but worth a try all the same.

What had she got to lose? She had lost it all already.

She could have a free try-out.

Within the week, Sid's knock brought forth a scruffy envelope, with miniscule, blue pills inside, stuck in the very corner of the brown paper. She took the first with him there, like a security blanket, both alone watching crap, American, sitcom hell in silence. As she had descended into a warm and hazy heaven of non-recognition and a spreading peace, he had kissed her forehead and left the room.

She only needed them once in a while.

When the thoughts flooded in.

When she couldn't keep out the constant, relentless barrage of former life – life she needed to keep out at all cost for her sanity.

They allowed her to function.

Unlike the prescription tablets – which just numbed her, took off the edge – they made her feel secure, made her not care. She did find herself holding the odd, unusual conversation, where it was as if she was listening to someone other than herself as she talked – someone much freer, funnier, and more popular with people.

They made her feel brave.

She liked it.

When she needed more, Sid duly obliged. But he could not continue to get them for her without any payment. The man he was getting them from had owed him a favour. The favour was now repaid. She would have to find money for them…not much money, but some.

Robyn tried without them once more.

But they had been a tiny chink of light in the darkness. *A reason to carry on.* They had helped her be normal with people, to talk to them without the fear that they were judging her, knew her past, knew it was all her fault for raising her son in the way that she had.

She needed them to get through.

He could get the bloke to come round to see her, Sid said. But she would need to pretend he was another Doctor, or Mary would catch on and involve the police – and this man was not a man to be messed with. She would need to get some money, need to give him something in return.

She had nothing.

But perhaps this man would understand her position, take pity on her.

There were people out there with compassion, as sure as there was a God in heaven.

There had to be something she could give him.

Chapter 25

He had come into her room, brought into the gloom by Mary, into the four small, bare walls that were now her life.

"New doctor to see you, love," said Mary, a familiar look of concern on her face. "Is everything all right?"

****

Still riddled with worry about Robyn and her reclusive ways, Mary had done her best. But after the initial glimmer of hope, when Robyn had told her all, Mary had, with her unseeing eyes, watched her retreat once again into endless hours of watching television, avoiding reality.

She had found Robyn several jobs, part-time, helping others, doing good things, things that she had thought would remind her of past times, in a positive way. Robyn had been unable to stick at any of them. She was completely disinterested in everything, everybody, life.

Robyn, these days, seemed in a haze, beyond contact – except for her odd and tenuous friendship with Sid.

Mary's place was not one of permanence.

For a few, who were beyond any hope of rehabilitation into the real world, it was their home and refuge for years at a time, until eventually Social Services re-homed them permanently, into somewhere that they could stay forever, in whatever mental condition they were in.

Mary sometimes ignored it when people had been there for far too long, if she still had some hope of a normal life for them – gave them a little longer, time and time again, until they were almost permanent fixtures, like the taps and the toilets and the disintegrating kitchen.

But this was strictly against the rules and was only possible because Social Services were so overrun with work, that the odd one slipped through the net, or she could fight for a little more time for them.

This she had done for Robyn on many occasions now, in the hope that this enormous depression may pass, lift slightly – just enough for her to start to function normally again, cope on her own, return to the land of the living.

But she soon would have to be housed somewhere permanent, somewhere that she could cope mentally. And as things were, this would not be without someone to care for her. She would probably end up in some kind of institution, with no help for her mental state, except a passing visit every now and then from a well-meaning, but overworked psychologist.

No help at all really.

Mary had experienced it time and time again.

She felt, in Robyn, something that she recognised in herself a long time ago – a glimmer of hope.

But she was on borrowed time.

Perhaps this new doctor was a good sign.

****

Robyn had not asked her to make the call, this time. This visit she had obviously arranged herself. *Maybe this was a turning point, the start of something new.*

She left them in peace.

When the door quietly shut, and Mary's footsteps receded into the dim distance of the damp and peeling hall, Robyn said,

"Hello. Did Sid send you? Or Mary?"

"Sid. Not Mary. I hear you are having difficulty with your G.P. and the pills. I may be able to help."

"I have no money. But I need them."

She looked down, eyes dark with sadness. Despair filled her heart as she realised that she had nothing, absolutely nothing, to offer him.

"I have no money," she repeated.

"One last pack," he said, kindly. "And then you will have to make your own arrangements. I am not a man without a heart. I see this as a public service."

The old bag was quite attractive, in her own way.

Sid had been right.

This woman was hooked.

It would be interesting to see how far she would go to get the money for them.

It was his little game, his little sniff of power. And he loved to have a bit of power.

It made him feel important.

He liked that – *especially when they reminded him of his own mother.*

"I'll come along next week and see how you are getting on."

He would make sure that he left it for just over two weeks, until she was desperate.

It was the only way people truly realised his worth, valued what he did – once they had gone without, for a bit.

Then they were truly grateful.

Always helped up the price.

He was providing a rather unique service, after all.

161

Chapter 26

Cath had been searching for weeks.

Every sodding beauty salon she rang had never heard of Cherry.

She had had three haircuts out of embarrassment. And now a mole-like helmet of black hair replaced her long locks.

Ah well, maybe a new image would help her shed the memory of John.

A fresh start.

A wake up call.

It was a bit chilly with all her barnet missing.

The calls to Cherry's parents had not been met with any luck.

She had left countless messages, but they had never returned her calls. She had tried all of their past friends – friends long since forgotten in the excitement of breaking away. But she had drawn a blank. *Several hundred blanks, in fact.*

It was no use.

There was no way she would ever find her.

****

Since leaving her beloved job in the film company and everything she had worked so hard for, in the midst of her heartbreak, she had started to work, freelance, as a director. She had had no choice. She couldn't face losing her apartment on top of everything else.

She had not expected any work. But she was good. So slowly, her diary had filled with exciting projects, which helped fill the void after the affair and soothe her wounds.

Her confidence was growing. Her daily rate had rocketed. But she was filled with desperation to connect with her past, to find her old friends.

****

One evening, when she hit the "MESSAGE PLAY" button of an Ansafone so antiquated that it virtually ran on steam, there was a message, from a familiar voice.

It was Cherry's father. He had never forgiven Cath for absconding with his beautiful daughter, all those years ago.

He felt certain that it was all Cath's doing.

His little angel would have never come up with an idea like that on her own.

Cherry, over the years, had never contradicted his theory, of course; and had been given the welcome of the female version of the prodigal son, on her return to the fold of her family. They had grown accustomed to the fact that she would never return from London to the dizzy delights of Scunthorpe again, but had forgiven her for her transgressions and worshipped the ground she stood on, once more.

Cherry's dad had become more than a little weary of the monthly phone messages from Cath, enquiring as to the whereabouts of Cherry; and nine years later – having met Cath's parents inadvertently in Lidl (while they both lunged for the final remaining pack of value mince that wasn't tinged with too much green, in the reduced section) and hearing from them how lonely she was – felt a bit guilty for his years of anger and left a message on Cath's Ansafone, to tell her where Cherry was working.

Time to let bygones be bygones.

Cath's heart nearly stopped when she heard the message.

Sleep that night was something elusive. She drifted in and out, dreaming about shagging one of her old primary school teachers; the one with the ginger hair, bow tie and custard-filled boils who drove a bright orange estate car with furry seats – waking only when he mutated into a Smurf and started trying to fish out her eye with a knitting needle.

She had jumped out of bed as though catapulted when the alarm had gone off; relieved that the ordeal of last night had, in fact, just been a dream, induced by eating too much cheese and downing three-quarters of a bottle of cheap, Spanish plonk, in front of a re-run of Wags' Boutique, before bed.

She felt nauseous.

She had longed to see Cherry so much, for so long, that now she knew where to find her, she wasn't sure if she actually wanted to.

Would it turn into one of those hyper-embarrassing events where you meet an old friend and realise that you have nothing in common whatsoever – except for the fact that you are both still alive? With nothing to talk about? And what would Cherry's reaction be? Their friendship had hardly been left on a good note. Yikes.

She would make herself look nice.

The last time she had seen her old friend; she was still lard-arse Cath, with the frumpy clothes, acne and air of desperation.

With Elvis grinding away on top of her.

The least she could do for her own sense of self-esteem was not to meet her gorgeous and stylish, old friend looking like a troll.

She had some pride.

John had bought her a few nice things, when they were together. Bloody lovely things, in fact. Things she could have never afforded herself. From shops that nearly called security at the very sight of her entering.

She had loaded them all into a large bin bag, but never managed to quite part with them. It would have made her sick to donate them to a charity shop. And then spot someone else in them.

And she had resisted her initial compunction to shred and burn them.

It seemed a shame to waste them.

She plucked a Balenciaga, pom-pom-encrusted shawl from the depths of the black plastic and threw it on top of an amazing Miu Miu peasant skirt, over-the-knee socks and some killer-heeled ankle boots. Hot peasant, with a twist of Mary-Poppins-gets-kinky. *Perfect.*

She arrived outside the Sloane Street salon where Cherry's dad had said that Cherry worked – in location, at least, her old friend seemed to have come full circle – and hovered outside the vast, state-of-the-art exterior, trying to peek through to catch a glimpse.

The salon was crammed with faces that she recognised from the telly and gossip pages. One of the wives from a Wags'

Boutique repeat the night before was having half a sheep's arse of blond rats' tails glued into her bleached, woolly barnet.

Permatanned stylists laughed and gossiped and savaged people's hair with outrageous flourishes, whilst looking like they themselves had been coiffed by Edward Scissorhands on acid, using a blunt and rusty steak knife.

Cherry was nowhere to be seen.

Cath, in a moment of bravery, entered the fray and tiptoed, nervously, to the counter.

"I'd like an appointment, please. With Cherry?"

"Hi," – a voice behind her. "Can I help you?"

Cath turned.

"Cherry?"

"Cherry's not here until two."

Thank the fucking lord. She knew it had been a long time and she hadn't been sure that she'd recognise her friend…but she was certain that a sex change would have been mentioned.

Cath arrived back at two thirty-three, having spent a morning spending money in Harrods as though it was going out of fashion, on things she didn't need, or even like, just out of sheer nerves.

She could see Cherry attacking the head of a very strange, Mrs. Slocombe-type, old, mess of a pensioner, who was shaking as badly as a jelly on a spinning washing machine – and who looked about as out of place in the salon as a fish at a cricket match. Unmistakeably Cherry.

She approached from behind, aware that she was visible in the huge bank of mirrors.

Cherry glanced up and then away, with not even the faintest hint of recognition.

Cath was sat down in an adjacent chair and a black gown placed around her shoulders.

She had made an appointment for a haircut.

With Cherry.

God, she wished she had just said 'hi' and asked her to come for a coffee. Now she felt really bloody stupid. And would be stuck in the chair for at least an hour, having a haircut she didn't want, at the hands of someone that used to be her best friend, but had fallen out with her in a spectacular fashion.

It wasn't like she had any hair to cut, anyway.

What was she going to ask for... a perm?

Her hair was as close-cropped as a small, black velvet helmet and was clippered, ruthlessly – in the privacy of her own home, with her own clippers – once a week.

She hated the hairdressers – ever since, when her hair was long, she had gone into one requesting to have a loose, hippy-type look and emerged looking like Brian May.

She watched as Cherry dusted off the old lady's shoulders, hauled her unceremoniously out of the chair and kissed her warmly, before guiding her onto her Zimmer, in a pair of outrageously unsuitable heels – and after a few, shuddering steps bunging her clumsily into another chair, where she was to have her old, grey claws seen to.

And then Cherry turned.

And looked at her full in the face.

And stared.

And began to laugh.

"Oh, my God! Oh, my God!" Cherry broke into a trot and charged at her friend, with a smile wider than a chimp at a tea party and her arms outstretched, in the style of something from a rotten, American, tear-jerker-reunion scene. And then she fell upon Cath's neck like Dracula, making strange, strangled noises, holding on with a grip more befitting a sumo wrestler. Cath realised that the feeling of moisture on her shoulder was tears – and that Cherry was sobbing; huge, comedy sobs. She wouldn't let go.

It was all going to be all right.

Chapter 27

Mary had had no choice. She had tried everything for Robyn. Kept her at the refuge, tried to help her, looked after her.

She had realised that the so-called doctor that had been visiting was not what he had appeared to be. She had rung the Medical centre, to be told that no G.P. had been to see Robyn for weeks.

And then she had realised what was going on.

She had been forced to give her a simple ultimatum.
Stop the pills.
Or get out.

Robyn had left that night, without leaving a forwarding address, or even speaking to her.

Mary had felt her way down the corridor, every inch and crack in the plaster as familiar to her fingertips as her own face, and knocked on Robyn's door.

Robyn had not answered.

Mary asked everybody in the refuge, frantically worried. But she had gone. Nobody knew quite when.

The police had been no help at all.
They had filed a Missing Persons Report.
And then there had been nothing.

Chapter 28

"Oh my God, when did you get so skinny? I've been starving myself for weeks and still have thighs like tights stuffed with cauliflower florets. You look amazing!"

"It's called loveless and lonely. Don't try it."

Cath and Cherry had abandoned all attempts of haircutting the unhaircuttable and – after appalling excuses about a fictitious, family trauma – Cherry had managed to skive the afternoon off.

Even though her day had only started at two.

They had spent the afternoon getting horribly inebriated at a Spanish bar, eaten all the tapas on the menu and were both now languishing in the basement, on a voluptuous, balding, red velvet sofa.

"So what became of you and Elvis?"

"Well, after you abandoned me by running off in that brutal manner, we were together for a full seven weeks. Until I finally found somewhere to run to. In Elephant. I'm still there. You bitch." Cath began to laugh and slapped her friend a little more than humorously – and rather painfully – on one slightly rippling thigh. Cherry instantly moved away.

Cath briskly withdrew her hand.

There was an uncomfortable silence.

The question hung silently in the air between them.

"So. Now I have to ask. Let's just get it out of the way. Why?" Cath was unable to make eye contact as she spoke.

"Because of his delightful personality and deeply disturbing, personal hygiene issues."

"No it wasn't. He always had them. Why?"

"You know." Cherry was reddening, shifting awkwardly.

"No, that's the thing – I don't."

"Oh, bloody hell, Cath. You do know."

"No! Tell me. I went through hell because of you. Put me out of my misery!"

"You…you crossed the line."

"What bloody line? What line was it that we hadn't already crossed?" Cath was genuinely confused.

Cherry put her head in her hands, looking at a spot of ground-in gum on the sticky carpet, avidly; trying to will herself out of the situation. After a while, she spoke, eyes still focussed firmly downwards, embarrassed hands tensed against velvet.

"You tried to come onto me."

She looked up.

Cath was sitting, staring at her, incredulous. "What?"

There was a snort and suddenly Cath was laughing, unable to stop.

"You think if even if I was gay I'd ever fancy a big-headed cow like you?"

Cherry winced, suddenly guilty. Suddenly seeing things slightly differently to the version she had embedded in her brain all these years.

She remembered what a great team they had been.

She realised she had left Cath in the shit, against her will, with no explanation. And that her judgement had been coloured by her disgust at herself – at the mess they had both spiralled into.

"Sorry." Short. To the point.

And a word that wiped away many years of guilt, sorrow and loss all at once.

They sat in momentary silence.

"I wonder what he's up to now."

"Shall we find him?"

They looked at each other and sniggered, any embarrassment gone, a terrible team once more.

"I think not."

For the rest of the afternoon, they covered over twenty years of friendship, unfolded the secrets of their souls with no detail spared, as if it had never been any different.

Chapter 29

Jude had just finished in excess of one hundred press-ups. His pectorals were actually burning. *It felt good.*

Another long and boring day stretched out ahead like a threat.

It was only 8.30 in the morning.

****

Three weeks ago, he had asked for a bible. He wasn't planning on topping himself or, *God help him,* of becoming religious all of a sudden.

But he was intrigued.

Surely it was a load of old bullshit?

A newspaper of former times, the equivalent of The News of the World *in a previous world – ninety per cent rumour, with a small smattering of the truth thrown in, for good measure?*

But his Dad had lived by it. Really believed it. Had Jude been missing something all these years?

Although, it seemed, his father's unwavering faith had not done him much good; his belief in good had not stopped him being cut short in his tracks.

Jude missed his father with an intensity that was impossible to explain. His departure had left a great, yawning chasm. He missed his mother. He missed his daughter. He missed life, freedom, choice.

He missed all the difficulties that normal, un-imprisoned life threw at everyone, every day, against their will; the bits of life that people saw as hard, inconvenient, a chore. Like having to get up in the morning to go to work, decide what to do with the off food in the refrigerator, worrying themselves sick about the mortgage, their kid's bedwetting, their lack of love life.

All those were joys he wished he still had, with every bone of his body.

It had been an interesting read, the bible
He could see what the old man got out of it.

It was history: a mass of stories with a past and an ending that taught you a lesson. The lessons were good. They meant something true. It was just their context that was sometimes a little skewed.

And screwed.

And unbelievable.

It was a great book.
But he was finding the forgiveness bit really hard.
Forgiveness was, surely, just letting people get away with it. It seemed that the bad truly won in this life, got further than the good.

Like Connie's mother.

He thought about Sam, long and hard.

And he thought about his poor child. *His Connie. Still with her mother, enduring her indifference, her lies.* And he paced, his head mad with conflicting thoughts, trying to make sense of it all, trying to understand.

****

Jude went to the computer suite and typed a word into the keyboard.

PSYCHOPATH.

"A psychopath is defined as a person having no concerns for the feelings of others and a complete disregard for any sense of social obligation. They seem egocentric and lack insight of any sense of responsibility or consequence. Their emotions are thought to be superficial and shallow, if they exist at all."

That certainly described his ex-wife.

"They are considered callous, manipulative, and incapable of forming lasting relationships, let alone showing any kind of true meaningful love."

That described her as well.

"They can show a fictitious love based upon their observations of true love in others. They typically never perform any action unless they determine it can be beneficial for themselves."

And so did that.

By now he was becoming anxious enough for the shaking of his hands to be making the mouse dash from side to side on the page, as if in escape from some snarling, imaginary cat.

He read on.

"Since psychopaths cause harm through their actions, it is assumed that they are not emotionally attached to the people they harm; however, according to the PCL-R Checklist, psychopaths are also careless in the way they treat themselves."

That sort of described somebody so fucked up that they would murder.
For a small amount of cash.
For their own heroin addiction.
But not in quite graphic enough terms.

"They frequently fail to alter their behaviour in a way that would prevent them from enduring future discomfort. Dr. Joseph Newman contends that the behaviour displayed by psychopaths is the result of 'an inability to process contextual cues'."

She had had an inability to process cues of any kind, contextual or not.
Bloody hell.

"It is thought that any emotions which the primary psychopath exhibits are the fruits of watching and mimicking other people's emotions. They show poor impulse control…"

Poor impulse control? Stabbing an innocent man with a chisel was a fairly poor control of impulses! He was filled with renewed hatred for her.
Her.
It.
The mother of his child.
The killer of his father.

His wife.

"… And a low tolerance for frustration and aggression. They have no empathy, remorse, anxiety or guilt in relation to their behaviour. In short, they truly are devoid of conscience. However, they understand that society expects them to behave in a conscientious manner, and therefore they mimic this behaviour when it suits their needs."

She had squeezed out a few tears, as he had been led away.
The bitch.
He felt sick.

"Most studies of psychopaths have taken place among prison populations."

And Jude realised that it was why so many of his inmates never improved, stayed bad, were just biding their time to get out and repeat their actions.

And why the bible made so much sense.

It was an attempted explanation of the actions of those whose actions were inexplicable.

It was an attempted cure for the incurable.

Psychopath.
Sweet Jesus. It was how people thought of him.

Chapter 30

Cath had by now met The Pilot on numerous occasions.

Joe.

Bloody arsehole.

On the first meeting, they had struck up an easy hatred of each other, much to Cherry's dismay. Their meetings as a threesome were fraught with anxiety for Cherry. There was a sense of competition between them that neither of them could just ignore.

But neither of them would back down.

Cath was sure that he was a seasoned bullshitter; with an intrinsic inability to not let forth a monumental porky-pie every time he opened his gob. She spent every occasion they met grilling him, trying to catch him out.

She couldn't handle his pomposity, self-importance and severe, humour failure.

What's more, he was incredibly, mind-numbingly, nauseatingly dull. In a duller than dull kind of way. Tom Cruise after a lobotomy.

His sense of misogyny meant that he was totally unable to deal with her sharp and cutting wit and the self-assertion that years in her industry – and bad treatment at the hands of her ex – had given her.

They had both developed a juvenile way of trying to outdo each other, in terms of history with Cherry.

Joe plainly felt that he had the upper hand and that Cath was a new arrival, since she had only recently reappeared – and he was already well in there.

And what was with that fucking hair? She looked like a bloody prepubescent boy. In clothes put together like someone who'd run through a jumble sale, covered in superglue. She had daft tits too. Tiny. Like two poached eggs. Infantile. There was no need for that in this day and age. There were operations to sort that out. He was half tempted to offer her the money. Perhaps she'd be almost screwable if her jugs were sorted.

Cath had come to the conclusion that he must be compensating for something. *Maybe a tiny, useless knob. He was the equivalent of a midget sitting on several phone directories so he could see over the steering wheel of his new Aston Martin.*

She couldn't see what her friend even liked in him. Except for his astronomical good looks that was.

If he'd had a brain to go with it, instead of an excess of arrogance and a wit that didn't even reach the half-mark, she could have almost fancied him.

Probably always been told how gorgeous he was.
And now the prat obviously believed his own hype.
Nauseating.

Cherry invariably had to sink at least three-quarters of a bottle of red before she could stomach either of them, when they were all together.

Her inebriation made her intolerance of the situation worse.

Which only lead to more wine.

To dull the pain.

The occasion when she realised that the combination was quite intolerable – and simply could not continue – was when she had purposefully got all three of them extremely pissed, several weeks before.

None of them had quite got up the guts to drop out, or could come up with any semblance of a reason to do so that quite held itself up in terms of believability.

Cath had the tendency to crank up her volume and lose all inhibition to a terrifying degree when pissed, these days – and to increase her Northern tendencies to excruciating levels.

Blunt was not the word.

Brutal was distinctly more accurate.

And she seemed to have developed a malicious streak. Cherry had begun to think that meeting up again might not have been so wise. But she loved her.

He had begun this particular dreaded evening with the usual round of 'do you remember whens', trying to out-remember Cath. This time he had chosen the 'do you remember the time you got so pissed in the restaurant and I had you in the ladies?' shocker. He had nudged Cherry, for reinforcement that this was a comedy occasion – to have been met with a look that could have curdled cream and her awkward silence.

A silence that was then filled by a shrieking Cath, retorting, "Oh, yes, I know all about that one. How is your arse these days, Cherry? Recovered? Nice work, mate. Bet you're really proud. Cherry is. Can't you fucking tell?"

Which again had been met with silence.

Cherry's toes had curled so far inside her shoes that they had been in danger of breaking their way out.

It was a topic that she had never brought up with him.

Avoided it at all cost since the incident.

He had never brought it up either – and if the mere mention of that part of town had come up on any occasion, they had both changed the subject rapidly.

His memory, from this particular description of events – as one of hilarity – obviously did not tally with her own.

In any shape or form.

A bit like when her Auntie Ethel had witnessed her Uncle Ed (on a romantic trip to Scunthorpe) with his hands firmly rummaging down a nubile waitress's top – and his version was that he had slipped on a piece of asparagus on the floor and had a very unfortunate landing. He had threatened to sue.

"Is there nothing about our private life that is private?" he had snarled before storming out.

That seemed fresh, coming from someone who had been determined to have every movement, in its full glory, recorded for posterity on the CCTV.

Cherry had shuddered. And then risen to her feet, in a feeble, abortive attempt to stop him from leaving – a failure further compounded by Cath, shouting, "Going to disappear to make a few more hundred phone calls to your fictitious mates are you? Pervert!" – at top volume, a large lump of spit flying like the wind from her lips.

The door had slammed hard enough for the ironic prints on the walls of Cherry's flat to vibrate, along with half the sixties' glasses, lined neatly behind the white, padded bar.

"Told you he was dodgy."

"And you've got a mouth like the Mersey tunnel."

Cherry had slumped back into her chair, defeated. There was no point in even arguing. Cath was in her own, personal, beer-hell and there would be no shutting her up. Joining her in the slide to semi-consciousness and liver-damage was the only answer. The rest would have to wait until the morning.

And that was the way that the evening had ended.

They had not met up as a threesome since, which was a relief.

Cherry had long since given up the thought that they would ever suffer each other's company again and had spent a great deal of time defending each of them to the other, to no avail. Joe despised Cath. And Cath loathed Joe.

Cherry tried, again and again, to explain to Cath his redeeming features. *She was in love with him, for fuck's sake. Why couldn't she see how lovely he was, underneath?*

But there were certain doubts in her mind.

She tried not to think about them.

She had still never met any of his friends – and yet he spent his entire life on his mobile to them. Or so he said; he always moved out of earshot, so she couldn't hear the conversations. *Oh God, perhaps he was married.*

His moods changed wildly from anger to jubilation.

Unpredictability didn't even touch on it.

He was totally hardcore.

It was half the challenge of his moody ways that she enjoyed.

He had also been very evasive about his parents.

She knew they were high-flyers; that he had a critical mother and a father who was something important in something or other – and had moved schools numerous times in his youth, due to his father being posted all over the place. She had assumed some of his weird ways were down to that.

She knew that he had not seen them for years – there had been some enormous problem that he refused to discuss. Even mentioning them was strictly out of bounds.

But then lots of people fell out with their parents.

Perhaps it was his invisible friends that worried her. *There must be one of them he wasn't too embarrassed to introduce her to? She wasn't that bad, surely?*

She was no longer sure.

Chapter 31

The old prostitute was walking back from her usual, lunchtime, liquid meal at her local.

A bit pissed, limping with her crutch, stray hairs escaping from her elegantly unexpected French pleat, she cut an unusual sight and, as always, passers-by tittered as she lurched past them.

Her hip was killing her today.

There was nothing else that the NHS could do for her; and since she was no longer turning tricks, private treatment was out of the question.

It was just life.

Another of the long list of hardships that hit you, one way or another. If you were sad, stupid, Sadie.

She had long since learned acceptance of many things.

As she hobbled, wincing, along the cobbled mews towards the street where her tiny, but immaculately tidy, devoid-of-possessions flat sat high in a crumbling mansion block, squinting in the sunlight at the traffic ahead, Sadie saw *him*.

Her heart nearly stopped.

Her pulse raced and she drew back, flattening herself to the wall, waiting for the sound of the hot rush of blood in her ears to die down so that she could hear – for her brain to reorganise itself into a logical order. She was immediately and horrifyingly sober.

He had pulled up in a car at the end of the mews, opened his door and walked around to open the passenger door to a sweet, happy-looking young girl, who was laughing and smiling.

He helped her out. He kissed her and got her bags out, handing them to her. They talked for a while.

Sadie could barely breathe.
Perhaps he had changed.

****

Memories flooded her brain. She was petrified.

Memories of facing him in terror. Memories of an unbearable pain in her leg and chest as she fought to get away from him, fought to save her own life – pain like a blow from a falling tree. Memories of falling, the sound of a car door slamming and the screech of tyres, the sounds of people running, their voices getting fainter.

And then nothing.

She had awoken in hospital.
She had been unconscious for nearly three weeks.

The shots to her leg had caused the most damage.
The shot to her chest, although intended to kill, had missed every vital organ and passed through her into a nearby building.

Her hip had been smashed beyond repair, severing her femoral artery.

Her knee was no more.

She had lost more than her entire blood volume twice over and had been transfused until the surgeons had nearly lost all hope. But she had survived; had a brand new hip, and knee – had made it. Against all the odds.

She had not been able to tell the police what had happened. There was no point.

With her past, why would they believe her? Just another old prostitute.

And with his mother, it wasn't worth the bother.

And if he ever found her again, he would surely finish the job.

After all, someone like her should not have humiliated a man like him.

He had his position in the community to think about.

His fantasy world.

Being beaten regularly, on the backside with a ruler, by someone old enough to be his mother, on a regular basis – while dressed in nappies – was not something somebody as important as him needed to have exposed. The papers would have had a field day, if it had ever got out. *Just as well she hadn't had the energy or inclination to spill the beans. And had valued her life a little more than to even attempt to give him away.*

****

It had not been her fault, really.

He had summoned her to where he was living. She had only done as requested to keep him calm, keep her supply of drugs coming, maintain the status quo.

It was because of the baby monitor.

He had wanted it as part of his fantasy.

How was she supposed to know that she should have switched it off? Or that his mother would come round unexpectedly and had a key to let herself in? Or that his mother was a government minister and was the real source of his amazing cash flow? No wonder he had problems...he was still tied to her purse strings – not so much her apron strings.

His mother had been silently in the kitchen, as the old prostitute was beating the bejesus out of him; this time with a leather paddle that he had bought expressly for the purpose from Anne Summers. He had been shrieking like a banshee, "No, no, no," and she had stopped, momentarily, before he had wiggled his arse at her again and she had realised that he meant 'yes, yes, yes.' She had continued to thrash at him as he had pushed back against the force of the paddle. Welts were appearing on his thighs and she was trying to stifle laughter at the pitiful sight.

"You nasty, mean, fucking bitch, Mummy!" he had cried.

"You slut! You filthy whore! Stop hurting me, Mummy!"

He had been in full flow then. She had continued furiously pummelling him, turning the implement round to use the handle for a bit more variety. *It was getting boring now. She just wanted him to finish, so she could go and recover with a cup of tea. But he'd taken a truckload of Viagra and at this rate she was going to be there for hours. Her wrist was giving out. It was her hand that needed the Viagra.* She had tried to remember if her arthritis tablets were somewhere in her handbag.

He had sunk further onto his shoulders, face down and had started to part his buttocks for further punishment.

Oh sweet Jesus. Surely not? Not with her hand, anyway!

She had reached for the small dildo she kept in her bag for such emergencies and started to poke it into his greedy backside, as he howled with unabashed glee. As she had cranked up the pace, with her eyes shut to block out the repulsive sight, he had

187

finally come with an ear-rending "Aaaaaarrrrrgggggghhhhhh!" and she had removed her instrument of torture with relief. There had been a piece of undigested carrot left on the end.

In the ensuing silence, they had both been startled by the sound of a female throat being cleared, behind them.

It was his mother.

His mother had sat, head in hands, in his immaculate kitchen, listening to the horrifying sounds emanating from the floor above, via the baby monitor. Thirteen minutes worth of him begging for all sorts. Swallowing hard against her snowballing nausea, the rising volume of his shrieks – recognisably joyful – had driven her to the point where she could no longer remain downstairs.

She hadn't expected him to be with an old woman.

Or to be shouting, "Mummy."

And she hadn't been able to make a sound, to stop them, to tear her eyes away from the vision of her son being brutalised by a dishevelled, old harridan.

And him loving it.

She had been watching her own son being degraded – degrading himself, degrading her, degrading his family name. She had witnessed first-hand the filth of her own son's inner mind. *It had to be stopped.*

He had reeled with shock at the sight of his mother, tried to stand up, covering his knob with his hands; but the terry nappy still pinned around his ankles had shackled him like a prisoner and he had fallen sideways off the bed and lay, prostrate, on the floor at her feet, eyes as wide as dinner plates.

He was wearing lipstick?

He had tried to say 'it was the first time' and that 'she had forced him to do it'.

But no-one in their right mind who had just witnessed a scene from the most appalling porn film, starring their own son, was going to believe that; so the old prostitute had resignedly explained to the poor woman (who was about the same age as her) that this had been going on for two years. And was just his little way of expressing himself. And that perhaps it was a result of his childhood; that perhaps he needed help.

This explanation of events really hadn't helped, under the circumstances.

His mother had then told him quite categorically that she no longer accepted him as her son, would never help him again, that his money was no more – and left.

The rage that ensued was something to behold.

He had cleared himself up, grey with anger and fear; exposed, shamed – and not for the first time in his life.

But never before quite on this scale. And it looked as though his mother really meant it this time. She had washed her hands of him. And that would be extremely inconvenient. His varying lines of work did not provide sufficient funds for his very particular needs. Fuck. He was ruined.

He had dressed, coldly, his breath hard and fast and coarse, shaking with fury and angry humiliation. His teeth were clenched and grinding furiously, beads of perspiration swelling on his forehead and the blood drained from his face.

The old prostitute had been fully clothed throughout the proceedings; and had quickly taken refuge downstairs in the kitchen. Listening to the sounds of him still dressing, through the baby monitor, she could hear every breath. And she realised that his mother had been able to hear every, last, gory detail. And that despite looking smaller in the flesh, she had recognised his mother instantly, from interviews on the television.

The enormity of the situation hit her like a mallet.

She was now in big, fucking trouble, with a capital T, written in luminous letters and underlined in red.

He was bad. Really bad.

Through and through.

He was going to make her pay.

In the past two years, she had witnessed his violence towards others – his cold and savage cruelty – time and time again. He had had a soft spot for her, she knew. Treated her not as badly as the rest. Fed her. With more things than food. Put a roof over her head.

But she had had to pay for it.

With her body.

And not just with him. There had been so many others. She had degraded herself to the point that she no longer cared. Days had come and gone, each bringing new humiliation. But she had needed him. She had nothing else.

She was ruined already.

What more shame could life have brought, that she had not shamed herself with anyway?

She didn't even know his real name.

He had used many, many names in his dealings, in his selling of women's bodies, in his selling of drugs. Even this beautiful maisonette, in which she visited him now, was paid for weekly in cash to cover his tracks; was filled with state-of-the-art furniture paid for with a card which did not bear his name – the food bought with a credit card bearing yet another name. It was always the same with him. He never stayed anywhere for long.

She felt frozen. Sitting on a cold stool in the kitchen, she didn't know what to do. Her thoughts were getting scrambled, fear was taking over; nothing rational was going through her brain.

Her mind, instead of telling her to run, had turned to throw at her a fleeting memory of happier times; of a holiday to Brighton, when she had gone to see Paul Daniels with her husband, in a former life – and the magician had stuck him to a chair. *God, he'd been annoyed. Had totally believed this to be impossible. Had only gone up on stage to prove, in some way, that he could not be affected. But had then been stuck there with imaginary glue, trying to rise, puce with annoyance.*

It had been one of the only times that she had ever seen him angry.

She could hear the rattle of car keys now, from upstairs. Perhaps he would just drive away and leave her be, until he calmed down. Fat chance.

She had then heard a sound that made her stomach turn and her heart stop, for what felt like seconds. He was moving the bed. And the unmistakeable sound of a floorboard being lifted rang true and clear, in the quiet of the kitchen.

It could only mean one thing.

He was retrieving his gun.

And she was running, out of the door, into the road; the door swinging shut, gasping for breath, her breath heavy in her chest like breathing in treacle, her legs heavy with terror. *She was running through quicksand, her whole body juddering in terror, filled with an adrenalin rush that rendered her incapable of thought or motion; running, running, running, running, but getting nowhere.*

Slower now, slower, stumbling, out of breath, her mouth dry, she felt herself giving up as she heard the door open behind her. *No, keep going, keep going.*

The voices of children in the next-door garden were shrill and almost comforting – *a nice sound to hear before you died.*

He had shot her knee.

She wasn't aware of the bullet. The pain had been instantaneous and like fire tearing through her bones. She had fallen heavily – the sound of impact like a dull crunch as her head made contact with the grey slabs – and lay there staring back at him, on the cold, rough hardness of the pavement, waiting for him to finish her off. It was inevitable. She had shut her eyes.

She could still hear children playing in the garden next door.

A second shot.

The children were silent, now.

A third shot.

She had arched and gyrated with the new impact. The pain was so intense that the third shot brought nothing new, except the sensation of drowning. *Her adrenalin was fizzling out now; her blood felt like syrup in her veins, she was drifting, floating up, the pain wrenching her guts from her body like a giant fist.*

And then the world had gone black.

He had never been caught.

She had discovered he had registered the flat under yet another fictitious name.

Photofits on the news had brought many sightings and reports of potential suspects.

But he had never been caught.

There had been no chance of police protection. They had far better things to do. Like stopping people in cars who appeared to be twelve and four-foot-two.

And protecting his mother. The old prostitute had known her face instantly. And seen the disgust etched on it as she looked at him, with eyes the same green as his.

But who would believe her?

She was a hooker.

Dirt.

Not to be trusted or believed.

And if she gave him away, he would find her.

He would kill her.

And she felt for his mother; a person of responsibility, a supporter of humanitarian causes, a leader.

She felt for her and her burden.

So the old prostitute had disappeared, reformed her ways, changed her name, taken it as a sign that yet again life would have to change.

But this time for the better.

She had been given another chance.

She had become 'Sadie'. She had detached herself, firmly, from all that was past, all that was ill with her life.

She wanted to do something positive to repay God for his kindness in preserving her. Instead of hating him for the ill He had done to her. She wanted to start anew.

****

And now, here she was, years on, looking at him again. Unmistakeably him. Older. Greying. Glasses. But him, without question. In her part of town.

193

He was now getting back in the car.

Maybe he was a reformed character?

But just as he wound down the window to say a final few words, she heard his parting shot to the young woman he was supposed to be in love with.

"Fuck off, you stupid, cunting little bitch. Or you won't know what's hit you."

He hadn't changed at all.

She waited for the car to disappear and hobbled, super-quick-speed, in the direction of the young girl she had seen get out of it. *No-one deserved to be on the receiving end of him.*

She had heard that he was getting married. Presumably this was his betrothed.

Poor girl.

She had to stop it.

The girl had stopped to look in a shop window.

As Sadie staggered up to her, now so short of breath that she could barely speak, the girl looked up and smiled.

"Do you want a fag?" she asked, kindly. "Or some money for a sandwich?"

Sadie paused, taken aback. *My God, she must look bloody appalling.*

"I'm not a vagrant, you know," she said. "I need to talk to you. It's probably the most important conversation you'll ever have with anybody."

"I don't want to become a Jehovah's Witness, thanks…"

"Not that!" – impatiently now. "Not that at all. This will save your life. It's about that young man whose car you just got out of. He tried to kill me, a long time ago. Shot me. He's hurt lots of people. Lots. I don't know what he's said to you, but it will be all lies. All of it. He is a… "

194

"Sod off, you deranged, old bag, I was trying to be nice to you!"

The old woman pressed a piece of paper into the girl's hand as she tried to get away from her.

It was all she could do.

The girl ran off, Sadie shouting madly at her in the background, but unable to keep up.

At least she had tried.

Chapter 32

"God almighty, Cath. You'll never guess what just happened to me!"

Cherry was short of puff, having mountaineered her way to Cath's palace in the heavens.

Well, condominium in Elephant.

But it was about a million floors up and she hadn't got the lungs for it. Or the shoes.

Prada's new sculptural heels weren't designed for lifts that did not work. Or walking. One heel seemed to be hanging on by a thread, which had made the last fifteen flights all the more precarious.

She flopped onto a moth-eaten, old Chesterfield, which had its stuffing hanging out like the gory remains of a half-eaten carcass at the zoo.

She caught her breath just long enough to light up another fag and turned to check that she had Cath's full attention.

It was a prerequisite; the drama would be somewhat lost if she wasn't holding court one hundred per cent successfully.

Cath – out of a long-standing habit that had reappeared as soon as they had renewed their friendship – stopped stirring the thick gloop that promised to transform into Bolognese according to the instructions and turned to face her friend, giving her her full concentration.

As usual, Cherry had come for a meal empty-handed – no wine, no flowers, no chocolates – no nothing. And was about to launch into some new and unbelievable saga, whilst necking all her booze. Some things never changed.

Cath smiled.

Cherry regaled the tale of the old bag.

"Blimey. Do you think she's fucking barking – or does she know something you don't?"

"Plainly insane. But why do I always get 'em? Either nutters or prostitutes. Always coming up to me. Every tube I take. Every bus I take."

"Every step you make, every breath you take, I'll be watching you!" sang Cath.

God she could be irritating. Cherry huffed and looked like thunder. *Cath was ruining her story. And didn't she realise this was of great importance?*

"Stop, you witch."

Cath realised her blunder, mumbled a non-meant apology and returned to her pot-stirring. The air was thick with angry silence.

After a minute or so, she turned to Cherry, to renew the conversation – as though nothing had happened and she hadn't fucked up.

"Are you sure you want to marry him?"

A pause. For a great deal too long.

Oh dear. Not a good sign. This could be a long evening.]

****

He had not got down on bended knee.
He had not even really asked her.

He had taken her to an art event, in the country and had been obnoxious and rude all the way there, in the car. Sitting with a face like thunder and driving erratically – the epitome of road rage – he had forced Cherry into an uneasy silence, dread filling her heart.

She felt sick.

There had been so many of these incidents – always uncomfortable, always filled with her anxiety and his inexplicable, unpredictable, unwarranted anger.

Never for a reason.

This time, he had picked her up already angry; and as she had climbed into the car, she could almost reach out and touch his hostility. The air was thick with it.

She had asked him what the matter was, immediately assuming that it was her fault, that she had done something; wanting to make amends, to make it all all right.

But his rage was always an impenetrable barrier, a wall of silent wrath. He always made her shake when he was like this, made her heart rate soar, her palms sweat. And she would always make it worse with some inane comment, trying to appease, to alleviate the tension, to make it all OK.

It would be better if she stayed quiet, didn't antagonise.

It had been a long journey. As time had gone on, the silence had grown thicker and denser, until it was as if they were sitting in fog. The silence gave her much time to think.

It was the injustice of it all.

She had begun to feel angry herself, as the minutes ticked away and she became victim of his terrible, anger-fuelled driving on top of his general air of displeasure. When he pulled up to the bumper of the car in front, on the motorway, at 80 miles an hour and started flashing his lights, bawling, "Out of the way, you fucking stupid, old cunt!" at the top of his voice, she had become frightened for her own safety.

The man in front was a pensioner who was driving perfectly well; not breaking any rules, undeserving of his rage. Just a bit slow.

And at this rate, because of Joe, they were all going to die.

"Stop the car," she had said quietly. He had ignored her.

"Stop the bloody car!" – louder now, her patience worn as thin as paper. "I will not sit in here any longer, with you driving like this. You're going to kill us all. Let me out, you moody shit."

He had then slowed down to a ridiculous crawl in retaliation to her request, veering across all the lanes onto the slow lane and braking hard, driving at little more than 30mph.

"Satisfied?"

And then an anger of enormous intensity had risen up like a monster within her, bubbling and boiling from weeks of suppression; and she had spat at the side of his face as he drove, her fear all gone, replaced with a venom even bigger than his own.

He had not pulled over.

He would not let her out of the car.

He would not speak.

She was absolutely enraged.

They had arrived at the venue and pulled into the car park.

And she had let rip with a tsunami of pent-up emotion, which had been swelling within her heart for longer than she cared to remember.

"AFTER THIS, I WANT NOTHING MORE TO DO WITH YOU! NOTHING! DO YOU UNDERSTAND ME? YOU VAIN, SELF-ABSORBED, ARROGANT, IGNORANT CUNT! PISS OFF!" she had screeched, in a voice she barely recognised as her own. "Let me out of the bloody car – now – you selfish, nasty loser," she added, a little more quietly, realising she was pushing her luck – and that the tirade of expletives all queuing up inside her brain, bursting to get out, were going to do nothing more, now, than add to his fury and her impending doom. *Time to just shut up, before she bit off more than she could chew.*

He had got out of the car and stood outside it, leaning on the bonnet, his back to her – as she fumbled with her seat belt and then couldn't get out of the car door because of the child-lock.

He eventually released her and she climbed out, still shaking and slammed the door as hard as she could, hoping it would fall off its hinges.

"YOU'D BETTER HAVE THIS THEN! STUPID COW. ENJOY!" he'd shouted back, hatefully; hurling a small box at her with all his might, so that it hit her mid-stomach, the shock winding her, slightly. He had then stalked angrily off inside the venue, without even looking at her, without so much as turning back.

When he had gone, she picked up the box.

She had wanted so much to leave it where he threw it, not touch it, make her way back home and disappear from him forever. She had wanted for him to come back out of the exhibition to find it left, exactly where he had thrown it; to know that it was all over, that she had meant what she had said.

But she also wanted to see what it was that he had thrown at her, make sense of something, anything. *And it might be something nice. And, more to the point, she was miles away from home, with no money and no means of getting back. Bollocks. She'd have to thumb a lift.*

And she so was full of confusion.

She loved him; of that, she was sure. But it seemed that her feelings were not reciprocated. She had had enough of it all.

Inside the box, was a beautiful, antique, diamond ring. *Fucking huge. Incredibly classy. Befitting Elizabeth Taylor, at the very least. Must have cost an absolute arm and a leg.*

Of course, she had to try it on.

It fitted one finger alone. Her wedding ring finger.

In fact, it fitted so well that she was unable to get it off.

Oh fuck.

She was awash with dilemma.

She leant against the side of the car, tearing at her finger, trying to remove it. Still so full of spleen towards him, she wanted to take it off, put it back in the box, place the box back on the gravel – sans fingerprints of course – to be able to pretend that she had not even been interested enough to look inside.

She spat on her finger, trying to use her own saliva to lubricate her digit, in order to remove it.

Her finger was swelling now.

There was lip-salve in her bag.

That would do it.

It would bloody have to.

She rummaged for it, frantically, and found it, already opened in the murky depths of the leather, stuck with grit and dirt and some kind of suspicious fluff. She smeared the grease, panic stricken, in huge, gloopy lumps all over the ring. It was a shade of 'orgasm pink, long-lasting formula' and removing it from the ornate, Art Nouveau, platinum mount was likely to prove a bit of a bugger. She turned to check that no-one was observing her... anyone watching would think that her behaviour was that of a lunatic.

Oh shit, he was coming out.

She had ducked down behind the car, heart racing, still fighting with ring and swollen digit. She started to crawl, on her hands and knees towards the shrubbery, like a deranged Spaniel in search of an elusive biscuit. She could hear his feet crunching, ever-closer on the gravel.

She made it into the bush behind his car, still out of his sight and sat, trying not to breathe, feeling foolish, beaten.

He would know, by now, that she had picked it up. Damn. Her opportunity to really teach him a lesson, be on top for once, was ruined.

At least he would now think that she was gone – she would have some semblance of pride left.

To her left, she heard the sound of somebody urinating close to her, flies having been undone. In fact, she was being splattered with a fine mist of urine from an incredibly strong-smelling, jet-propelled wee. "Bloody hell! Yuck! You dirty..."

Then a voice, "Oh dear, I'm terribly sorry, madam. I didn't know anyone was there… " She still had her eyes shut, wiping at her mouth with gusto; hoping none had gone in.

The bush rustled. She became aware that the voice was still there, the gaze of the man now directed at her, looking at her crouched in the hedgerow.

"Are you all right, madam?"

Oh shit shit shit shit shit, she had been discovered hiding in a bloody shrub. Could things get any worse?

She looked around to see the face of an old man, looking quizzically at her, bending towards her, a worried but slightly amused expression on his face. He had zipped up and was flushed with embarrassment.

"Go away!" she hissed and ducked down even further.

He disappeared, rapidly.

She had remained motionless, breathing quietly.

Her legs were beginning to cramp.

She needed a wee herself come to think of it.

Desperately.

When she had been able to hear nothing else, she had tentatively emerged, silently peering to check that the coast was clear.

"I hope it's a good fit."

He was there, standing by the car, watching her. Laughing at her.

"Yes," she had said. "Can we go home now?"

****

But today, in Cath's kitchen, she felt sure that it was the right thing to do. Nobody had the perfect relationship, did they?

She adored him, didn't she?

He made her go weak at the knees and soggy in the knickers, even after all this time.

When things were great, they were really great – better than anyone she knew who had a relationship. He made her laugh, could be warm, passionate, needy, silly. She was still excited every time he rang her. He was like no-one else she had ever met.

She could tolerate the bad bits. He didn't mean anything by his actions. *He was just troubled.*

It wasn't really his fault.

"Yes, I do want to marry him," she said to Cath. "Sincerely. He really does love me."

"He has a pretty funny way of showing it, honey. Nice ring and all that. But he's a bloody arsehole. You've said so yourself. Marriage is a huge, bloody commitment. You need to be absolutely sure. Otherwise you're stuck with him just because you like a big rock. Or should that be a big cock? And you can take that as you will."

"I know you don't like him."

"Just don't make a mistake. You don't need to get married to him. Wait to see if he can sort out his temper first."

Cath piled the mountain of overcooked Bolognese onto plates and they tucked in.

This evening, however, Cherry could not shift the small atom of doubt at the back of her mind. She was beginning to wonder if her friend – and indeed the bizarre, old lady – was onto something.

Chapter 33

Connie would have been bonny lass, had she not been so thin.

And bruised.

And it wasn't fair what the other kids said at school about her, when they pushed her out of the way, shoved her about, said she smelled of shit.

It wasn't her fault.

She tried to wash her own clothes in the sink each night. She wasn't allowed to use the washing machine. Her mother wouldn't let her into the kitchen. Not unless she had already passed out, anyway.

She wasn't at school much.

"On account of the bullying," said her mother, when Social Services had come round to make gentle, initial enquiries. The school had 'concerns'.

Connie had missed the first meeting that she was due to have with them, as her mother had made her hide in the cupboard under the stairs.

She had heard the voices, listening from the dark, in the stench of damp and the choking dust. She heard her mother saying that Connie had 'gone out to play, would be back later. They would have to come back another time'.

Another appointment was made, but the story was the same.

Until they'd threatened Sam with court.

On the final occasion, there had been three weeks' notice.

Enough time for the bruises to vanish. But Connie's spirit remained bruised.

She was too frightened to tell. Her mother said she would kill her if she did.

It was best not to say.

It was Miss Appleton's fault.

She had betrayed Connie. Connie had trusted her. And Miss Appleton had let her down. She couldn't trust her again.

And now, there was no-one left to talk to.

Except for their old neighbour who ran the sweetie shop. And even then, she couldn't be sure. What if he said something to Mummy? She had to keep her mouth shut. It was for the best.

Miss Appleton knew that others pushing Connie about in the playground had not been enough to cause that kind of bruising.

She had been looking out of the staffroom window, when it started. They circled Connie, pushing, laughing at her, calling her "Pikey shit!" as the frail, little girl crouched, hands over her ears, eyes shut, waiting for it to all stop.

Miss Appleton had rushed down to the playground, skidding down the stairs, heels sparking, hands burning on the handrail – and they had all run at the sight of her; laughing, leaving Connie still, too afraid to move, eyes closed, waiting.

She had led the petrified, little girl into the staffroom, just as the bell went and a sea of teaching staff, anxious to get the afternoon over and done with so that they could make their escape, evacuated it.

It had taken Connie a long time to talk, to confess the bruises had not just happened. But she had finally caved in to the words of kindness, the comforting arms held tightly around her shaking body – broken down; her story gushing, tumbling from her lips. Desperately begging, "Please, please don't tell, it will all be worse."

For months, Miss Appleton had kept her promise. And Connie had finally had a friend.

But the promise had been broken after an unusually long absence from school.

Miss Appleton had gone to Connie's home, after school one day – and as she had raised her hand to knock at the door, she had heard the sound of Connie's voice whimpering and pleading for it all to stop, from behind the battered wood of the front door.

And then there was nothing.

She had started to shout, "STOP!" through the letterbox. "CONNIE! ANSWER ME! OPEN THE DOOR!"

There was the sound of running on the stairs.

Muffled voices.

The slam of a door.

She had just got out her mobile and was frantically dialling 999, when a window opened, above her.

"FUCK OFF! MIND YOUR OWN BUSINESS! WHO THE FUCK ARE YOU, ANYWAY?"

"Connie's teach… "

The window had slammed shut.

She had told the police, alerted Social Services and broken her promises to the little girl.

Connie had returned to school after a few days, smaller, thinner, paler than before, black circles of tiredness underlining her miserable, terrified eyes. She had remained silent after that, refusing to talk to her teacher again – except once.

"Please leave me alone," she had said.

Fear was a funny thing. It brought you full circle. It made you actually believe what you knew, inside, was wrong. And *then, eventually, it made you believe that **everything** you had been told, for your whole, entire life, was not right. Not the truth. A lie, like everything else.*

But you couldn't say. You couldn't even ask the only one who knew. Because the very question would result in punishment so bad that you couldn't breathe.

Connie still said that everything was fine when the burning started.

She had walked in on her mum as she was in the kitchen.

She had only wanted a glass of water. She was so very thirsty.

She had crept, terrified, down the stairs in the silence of night to get some. It would momentarily fill the empty cavern of her stomach. She had not been allowed to have any food that evening.

She had been a bad, bad girl.

Her periods had started that morning and she had been too frightened to say, too terrified of getting yet another thing wrong.

It was the only thing she was good at – getting things wrong. But Mummy had seen the blood in her knickers as she tried to wash them out in the upstairs sink.

"Disgusting. Slut. Filthy, little slut."

When Connie had arrived in the filthy pit where the kitchen sink was, the familiar, rancid smell of burning chemicals had hit her and she realised, too late, that her mother was using.

Again.

She hoped her mother had already had her fix. She knew that if she had disturbed her when she was desperate, before the narcotics had hit her system, she would be punished.

But her mother had not yet filled the needle, was glazed and angry.

She turned on Connie.

"You little bitch. Get out. Get upstairs. I fucking told you already to not come down here! NO...STAY THERE, YOU LITTLE COW! DON'T TURN AWAY WHILE I'M TALKING TO YOU!"

Her mother was lurching towards her in the dark now, shaking with anger.

Connie knew what was coming.

Sam grabbed her by the hair and began to kick her; stomach, back, kidneys, chest, legs – until she fell to the floor in easy submission, too frightened to even make a cry.

The back of the spoon, fresh from the gas hob, provided a pain more intense than she could bear. But she knew that a single sound would make her agony endure for longer, as her mother went from anger, to blind, inexplicable rage. The pain was like a white light in her brain. It came again and again and again.

When the iron grip finally loosened, Connie ran – ran from the room, up the stairs, stumbling; the gripper treads, where the carpet had been removed, slicing into her toes.

She ran into her room and sat in the darkness; back braced against the door, knees to chest, breathing quickly, shallow, terrified breaths, listening, listening, trying to calm her breaths so that they didn't drown the sounds from downstairs – so she could hear what was happening.

It *was OK. Mummy was still downstairs. She was not coming.*

And there she sat, all night, not daring to go to sleep.

Chapter 34

They had just come out of the fair on Blackheath.

Cherry, tired of tedious and lengthy visits to art galleries, had forced him to go for some light relief.

It was a test, a last chance.

She loved him. He made her heart lurch and gave her butterflies. She felt lucky to be with such a strong, beautiful-looking man. But the frequent bad moods, the soul-destroying rows and bad words were wearing her down. And she hated the fact that her nearest and dearest could not see in him the good bits she could see. It filled her with more doubt.

And there were the lies. Stupid, small, inconsequential, unnecessary. They were not important untruths, but he slipped up on occasion – gave himself away. It was usually in front of her friends, trying to impress, trying to make himself look important, trying to make them like him when he knew they did not.

It made him look stupid. She couldn't understand why he did it.

She had learnt not to challenge him when the discrepancies arose. His embarrassment would lead to anger. And Joe backed into a corner was not a pretty sight.

He had met a group of friends from her work, once.

Cherry had been talking about him, for weeks, since the engagement. She and Joe had been excitedly making plans for the future, having fun. She wanted to show him off.

It had been a simple drink, in a simple pub, where the girls were giggling with Joe, excited to finally meet him. At the end of the night, just as Cherry was about to leave them all to continue their fun at a club, one of the girls had grabbed her in the toilets.

"Oh, Cherry! He's gorgeous! Aren't you lucky!"

Cherry had blushed, happy with some rare approval.

"He told me about his award too. You must be so proud!"

Cherry's heart sank.

He'd tried that one before. Excused himself, later, when Cherry had asked him about it in excitement, asked if she could go to the ceremony; blamed Cath – said she'd heard wrongly. It was the noise in the club they were in.

"Yes," she said, "I'm really proud of him."

Later, they'd gone back to his flat.

"So, Joe. The award. For bravery. Susie told me all about it."

Cherry had hoped he'd tell her it was true.

They had fought for hours. She had blinked back hot tears as he ranted, millimetres from her face – his breath warm on her mouth, his words cold in her ears, his eyes burning into hers.

She had listened to herself apologise for not believing his lie.

And there was the fact that she felt somehow wary of him, of his temper. He had never hurt her. Most of the time he was loving, attentive, sweet.

She couldn't mention it to her friends. She knew what their reaction would be. And she loved him, wanted to be with him.

When she had told him of her encounter with the old lady, he had flown into the worst rage she had seen him have.

She had only mentioned it.

There was no reason for her to keep it from him.

She had thought he would find it funny.

But it wasn't surprising, his anger.

She was supposed to love him.

Even mentioning it was to doubt him.

And look at all he'd done for her. Educated her, taken her to nice places, bought her expensive gifts. And didn't she know how lucky she was to be with him? It wasn't as if she had that much to offer, was it? There were plenty of women who would jump at the chance to be with him. Oh yes, there had been plenty of offers.

He was in full flow now, getting progressively more foul as he whipped up momentum towards a crashing finale of abuse. She listened, without contradiction, as if she was having an out-of-body experience.

She was a fucking stupid, old bitch who had let him down, betrayed him by even mentioning such toss. A two-bit waste of his breath, a fucking terrible shag. And he was too embarrassed of her to let her meet his mates. Oh no, couldn't do that. He'd be a laughing stock! They were all dating models and 'it-girls', while he was wasting his time with her! Anyway, perhaps she should just go off and listen to a few more Alzheimer's nutcases with mad stories to tell and fucking leave him alone! PERHAPS HE SHOULD JUST LEAVE HER TO CRAWL OFF WITH SOME BLOODY NORTHERN BRICKIE WHO WAS MUCH MORE HER LEVEL! SHE'D BE LAUGHING THE OTHER SIDE OF HER FACE THEN, WOULDN'T SHE? THEN SHE'D SUDDENLY REALISE WHAT SHE'D THROWN AWAY, FUCKING HIM OVER BY BELIEVING SOME OLD COW AND HER LIES!

She had remained silent, dumbstruck by his words. She had never, ever heard such filth, such hatred. She had stood, shocked, unspeaking, tears welling, until his volume gradually reduced, until he had calmed down a degree – too frightened to respond in any small way in case his rage increased once more; fearful that those clenched fists might actually be put to use, although he had never gone that far before.

She had never seen him so angry.

He eventually ran out of venom and across his eyes passed quite a different emotion.

She could not quite place it.

He had then stormed out of the room, leaving her standing in the corner, shocked and speechless – and she had locked himself in her bathroom where she sat, rigid with shock. She rummaged, with shaking hands, through the bathroom cabinet for her 'emergency' fag, finding two in the packet, breaking three matches trying to light one cigarette. She looked at herself, long and hard, in the mirror – at her own pale, drawn, haggard face. *This could not go on.*

Later, much later, when she had emerged, half wondering if he had let himself out – and had quietly gone to sit down, not daring to even make a noise in her own flat – he had reappeared, slightly clammy, with a perspiration-beaded top lip and walked towards her. He had thrown himself on the floor, at her feet and sobbed and sobbed and sobbed, clutching her ankles.

Eventually he had looked up, lips quivering, a myriad of emotions crossing his face, judders of fear contorting his mouth, making his lips squirm and wobble.

"Sorry," he had said, simply. "Please, please, please forgive me. I didn't mean any of it. I didn't mean what I said. I'm just a fuck-up. Give me another chance."

He had begun to sob again, a pitiful trail of snot from his right nostril making a shiny, vibrating line, as it stretched to her thigh. He was face down on her knees, looking up occasionally at her face, begging, "I love you so much. I can't bear the thought of you doubting me."

Eventually, Cherry's kind heart had got the better of her and she had silently cupped his face in her hands and looked at him, full in the face.
"Stop it, now. It's OK. But never again."

And then he had tried to kiss her. She had brushed him off, still stunned by his cutting words, yet wanting to forgive, wanting so much for it all to be OK, trying to rationalise his awful behaviour.

He never really meant it, did he? He just felt betrayed. He couldn't help himself. They were only words. Disgusting words. He did truly love her like no man had ever done before, didn't he? And she adored him. Most of the time. He just had problems. Huge problems. Not his fault. He needed help. Needed her help.

But still, ever-increasing doubts filled her mind, which she hurriedly pushed to the back; she boxed them, wrapped them and put them in the segment of her brain marked "trash".

****

It was a test, a last chance.

Blackheath fair was always great. She had first gone in those heady times when she had first set up camp with Cath and Elvis. It had been like going to the country…vast expanses of green in a village setting; a small glimpse of a life back home in the country, a vision of large sky, open grass, the things that she secretly missed, but could not confess to wanting back.

And they had had fun, such fun, playing open-air bingo on small, slippery seats domed like mushrooms, having taken acid which had appeared not to work – until they had got down from the big wheel and collapsed on the grass, drunken legs unable to support them, feeling dizzy still from the ride, although everyone else around (unencumbered by drugs) was walking with no problem.

They had laughed and laughed, been thrown out of the bingo for creating a rumpus and then lay on the grass, picking magic mushrooms that were, in fact, normal mushrooms.

Going back to the fair had brought back such great memories that she had been excited for the whole weekend in anticipation. He had certainly been much better behaved since his meltdown in the flat; his realisation that he had pushed it way too far, that his actions had threatened his relationship with her in a near irreversible way, had softened him somehow. He had even tried to be civil to her friends in his own useless way. *But she still had to prove to herself that they had a future – that they could have some bloody fun – rip-roaring, side-splitting, daft fun.*

So this afternoon was his trial. He had to prove to her he could love it too; it would be a sign that she was not mistaken, that Joe was the man for her.

And she had been proved right.
It had been the best afternoon she had ever had with him.

He had giggled like a child, whooping and yelling on the rides, hugging her close, kissing her madly behind the Ferris wheel, telling her he adored her. Hand in hand, they had meandered, drunk with a shared happiness that had never quite existed between them before, across the heath, back to the village, towards the train home.

They had stopped outside an estate agent and he had suddenly started gabbling at a hundred miles an hour about the future – making plans, pointing out houses; houses where they might live together, make babies.

And then it had all gone horribly, suddenly, maleficently wrong.

"Spencer." – A woman's voice behind them.

Cherry had ignored it, the name meaning nothing to her.

But he had spun around, freeing himself of her hand and stood, facing the owner of the voice – and then he had rapidly begun to walk away, to leave Cherry there; *no explanation, no word – no nothing.*

The woman looked strangely familiar. In her sixties maybe, immaculately dressed – suited, nice shoes, Margaret Thatcher handbag.

"Hello," she said to Cherry.

Cherry turned to watch Joe, who had now turned back and started to rush back towards them, his face showing an agitation that she had never seen before. His face was curdled in an expression of confusion and horror. He started to call her, "CHERRY! COME HERE NOW!"

Cherry looked back at the woman, who was now proffering a manicured hand for her to shake and saying, "I think we need to talk."

Cherry began to giggle, confused and shook the woman's hand.

"Are you Spencer's girlfriend?" the woman said.

"Who the fuck is Spencer?" Cherry looked around for Joe, but Joe had gone.

"Spencer," she repeated, as if that was going to help. "The man you were with. He's my son."

Cherry was no longer laughing.

"I think we should go for a cup of tea," the woman said.

Chapter 35

Jude had bid farewell to Arthur a few weeks previously.

He missed the old man. He had been one of his only friends – a lovely, frightened, old man who had been imprisoned for life, way, way back and was by now so institutionalised that he had purposefully postponed his release, time and time again, with pre-arranged 'attacks' on other inmates.

All the men liked Arthur.

They let him act out his assailments on them, prior to release each time, with good grace; each of them knowing the old man's only friends were inside, that he knew no-one outside, that he would be unable to cope.

Arthur liked prison.

These days, it was all he knew.

It would be different on the outside.

People weren't the same as they had been, back in the day.

He watched youngsters come in.

They had no honour, these days, and no sense of loyalty.

They talked of a strange thing called "respect", which bore no resemblance to the word that he had known; did not seem to need to be earned, these days – but was expected, by people who deserved no respect, who did nothing to warrant it.

He was frightened of the world out there.

He had spent years playing cards and talking to Jude.

****

His crime had been a crime that did not necessarily warrant the time that he had spent in prison.

He had, once, been the proud fiancé of his childhood sweetheart.

She had become pregnant.

It was too soon, but he loved her, wanted to stay with her, support her. They had both become accustomed to the idea and started to even look forward to it.

They had returned from the pub, one night, to be met with angry, young men in a darkened underpass. They had threatened them, cornered them. The blows had started.

Arthur had run.
He had run and run. *Cowardly. Gutless. Weak-kneed.*
He had run for help.
But she had not followed.

When he arrived back at the spot where it was happening, with the police – alerted by telephone from the house where somebody had finally answered his screams at the door – there was a small crowd.

Crowding around a body.
Her body.

She had been brutally raped, his love. Her face was smashed; one side of her head caved in by the brick that now lay beside her, thick with her blood.

His love.

He had run over and then stopped and spumed vomit, through his fingers.

She was gone.

Gone.

Gone with the small life inside her, blood oozing from between her legs.

It had taken weeks for Arthur to find them.

People had told him where they lived; knowing Arthur would never give them away. He was an honourable man.

Everyone was behind him.

It was the guilt that did it.

Had he stayed, had he not run looking for help, it would all have been different.

He had not had time to say goodbye; had left her – alone, petrified, being brutalised, without him there to protect her, to be killed with her.

Because that would have been much better than being alive with this guilt – this overwhelming, all-consuming, penitence-filled loss.

He had killed two of the men, cold bloodedly, lying in wait with a pickaxe handle. The first had been killed with one blow; the sound of a dull 'thwack' resounding through the night, after the whistle of displaced air. The other had taken a little more time – a look of surprise and shock and confusion in his eyes, as he dragged himself along bitumen, leaving a thick blood-slick in his wake. Those sounds and images had recurred to Arthur, night after night since – the memory making him sick to his bones. He was unable to escape from them, even in his dreams.

Arthur had been caught.

And punished.

It was perfectly fair. In fact he'd waited patiently for the police to turn up, sitting by the bodies. He didn't care any more.

Arthur welcomed his punishment. Accepted it. Needed it. For not protecting his wife-to-be and unborn child.

****

But now, he was to be released.

They all knew he was not dangerous.

He couldn't get away with his attempts to stay incarcerated any longer.

He was led, blinking into the sunlight, one spring morning. He had been provided with a roof over his head, some work. He was to be looked after.

After a few weeks of freedom, he could take no more.

Everything he knew had changed out of all recognition. He knew he had to get back inside, where his friends were, where he was accepted, popular, where he felt at ease. He didn't want to hurt anybody, or frighten anybody. He wasn't that kind of man. His killing had been specific, was needed. He hated no-one except himself.

He had tried for voluntary work in the prison. But they would not allow him, said it would impede his rehabilitation into normal life.

Normal life? They didn't know what they were talking about. There was nothing normal out here, any more.

The solution came as he was walking past window dressers, dressing women of plastic – mannequins – in a department store. Years of early mornings meant that he was always awake by 5 a.m. and, unable to stand his own company was, in these few weeks since his release, compelled to walk the pavements early each morning; finding some comfort in the commuter-rush, of shops opening, streets being swept – a little company to fill his loneliness.

It had been years since he had seen a naked woman.

In fact, he had only ever seen one.

He felt a familiar stirring in his groin.

Plastic as they were, they were having a very unwelcome effect on him – even with their missing limbs, their lack of genitalia.

Indecency.

That was the only way.

Nobody would get hurt.

Nobody too frightened.

He would not affect anybody's livelihood, not take anything away from anyone.

But it would be totally unacceptable, all the same.

Perfect!

He began to laugh at himself and – winking at the shocked girls as they dressed the mannequins – he began to masturbate against the window, passers-by tittering and nudging and shaking heads. It was a pathetic sight – a dirty, leering, old codger with a long-since-forgotten, old penis, furiously thumping away at it with a look of furrowed concentration until, after it was turning red-raw with unexpected use, it finished its deed with a pathetic drip.

The police had been called, of course. And he had promised to "never do it again".

But went back every day for the next week – same time, same place, so it would be easy for the police to catch him immediately.

When he had been finally been put back in prison, *(the man was an absolute menace to society. Obviously couldn't help himself. Was a hazard on the streets. There was only one place for him.)* he had seen the psychologist. After a few weeks of solitary and some customary, half-baked counselling, he had been returned to his old block, with his mates.

Job done. Much better.

They had all been thrilled to see him. None more so than Jude, who had been even more lonely than usual without him.

"You crafty, old bugger! Are you mad? That was your chance for freedom. I'd have given my right arm just for a sniff of that!"

'I'm not like you, Jude. What have I got left out there? My friends are here. My girl and baby I will never see again. And I'm too frightened to die. I won't be reunited with them. They're up there and I'm going down, down, down. And if I was, by some freak of circumstance, allowed upwards, she would meet me at the Pearly Gates hating me for letting her down. I left her on her own to go through all that, remember. I'm better off in here."

"Oh, fuck, mate. Don't know what to say. But the guilt I understand. Mine is for ever introducing my wife into my family. I caused the destruction of all of them by doing that. So it really is my fault too."

"Aah yes, but you will have the chance to make it all all right when you get out. To show them you never did anything. To start afresh. At least they're all still there. Mine are never coming back. I can't turn the clock back. But maybe you can, Jude. Maybe you can."

Chapter 36

Cath was at her flat, with Mabel.

She had grown to adore Mabel as much as Cherry did.

She was the most amazing, old woman she had ever met.

At first, the shaking and drooling had slightly scared her. And the inappropriate tardiness of Mabel's reactions had been tricky, until she became accustomed to them.

Mabel's facial responses – and indeed, verbal – were very out of the ordinary. Her Parkinson's did not only make her shake and trot rapidly in one direction, no hope of changing it – rendering her now unable to turn corners without several yards of preparation – but her reactions to conversation lagged several seconds behind, so that she often laughed at jokes way after the event, her face frozen solid like un-defrosted steak, beforehand.

On several evenings, she had laughed at Cath when the topic had turned to something far more serious and Cath had wondered if she was, indeed, insane.

But Mabel was far from insane. She was one of the most grounded, yet extraordinarily fascinating women Cath had ever met. Her entire life was an experience in variety and Cath was by now considering changing the whole documentary she had started to try to put together into one of Mabel's life.

Mabel baulked at nothing.

She was more open-minded than anybody that Cath had ever met. Nothing fazed her whatsoever and she positively enjoyed being shocking, joining in with these two youngsters who were so full of life and inexperience.

It was ten o'clock in the morning.

Mabel had rung on the buzzer, as promised, at nine on the dot – to no answer.

Cath had still been in bed. She had been dreaming of being at the bus stop, in nothing more than a pair of grey, marl leggings, in which she had wet her pants beyond any hope of hiding it. Just before the bus stop, she'd been in a small, dark orchard, in which there were multiple apple trees – each with a small, enamel, children's toilet with a wooden seat.

*The toilets were all full of leaves and crap and when she had finally found a clean one and started, with abject relief, to wee, **there was a bell sound** and she had realised that the orchard had simply been a dream and that she was, in fact at the bus stop, with the bullies from her school, who called her 'fat Cath' – and they were all pointing (laughing as the dark patch between her legs in the pale grey, grew and grew) and she was too humiliated to run and then **the bell on the bus**, signalling the doors opening, was **ringing loud in her ears**. But they were all ignoring it and wouldn't get on and all the passengers were laughing and pointing too **and ringing bells**. But then she realised that it was really a dream; and she was awake now – properly awake. But her face had changed since she'd started using that new face cream – and had scabs all over it which, **when the bell rang** she had to pick off. The scabs had little windows behind, with small chocolates inside, just like an advent calendar... and she'd only got to December 11th and there wasn't much face left **and there was a bell again**...*

She had opened her eyes with a start.

And realised, with abject relief, that the orchard, bus stop and advent-calendar-face had vanished and she was alone in bed; clutching between her legs, her aged, Mickey Mouse alarm clock having failed her, yet again. The tennis racquet had become stuck behind the yellow tennis ball and was making a strange, grinding noise.

But the incessant bell was real.

It was the sound of the doorbell – and it was still ringing.

Oh, Jesus. She was drenched. The weeing bit had obviously not been a dream, either. She'd overslept. Thank God it would be Mabel.

The lift had worked right up to the floor below Cath's penthouse and then stopped. Mabel had then hobbled the rest of the way up the stairs and was desperately ringing her doorbell. She needed to sit down.

Cath rapidly threw on yesterday's clothes – in a heap at the side of her bed, sunny-side-up. And she ran; smelling of fresh, warm urine to gather Mabel from outside her door, in the communal hall.

"It does rather reek of the gentlemen's urinal, in your hallway," Mabel said, looking full of disgust. "And I do need to sit down, dear. I need a biscuit."

"Sorry, Mabe, I think that may be me stinking!" Cath regaled the tale of her dream.

Mabel laughed. "Actually, it might possibly be me. I was merely trying to cover it up by blaming some unsuspecting lay-abouts," she said.

Cath's description of her dream left Mabel hoarse with rasping giggles.

"I think I may need to leave you with a small gift of my very special Tenalady. Eight times dryer than the normal pantliner. It allows you to live life and enjoy," she said, once she had regained her composure. "Honestly, young lady, it's a bit too early in your life for these kinds of moments. At least I have an excuse. Is there some traumatic experience setting off this bed-wetting extravaganza? Anything I should know?"

Cath and Mabel had scoffed a fantastic breakfast of dense, white bread and bacon sandwiches, grease running down their fingers to their wrists. Cath had only really just started interrogating Mabel – tape recorder on, pen in hand, taking notes for the documentary – when her mobile had rung.

It was Cherry on the phone, crying, sounding frantic; crying so much that Cath couldn't understand her words.

"Cherry! Cherry, listen! Get a cab, honey. I'm at home. With Mabel. Get yourself here, now."

As she put down her phone, Mabel's brows were raised in a silent question.

"God only knows, Mabe," said Cath. "It's Cherry. She's in some kind of mess. She's on her way."

Cherry had arrived an hour later.

Her face was swollen with tears, her eyes like piss-holes in the snow, top lip swollen and blotchy with crying. She looked as if she'd done nine rounds with Frank Bruno and had come off distinctly badly.

"Jesus Christ, Cherry! Are you hurt? What the fuck has happened?"

'N... N... N... No-OOO-oooo!" she wailed.

Cath and Mabel waited with interest.

Cherry had always been a drama queen, but this was obviously destined to be a performance of Oscar-winning proportions.

She was face down on the table now, huge 'boo-hoos' wracking her shoulders.

Cath held her, waiting for some degree of the histrionics to wane, while Mabel stumbled into the kitchen to boil the kettle – which was not a good idea.

So Cath sat Mabel back down too and arrived back a couple of minutes later, with fresh coffee and a packet of soft, gone-off Hobnobs.

At the sight of them returning from the kitchen, Cherry resumed her dreadful "Wooo-aaa-hhhhhh"-ing.

"Stop, stop, stop," said Cath, beginning to feel more unsympathetic as time went on.

Bound to be some other boring-as-arseholes saga about Joe. When would she ever learn? They were all sick of her tales of woe and then her insistence in staying with him. What did she expect? Same old, same old, blah blah blah. Dump him. Or put up and shut up. End of.

"Come on, Cherry. Can't be that bad can it? Just calm it down a bit. Here," she proffered a tissue, "Blow your nose."

Cherry rubbed her nose and eyes and took some deep breaths. She calmed herself enough to speak.

"He's not called Joe," she started. "I don't know what's going on! He's called Spencer and I met his mother and he doesn't work for British Airways. And he's not at his flat and his phone's dead AND THERE'S NOTHING IN MY BANK ACCOUNT!" She inhaled, gasping air in spasmodic rushes.

Oh fuck, she was revving up for another big one. Perhaps she needed a slap. Or a glass of wine and a fag. Bit early, but what the hell...

Cath shoved a mug of Chateau Neuf du Pape under her nose and a lit fag between her teeth. Cherry downed half the

booze in one gulp; the mellow flavour not even having enough
time to tussle with her taste buds.

"I'm so stu-uu-uuuupid," Cherry wailed. "He's gone! He's
taken all my money. Everything!"

"What do you mean, all your money? What money?"

"Forget the money," said Mabel, quietly, from the other
side of the table. "I'm loaded, dear. And have no-one to spend it
on. And can't take it with me. So forget the money, dear. That's
not the problem. But just tell your friends here what has
happened. How we can help. You're safe now, my sweet." She
sucked her Hobnob noisily; teeth out on Cath's clean table-cloth,
coffee dribbling out of one corner of her mouth – and put a
shaky hand out towards Cherry's, missing it on the first attempt,
but managing to redirect it over Cherry's clenched fist on the
second.

And Cherry, slowly, in a wobbling voice, began to explain.

****

She had accepted the invitation from Joe's mother for tea.

She had followed the woman, compliantly, as she led the
way; a sense of dread overtaking her heart.

She was so confused and anxious that, as they approached
the tearooms, she had felt the need to break the dreadful silence
between them. But she had been unable to bring herself to say
anything relevant to the woman and had, instead, started a tirade
of nonsensical small talk, about *'weather and wasn't it lovely on
the Heath and had she ever been up in a Ferris wheel when she
was younger, not meaning that she was old, of course, but she
obviously hadn't done it today, because she was in smart shoes
and had a handbag and had a skirt on and skirts weren't really
suitable for a Ferris wheel, because people could see your
knickers and that's why she'd worn trousers herself today,*

229

because she was really excited about the fair, so she'd got all ready with a picnic and everything and she and Joe had been planning it for ages...'

It had been obvious that Joe wasn't coming back for her.

Joe.

Not Joe.

"Spencer."

Cherry's hands shook as she sipped her tea, waiting for an explanation, no longer talking – there was really nothing else for her to say.

"A long time ago, I had a son. A son I was very proud of. A son called Spencer. I spoiled him. In fact, I ruined him. He never went without. He had everything a boy could possibly want," she said softly. "He was a nice little boy. But as he got older, things changed. I started to notice things. Little lies, at first. Small, silly lies that I ignored. But they got worse. He used to live in a fantasy world. He mixed with bad people, as he got older. And I couldn't have that. Because of my career. So I set him up in a flat. And then another flat. And another. Gave him money. Provided everything for him. To try to keep him away from... it all. But, you see, trouble followed him, wherever he went. He enjoyed trouble – he courted it. And I was always his passport out of it, when it got too much. And then he'd start again – every time, however much he promised. Promises were nothing to him; just a way of him getting what he wanted. And then he was right back to square one. Trouble. I only know some of it, myself. But I know there were drugs and girls and nasty, nasty lies. And every time, he promised he would change. But, of course, he didn't."

Cherry was aghast.

"But he said he hadn't seen you for years. Are you still giving him money?"

"No. I stopped that nearly four years ago. My money was only funding his vile habits and his filthy life. And I hoped that without it, the harsh reality of having to find a job would change him. So tell me… has it? What is he doing now?"

" He's… a pilot. For British Airways. That's why he has to disappear so much…" said Cherry, hoping to God that she was right.

But the woman said nothing for a long, long time.

"And how long has he been a pilot, Cherry?"

"For ten years. He's… he's not, is he." – a statement, rather than a question.

"No," – very, very kindly now. "Five years ago, he was still dealing drugs," she said. "And four years ago, he was selling women. Prostituting them for his own financial gain. But there's still a chance that things have changed, now. I hope so. I hope so for your sake and my sake. And if he's made a clean start, he wouldn't have wanted to tell you about his past. So there's a chance."

"There's not a chance, really, is there?" – again, a statement, not a question.

A horrible, self-explanatory, no-need-to-dignify-that-with-a-response, type pause followed.

"No children?"

"No children."

"Good," said the woman. "I've always been worried that it would be genetic."

She had kissed Cherry, given her her phone number – and left.

****

"I wandered round and round, trying to ring him, but his phone went straight to Ansafone. And I went to his flat. But there was no answer. And I went home again – and I rang British Airways and they'd never heard of him; so it's all a lie, a big, fat, fucking lie… and I feel so STUUUPIID!" She was shouting now. "And I should have listened! Not just to you, but to myself! There were so many things, things that didn't add up, but I wanted someone to be mine, someone who was mad about me and… he said he loved me! Cath! What do I do?"

"And what about the money?"

"My card was declined and I only got paid on Friday. So I got a statement and there's nothing there! NOTHING! And so I rang the bank, thinking it was all a mistake and they'd transferred it into my deposit account or something – and it's all gone. ALL OF IT! My savings. My inheritance from my Nan. Everything! Cath, what do I do?"

"I told you not to worry about the money, dear." – Mabel, softly, kindly.

"FUCKING CUNT!" – Cath, not softly, not kindly.

"You don't understand. That's not the worst…" Cherry was crying now, more than at any other time in her life, looking at them wildly.

"*I'M PREGNANT!*" she bawled.

Chapter 37

Sadie was brushing her hair, tearing at it bitterly.

My God, she was cold.

Heating was something that she would not waste money on... there simply wasn't enough. Her dole cheque had just about covered her bills. But then they had put up her rent.

The Social wouldn't give her any more. They told her she'd have to move somewhere cheaper.

She had gone along and begged, of course. Told them about her ailing hip, her bad knee, explained that she really couldn't move. Not now. Not after years.

They didn't give a toss.

She had been on the list for a council flat forever now; but always someone else jumped to the top of the list... young, pregnant girls, immigrants... everyone was more important than an old lady.

And besides, they didn't understand. This place was all she had, all she was ever likely to have. It was the only remaining piece of familiarity in her life, the only tangible thing that she had to cling to. Losing this place would be the end of the world.

She put on another jumper.

****

She had cut out the drugs. *Cold turkey hell, alone with it, wanting to die, her bones aching, unable to keep her limbs still – they had taken on a life of their own.*

Then the sickness had started.

She was too ill to even leave her flat to go in search of drugs then. Too ill to even get out of her bed.

Now, she was long past needing it.

Even though the past – that she had so successfully blocked out now, for so long – had returned, forcing its way into her mind, seeping in, vivid and purple and lurid in detail.

And she had stopped turning tricks too.

Although if she went on like this, she would have to start again, just to afford food.

She hadn't eaten well now for weeks. Her already thin frame was even more emaciated; hips jutting, cheekbones sharp, eye sockets dark.

All her money now was used on the rent.

There was nothing left for food.

She had found that on certain days, outside the back of an expensive and deluxe deli, fresh sandwiches were dumped by the bucket-load. They were perfectly good. Beautiful, in fact; with fillings that she could only dream of. She would wait for everyone to leave the shop at closing time and then close in for the kill, like a hyena, looking carefully over her shoulder to ensure that nobody else could discover her find and take it from her.

It felt like stealing, something that she had never, ever done, no matter how hard times had been.

That was not the same as using, or selling her body. Stealing, to Sadie, was wrong. *It could hurt other people.*

Sadie had never hurt anybody in her life. Except herself.

234

But others had spotted her, foraging in the bins. And now her source of nourishment was gone.

****

She carried on brushing and de-knotting, winding and twisting. It was such an automatic thing, something that needed no thought, something so familiar that it brought feelings of comfort, order – a ritual.

A French pleat.

She sat on the end of the old bed, in her window, watching buses stuffed with people go by; watching weary, glazed pedestrians communicating with no-one, going about their business, on autopilot, like ants.

Watching them made her feel less lonely.

She watched a handsome, young man go past, full of himself, admiring his reflection in a shop window when he thought no-one was observing; pulling his best face, the one he practised at home. And then falling, headfirst over a traffic cone.

She laughed out loud as he sprawled.

Oh, the price indeed for such vanity.

And then there was knocking at her door.

She froze, heart beating fast.

It wasn't rent day.

She had no friends.

The knocking started again.

Sadie put the chain on the door and opened it a crack. She couldn't see who was there... no-one she recognised. But somebody who was female and young.

"Who is it?" she faltered.

"You stopped me in the street, weeks ago. You gave me a piece of paper. I need to talk to you. Please..."

Sadie tried to think, not responding. *Who?*

Then, she remembered the girl.

HIS girl.

"I'm sorry about the spartan surroundings," said Sadie, as she let Cherry into the room. "There is a chair. In the kitchen. I'll get it."

The flat inside was neat. But devoid of all furniture, except for the bed, which was immaculate apart from the imprint left by Sadie's backside.

There were clothes neatly piled and pressed in the corner, an iron still plugged in – but not on – on the floor.

Cherry looked at the poverty surrounding her, at the pitiful state of the thin woman before her and winced.

"Let me take you out for breakfast."

Sadie's eyes lit up. *She was hungry, oh so very hungry. And what harm could it do? She was already salivating; her stomach had begun to growl, deeply with just the thought of it. Something hot...*

But then she reminded herself of the impending conversation.

"No," she said. "We'll talk here."

Sadie sat back down on the bed and waved a frail hand at Cherry to follow suit.

"What do you need to know?"

Cherry began to talk, her words chaotic, quick with consternation, her voice small and worried.

She was innocent. Oh, so very young and innocent.

When she had finished, Sadie sighed a long sigh.

"Now where do I start?" she said.

Chapter 38

Sam hated her daughter.

Hated every bone in her body.

But she had to be careful.

They were onto her, Social Services. That bitch from the school, fucking busybody, had said something. As if she knew what it was like to have a kid. Day in, day out, no reprieve, no let-up – relentless.

None of it was her fault. She hadn't asked for any of it. She despised all of them for what her life had become.

****

She had tried to see her parents, after it had all happened.

They had taken her in, *Sam and her bastard child,* for three weeks.

To Sam's mum, the opinion of the neighbours meant more to her than helping her daughter. Much, much more.

It was the shame of it, really. They had the lovely kitchen, the nice house, and the good children: all the trappings of decency and hard work. Their other children had never let them down. But this one, well – she'd always been trouble. It made them look bad.

She had ushered her daughter in, a look of anger on her face, checking that no-one was looking as she had shut the door with a slam.

Her husband had persuaded her to let Sam stay, against all reason, against everything she advised him.

He'd forced her hand, *after all she'd done for him all these years... all her wifely support, the nice home that she had made, the meals she had slaved over. For a daughter that was entirely selfish.*

He'd obviously forgotten what his daughter was like – all Sam had put her through.

They were better off without her.

Sam had gone to her mother, in panic, many times in those first, few weeks after *it* happened; asking for help, herself a child, wanting to confess all that had happened, wanting somebody to help her, make it all all right, love her.

But she had been turned away, coldly.

Until her father had intervened – forced her mother's hand.

Sam's mother found her own daughter disgusting.

And there was no reason why she should be expected to help look after her illegitimate child.

Sam had to learn.

Like she herself had.

She'd already done her bit – raised four children, sacrificed her life for them, kept the house clean, plumped the cushions, washed the floors endlessly, watched her own friends go out when she could not. Not been appreciated for it.

She was not going to do that again.

Not for anybody.

No bloody way.

On the last day that Sam had been at her parents, she awoke to find Connie wailing and her mother hoovering outside her door, bashing into the frame, loudly and purposefully. Sam hadn't slept all night. Connie had been having nightmares again, waking up screaming, not giving her any rest. She was tired. Sam started crying, silently, alone in her bed.

The hoovering had stopped and the door pushed open, abruptly.

"Your child is up and crying. It's 9 o'clock. What makes you think you're the only one entitled to a lie-in? The crying. I suggest you do something about it."

And then she was gone.

Sam was filled with the familiar dread and fear of her mother's wrath.

Since childhood, it had gone on for days. Not for any reason. She could go to bed one evening, everything fine – and get up the next to find that her mother was angry and full of hate again. It was always directed at her, the privilege of being the oldest – the one that had popped out and put her mother's life on hold. And then the others had come. But they were loved – they were all OK. They had not ruined their mother's life any more than she had already done. The hatred was reserved only for her, just as it always had been.

So this morning, Sam had gone for her fix. She had gone into the same room as Connie, who was still whimpering.

In front of her tiny daughter, fat arms outstretched, waiting for a hug from Mummy, needing some affection, glad to see her, *all better now*, Sam had put on the wedding garter, twisted it tight around her arm, waited for the circulation to stop and injected.

She had felt immediately better.

Connie was looking at her, smiling.

But the silence was broken by her mother's voice.

"You filthy, little whore. Get out."

She had crept in, seen it all.

"And take your bastard child with you."

Sam's mother had thrown their possessions onto the lawn. She had physically pushed her daughter and the little girl outside and watched, as they scrabbled to pick up their belongings, satisfied that her behaviour was justified. And she had closed the front door, firmly, behind them.

And then she had got back to the polishing, anticipating the moment that her husband got back from work – and she would, yet again, cry to him about how her oldest daughter treated her; *had never appreciated what she had done for her – and look what she had done this time! She could cry, she felt so let down. Again, just like every other time.*

Sam had run back to the flat she had first escaped to, after the killing. To life, alone with her daughter and the dealer who had put a roof over her head.

And then days had turned into weeks into months into years. And daily, her resentment of her own daughter grew.

Connie had gone from being a rambunctious, fat, pain in the arse, to someone who asked questions, wanted her all the time, needed her, sucked her dry, stopped her living, made her sick.

And then, the hitting had started. Just as her mother had done before her.

She didn't know how else to shut her up.

241

Chapter 39

Cherry felt sick. The new information confirmed all her worst fears.

All thoughts of herself gone, she had put her arms around this poor, frail, old woman and hugged her.

It all finally made sense.

The calls, the changes in mood, the lack of friends, the power struggle.

He had been evil, incarnate.

And she had been stupid enough to believe it all, push cold, hard fact to the back, pretend it wasn't there, ignore her doubts.

But at least he had not really done anything to her. *Except to lie. And take all her money. And make her fall for him.*

And get her pregnant.

And then she remembered the strange night in the toilets and the strange morning after.

And how frightened she was of his anger. And how small and pathetic and useless he enjoyed making her feel. And how she was actually rather frightened to finish with him, had she ever given it enough thought. But hadn't wanted to admit that to herself. Because that would have made her truly, truly pathetic.

And she winced.

But nothing was as bad as what he had put this poor woman through. Even though the thought that the man she had loved had shared a bed with her ageing bones was odd, to say the least. He had always been so critical and fussy about Cherry's appearance. *God knows how he must have made Sadie feel.*

They had been there for nearly three hours. Cherry had been quiet all the way through, as Sadie told her tale of how he'd taken her in, used her, abused her, and treated her so badly even her self-respect had been taken from her, until she'd felt she deserved nothing more.

And then shot her.

Cherry finally broke her silence.

"Let's get something to eat," she said. "I want you to meet someone."

****

Mabel and Cath joined them in a tiny, basement café.

Mabel had been desperately worried about Cherry, whom she absolutely worshipped and for whom, by now, she would have done anything.

Mabel listened intently to Sadie, nodding inappropriately when she should have been shaking her head and shaking her head when she should have been nodding. But it didn't matter.

"But how did he get away with it? Why did the police not get him?"

"His mother," said Sadie. "I watched for a long time as a blind eye was turned – as he tore people's lives apart, time and time again. He treated me rather well in comparison. But he got away with everything."

"How do you mean, his mum?"

"She's the Minister for Health."

Cath spat out a huge mouthful of bacon.

"You must come and stay with me, Sally." Mabel said, at the end of it all.

"Thank you, but no. I am quite happy where I am. And it's Sadie."

"No!" said Mabel. "You MUST come and stay with me, Sarah. It was not a request. And I am not a woman to be messed with. And besides anything else, I need someone to live with me, or they're going to put me into a Nursing Home."

"What?" – Cherry now.

"You heard, young lady. My kind G.P. thinks it will be for the best. I know it will kill me, but they say they can't send out any more people in the dead of night when I fall. So I either find someone who will look after me, or that's it. Finito. Nursing Home. And I'd rather die."

"Bloody hell, Mabel, why didn't you say before?"

"Pride, my dear. And I couldn't bear the thought of either of you offering. I find you both quite intolerable."

She winked.

Sadie made her excuses and left for the toilet.

Mabel leaned over the table with a conspiratorial wink and whispered – spitting specks of saliva as she did – "You do realise that was pure fiction, don't you? There's life in the old gal yet! But it sounds like Sandra could do with a bit of a hand."

"Sadie."

"Sadie, Sandra, Sally… who cares? I'm rather looking forward to the company. Now who's going to help me with the old iron railings? I need a poo."

"Railings?" Cherry and Cath looked at each other, puzzled. "Corset, my dear. Don't you youngsters know anything? Keeps in the hernia."

When Sadie got back from the loo, she sat back down, wearily.

They all looked round.

"I'm so sorry, Cherry," she said, "to tell you all this. But I'm glad for you that he's gone. It's better that way, believe me. I think I'd better go now." She started to gather her things.

"Oh no you don't," said Cath – who had, up to now, been unusually quiet. "I need a fookin' hand here."

Mabel was up on her feet and stumbling wildly, barely held up by Cath, who was purple with effort and puffing like a steam train.

"This is a three man job, I'm afraid – she's a bit pissed and she's in heels."

The three of them helped Mabel into the toilet, squishing her into the tiny cubicle and fighting with her undergarments, of which there were plenty. There wasn't room for all of them and Mabel was putting on the performance of a lifetime. She deserved an Oscar.

Cherry and Cath withdrew outside the door, leaving Sadie with Mabel.

"I needed that!" Mabel said, as Sadie turned green. "And I need you, dear. What's more, I think you need me."

She started to haul herself to her feet. "And so does Cherry."

Chapter 40

"Fiona. You've got to help me."

"Jesus, Cherry. Look at the state of you. What is it?"

Fiona was washing up, at the sink in their shared kitchen. Elbow length, pink rubber washing-up gloves with a marabou trim, a plastic apron with a bra and suspenders on the front and a pan-scrubber shaped like a hedgehog. She never did anything by halves.

"What do you know about abortion?"

Fiona whirled round.

"Oh my God. You're up the duff. But I thought you were happy. You're engaged... does he know? What's the problem? Is it someone else's?"

Cherry sat heavily on the kitchen chair.

"Sit down, Fi. This is going to take some time."

Cherry was by now quite numb with shock.

****

The news of the baby had produced quite a reaction from Sadie. She had started to cry. Crying what seemed to be years and years of tears – a river running down each cheek into the crags either side of her nose, matting her eyelashes until she was unable to see.

She hadn't made a sound.

There was no visible shoulder-heaving.

It seemed that an eternity of practice of stifling grief, hiding it from view, of making no sound as she sobbed, had meant that she could cry without moving. This was pure, unadulterated, chronic sorrow making its exit from her thin, old body; oozing out like an oil-spill, black and thick and relentless.

Eventually, she had taken Cherry's face between her hands and said, "Cherry, my sweet, little angel. You must not have this baby. However you are tempted, however much you want it, whatever you may believe in your heart about termination. I implore you."

Sadie was not what they had all expected her to be, considering her situation. She was well spoken, eloquent, educated. Her words were measured and considered, brimming with emotion. She knew about the world. It was astonishing that she had ended up in the mess that was her life.

"Years ago, I was absolutely against abortion. I went on rallies in the sixties, opposing it. I was wrong. Some people are never meant to be born. They take lives, they ruin everything that they see; once they are born there is no turning back. You would be joined to Spencer, Joe – David as I knew him; inextricably linked, forever, no going back, always in your life."

There was silence, all around.

"That's a bit harsh, isn't it?" said Cath, irritated, putting her arm around her friend. "Just because she's pregnant doesn't mean it has to turn out like him!"

"You have children, Sandy?" said Mabel.

"No. I don't," said Sadie.

"Then I do think your words are rather harsh and unfeeling, my dear. A little nescient, as you have no children of your own. And that's all I have to say on the matter."

****

And now, back in the sanctuary of her own, dingy kitchen with Fiona, Cherry felt utterly desolate.

Fiona listened to her friend, absorbed all the detail without comment or interruption: gave her time to bare her soul. She was good at this. Time spent talking to lonely clients – some of whom came to her more for a piece of solace, than a shag – had equipped her with just about as much understanding of human nature as a trained therapist. She sometimes wondered if she was barking up the wrong tree continuing with her law training.

Cherry's tale of woe made her feel sadder than she had been in a long while.

She was a great girl, Cherry.

She didn't deserve this.

Nobody deserved this: certainly not someone with such a sweet heart.

The two of them had lived in perfect harmony for a long time now and were in the habit of making sure that they at least shared a Sunday roast every week, once Fiona had got back from church. They had an easy friendship – no pressure, no grief, no expectation; just a natural and amiable camaraderie and a shared enjoyment of the macabre and the fun in their respective, daily encounters.

When Cherry had finished, Fiona leaned back in her chair, looked at the ceiling and whistled.

"Well, my friend. It's not so much what I know about abortion, but what you feel about it. How do you feel about it?"

"I don't want this thing in my body. I feel violated by it." Cherry looked up at her, pain in her eyes. "Does that make me a bad person?"

"No, honey. It makes you a very honest person," said Fiona, eyes crinkling into a smile. "But I want to prepare you for something. I felt the same as you, once. I got rid of it. But as soon as it was over, instead of feeling relieved, as I thought I would, I felt very, very bad. For a very, very long time. The father was a boyfriend. He didn't want me to have it. I was very young. And I still think it was the right thing to do. But you know, sometimes I look at people with kids and wonder what he or she would have been like. Not all the time, just every now and then. But that's bad enough. If you get what I mean."

"Yes. I get what you mean. Oh my God, what do I do?"

"What your instinct tells you."

Chapter 41

Both Fiona and Cath had gone with her.

The clinic had been a shock.

Mabel had paid for it.

Cherry knew that it was what she needed to do. She had been fairly sure that it was what she wanted. And several chats with Sadie, who was by now firmly ensconced at Mabel's Camberwell abode, had confirmed to her that she wanted nothing, nothing at all that could link her in the future to *him*. It would be a life sentence.

Yet now, here, within these walls, she felt more alone than she had ever felt in her life. Waves of conflicting feelings swept through her mind, confusing her, rendering her incapable of logic; love, hate, guilt, anger, fear. Past, present and future all merged together in a whirl of multicoloured options, all leading down polluted paths that seemed impossible to take.

The anaesthetist came towards her, notes at the ready, to ask yet more questions. The room was heating up like a furnace, going black, the sterile scent of the hospital choking her – and then Cherry's chair seemed to be moving of its own accord to a strange angle beneath her legs, tipping her askew until the floor rushed up towards her face.

The voices around her buzzed like faraway flies caught in an upturned cup – and then there was nothing.

She came round in a curtained off cubicle, Fiona and Cath both on the same chair next to the bed where she now lay.

They smiled at her, anxiously. Cherry felt a squeeze of the hand. But no-one spoke.

The waiting was the worst bit.
She was in a room with four beds – with four other women, all waiting, just like her. Through the door of the room was an impersonal corridor, leading to yet more rooms, just like the one she was in. At intervals, women were wheeled through it, one by one – and then later on trolleys, semi-conscious, back to their beds. Nurses were laughing and joking with one another, talking of boyfriends and holidays and *have you seen that dishy, new consultant and so-and-so's off sick again. It's her back.*

Cherry tried to distract herself. Her nails bit into her palms and she circled her surgical-stocking-clad ankles, her body tense. The hands on the old-school, electric clock on the wall moved with painful apathy, each rotation lasting an eternity, adding to her panic. None of the nurses had been to see her for a very long time.

She wondered if they were being taken to theatre in alphabetical order.
It had always been the same, even at school.
Woods was a dreadful name to have as a surname. Last for everything. School injections, school dentist, the Nit Nurse, exam results: she was an expert in waiting her turn at the end of the alphabet, her nerves building from a small fluttering into a crashing crescendo, as she customarily observed all – from

Adams, to Whiting – emerging from their doom, blinking into the light, shaking their heads to demonstrate how bad it was.

Perhaps they'd forgotten her.

"MISS WOODS."

They had come for her now. Fuck fuck fuck fuck fuck. She wanted her Mummy. And Daddy. And teddy. And answers, quick, quick, quick. She needed a message from above, a flash of divine inspiration – or divine intervention; it was her last chance to change her mind.

And then she was counting backwards as the world went hazy and her eyesight became like a tunnel with strange, little people at the end.

When she came round, the pain shocked her. Nobody had said there would be pain. Aching – a deep, throbbing, unending, crippling pain that sat in her guts, but lower, much lower. She prepared herself for the immense grief and regret that would surely now come. But there was nothing.

She felt relieved.

In fact she felt almost euphoric.

Perhaps there was something deeply wrong with her.

Perhaps even sleeping with him had removed her soul.

But the pain. Oh Jesus, no-one had prepared her for that.

The nurse bustled in with a small plastic pot. Two pills.

Her eyes crinkled into a smile. "You have some visitors. Are you ready for them yet, sweet?"

"Yes. No."

It was the last thing she wanted.

She didn't want to talk to anybody.

She didn't know what to say.

They were right when they said the hormones kicked in later.

The next morning the tears would just not stop.

Chapter 42

"There have been enough tears," Mabel had said. "We're going to have a little party. To celebrate Cherry coming home. And to help everybody get back to normal. And no arguments."

It was to be at Mabel's place.

Despite the long time that she had known Cherry and Cath, Mabel had only ever said that she lived in Camberwell. And had not invited them back, ever, 'on account of the mess'.

They had both assumed that she lived in a grotty, crumbling, old flat. They had joked about it, affectionately and out of earshot, on many occasions: *pungent pants hanging over three-bar-heaters to dry, sticky carpet, the aroma of old food and old age.*

"This must be the wrong address."

Cherry, Cath and Fiona were standing in the swooping, gravelled drive of a vast, Edwardian house overgrown with ivy.

"I checked it three times. It's the right number. Perhaps we're in the wrong road. Let's call Mabe."

An ageing, ginger tom writhed a sinuous dance around their legs; mewing loudly and purring like an old motor.

"Mabe? Is that you?" The phone had been answered.

"Yes, my dears. Oh, I can see you! Come to the door. I'll let you in!"

Mabel appeared in the doorway, struggling to open it. She had dolled herself up to the nines. The cat stalked past her, back arched, stiff-legged with arthritis, bell tinkling as she reached down to catch the fur with her gnarled hand. It vanished into the gloom of a wood-panelled hallway, behind.

"Don't mind him. No manners."

"Bloody hell, Mabel! What a house! You must be loaded!"

"I did tell you I was. You didn't appear to believe me. Iniquitous youths," she said, slurring slightly.

" I know you did, Mabe. But I thought you meant you'd got a bit tucked away for a rainy day! Not this! Wow!"

Mabel waved them all in, graciously.

It was a beautiful, beautiful house. Double fronted. Immaculate inside. A bit niffy, in that musty way that mouldy cheese and old school dinners smell; but containing a glorious conglomeration of antiquities and treasures.

The old man she always described as her favourite taxi driver appeared and took their coats.

Cath looked at Mabel, eyebrows raised.

"And the taxi driver moved in when, Mabel?" she exclaimed, rather too loudly.

"In about 1984, Madam," he said. "I am her butler. She has always loved a little jest, has our Mabel! May I take your coats?"

They went through to an immense drawing room with what looked like a medieval banqueting table in the middle.

"The food will arrive presently," said Mabel. "Now who wants a gin?"

"You really are a dark horse," said Cherry. "And I remember when we met, you said about your husband having to sell his motorbike to buy your ring. And about working as a

255

dancer and stuff. So what happened in between? Did you win the lottery?"

"Oh yes. I did. It's all true. Except the lottery part... I was always rich. My husband was very poor. And he sold the only thing he possessed to buy me that ring. And I knew how very much he loved me, because he had never seen my home before he asked me to marry him. And he knew nothing of the money. I made sure of that. And he had already bought me the ring before he came here to ask for my hand. Armed with only the address – a bit like you. He walked for six miles in the rain to give it to me too. He was a truly wonderful man. And I'll still never get over him." She had tears in her eyes. "And yes, I worked. I worked because it was fun and I met lovely people. And it was my bit towards a war that no-one wanted to fight. So us ladies were all fighting alongside our men really – although we weren't there, we were all doing our bit. And I loved that. It wasn't about money, my working."

"So why have you been so secretive about it all this time?"

"I have done nothing of the sort! We were brought up knowing it was vulgar to flaunt wealth in my day: no ostentatious jewels, new noses or silly, indiscreet breasts."
Fiona flushed and crossed her arms over her chest. Hers were for a good cause, she justified to herself rapidly.

They all sat and ate a proper feast.

Mabel hadn't spared the horses. There was an amazing pot-roast with a gravy rich and dark enough to batter the most discerning taste-buds into submission, troughs of chargrilled vegetables, creamy, mashed, garlic potatoes and baskets of crusty, fresh-from-the-oven, exotic breads. A lemon meringue pie of Brobdingnagian proportions with a mellow, brown, cracked-to-perfection-crust followed and thick, yellow Cornish cream. And then there was the cheese. A selection of the most pungent, pre-eminent cheeses of behemoth size was presented. In huge silver domes, each with a solid silver marker skewered through the top, bearing its name.

"Who does the cooking, Mabe?"

"Surely you don't? You can barely get yer knickers on!" Cath said, with her usual delicacy.

"Fortnum's darling. They deliver. It's all ready-made. I know the lovely man in charge."

They had all eaten in silence. In shock.

Cath had to lie down afterwards, with her trousers unzipped to help relieve some of the mounting pressure. She lay, gingerly on an exquisite Louis chaise longue, the ancient fabric stiff beneath her fingers, looking up at a chandelier that spanned five feet of ornate ceiling. Cherry and Fiona were propped below her, sitting on a vast, antique Persian rug that had long since lost patches of pile to moths, leaning back against her legs.

In the fireplace crackled sap-drenched logs, spitting charred fragments, the flames – sucked hungrily into the chimney – casting a flickering, orange glow over their faces.

Sadie was bustling-busy: clearing glasses and topping up nibbles. She finished making herself useful and sat gracefully in an overstuffed, leather armchair – horsehair spilling from one cat-claw-ravaged corner.

"How are you, Cherry?" she said, concern clouding her features.

"Better. Especially after all this wine. Much better."

"I'm so glad. Here's to the future," she said, raising her glass towards Cherry.

"Here's to men! Bastards, one and all!" announced Fiona.

"Here, here!"

"And to women!"

"And to men! Oh, we've had them already. Not all bastards!" added Mabel. "AND TO GIN!" She was laughing hoarsely, shouting at full volume and having a truly phenomenal time. "AND TO CHARADES!"

"Oh fuck, Mabel – NO!"

Playing Charades with Mabel was indeed a charade.

The heady mix of her Parkinsonian tremors and her malapropistic tendencies, together with the gaping generation gap and a splash of memory loss, made for a complicated version of the game.

"Seven words. Film. Second word!"

Mabel was in an incongruous, high-backed, PVC, standard-issue, NHS reclining chair in an insipid green and was waving her arms around like the conductor of a mad orchestra.

"Bird."

"Flap."

"Wings."

"Vampire."

"Fly."

"Arms."

"Flew."

"FLEW!"

"Seventh word."

"Sleep."

"Rhymes with dead."

"Head."

"Sleepy-head."

"BED! OK, next word. Sixth word."

Mabel was now finger-twirling, as though she was trying to wind spaghetti out of her right ear – but this was hard to decipher on account of her mad gurning and pill-rolling tremor.

"Mad."

"Nutter."

"Lunatic."

"Bonkers."

"Insane."

"Curly."

"Curly whirly?"

"Cuckoo?"

"CUCKOO!"

"Cuckoo's bed?"

They were all looking confused.

"First word. First syllable."

"Sky."

"Moon."

"Sun."

"SUN. Second syllable."

"Finger."

"Point."

"One."

"ONE!"

"Sun one."

"Someone?"

"SOMEONE!"

"Someone, something, something, something, something, Cuckoo's Bed?"

Time was up. Mabel had been given three minutes overtime to compensate already.

"*Someone Flew Out Of The Cuckoo's Bed!*" she exclaimed crossly. "You must know it. With that marvellous Nick Jackelson."

"Do you mean *One Flew Over The Cuckoo's Nest?*"

"Yes. That's what I said."

"It was Jack Nicholson. And it's six words."

"As I said, dear. Gin?"

259

It was a long night.

Sadie was by now putting on weight and turning into a rather wonderful looking, old woman. She had an unusual grace, despite her war wounds. And a small semblance of pride was growing inside her, day by day.

She loved looking after Mabel. Made her feel as if she had a purpose in life, was doing something good for a change, something worthwhile. It had been a long, long time since she had felt that sensation.

And the pair of them got along famously.

Maybe it was a generation thing. There were quite a few years between them, but they both remembered a time when, it seemed, people had been better people: more truthful, less greedy, less wrapped up in their own desires.

They both missed it.

Mabel had, in her usual moments of unabashed boldness, asked Sadie more about herself. About everything, in fact.

"So dear. The prostitution. What on earth made you turn to that as a profession? Not that I'm judging, mind. I'm all for a little how's-yer-father myself, don't you know! Do love a bit of hanky panky. And chaps don't do it willingly with a wrinkled, old bird such as myself. How long have you done it?"

"How long have you paid for it?"

"None of your business!" Mabel was indignant.

"Well then."

They had sat in an amiable silence.

Mabel broke it with a stupendous, record-breaking fart. It was almost loud enough to cause the crockery to rattle.

She didn't even blink in acknowledgement, or look vaguely aware that it had even happened. Although Sadie found it hard to believe that Mabel had not felt it.

"Family?" continued Mabel.

"What?"

"Family. Have you got any?"

"No."

"And no kids."

"No kids. You?"

"Nope."

"Family?"

"No."

"Looks as if we're a real sad, old pair then, doesn't it!"

"Gin?"

"No, thank you. My liver really cannot keep up with yours. I do need to thank you for your hospitality though, Mabel and to bid my farewell. It's really time that I got back to my life."

"And what life was that, my dear. Doesn't sound like much of one to me. And what am I supposed to do rattling around in this old cage without you? I'm used to you now, dear. And your cooking is quite lovely. And I don't have to pay you. Although I will if you like."

"No, Mabel. Payment is out of the question. But I don't want charity. I don't deserve it."

"And why's that. I can't imagine that you've ever done anything that bad, dear. And this isn't charity. I need you to wipe my arse."

Chapter 43

Jude's exemplary behaviour had meant an upgrade.

He had been transferred to an open prison in Kent, a far cry from the rigid, violent surroundings he had become accustomed to. He now had nine GCSEs and three A-levels under his belt and was preparing for a degree.

They were all pleased with him.

Maybe four more years, if he was lucky.

Four more years.

A lifetime.

He had already served half as many years in prison as his tender years when he had been sentenced. He could barely remember life on the outside.

He pined daily, still, for his sweet, precious daughter; wept for his beloved parents, felt a deep and foul loathing for his now ex-wife.

She had divorced him whilst he had been in there.

The court had already agreed it.

He was informed coldly, by letter.

Divorced for desertion.

Now that was a laugh.

God, how he loathed her.

There was no forwarding address for him to contact her, no way of finding out how his poor, sweet daughter; his life force; his innocent baby was. She had refused all access for him – no photographs, no letters, nothing, nothing at all.

All his letters to Connie had been sent back, unopened.

He had never stopped sending them, in the hope that one might get through, get past the clutches of her mother; to tell her he still loved her, thought of her day and night, a sweet, sickening pain always in his soul.

He hoped that somewhere in the child's heart, she could remember past the pain, past the lies that she was inextricably woven into, to the times he held her, cherished her, and protected her from her mother.

She had been so small, so trusting, however many times her mother had coldly pushed her away.

Did she remember him?

Did she remember running into his arms for comfort, comfort that was always there, given freely and with adoration?

Or had her very mind been perverted with false ideas of him, her loving father?

Round and round the thoughts, unending, a circle with no beginning or end, a mass of tangled memories spinning out of control in his mind.

Blantyre House was not unpleasant.

But Jude was not accustomed to this level of freedom. Freedom was something he had forgotten how to deal with.

He remained – as was his way – obliging, good-natured, quiet, respectful; liked by fellow inmates and prison wardens alike. Head down, studying, going to the chapel, helping new prisoners come to terms with their lot whenever they appeared, almost regal in his demeanour.

He was certainly no threat to anybody.

Many times, attempts had been made to goad some kind of reaction out of Jude – sometimes by fellow inmates, sometimes wardens with tendencies to bully and stir.

But it had never been any use.

Jude could not be incited into bad behaviour.

He had, on several occasions, been set upon in the early days and had remained curled in a ball until the kicking stopped, the punches ceased: turning the other cheek, as his parents had taught. He had developed a way of retreating into his own mind, deflecting the pain, trusting in God, using his long-awaited goal of freedom as a shield.

He had worked with three psychologists in his time inside, striking up a good relationship with all of them. His annual reviews were faultless, the action plans for his return to normality being the most difficult for the staff in the prison to set… there was really nothing to aim for.

Finally, having settled into life in an open prison for a further, endless year – occupying himself with study, rigorous, self-imposed, daily exercise regimes and visits to the Chapel – Jude's case, once more, was assessed to decide quite how much risk he would be to the public at large.

Psychologists, prison guards, education officers, the Chaplain… the interviews were endless.

The parole board finally came to their decision.

They were to allow Jude escorted absences, with a prison officer, into the town.

He was shocked. Pleased. Overwhelmed. Shaking with excitement.

On his first visit to the town, he was escorted by Doll, a huge, Cumberland sausage of a man who totally believed in

Jude's innocence. They had struck up a relationship of mutual admiration and respect, over the last year.

Jude had told Doll his tale, his feelings, his reality.

"Fuck, mate. I have to say, after all this time, I honestly believe you. You're not the first that I've thought was in here wrongly, you know. It's very rare. But it happens."

Doll drew long and hard on his fag.

They were huddled over a game of chess, which was supposed to be part of Jude's rehabilitation, but was really a welcome escape for both men.

Doll loved his job, most of the time. Loved working with the inmates, loved a challenge.

Hated the management sometimes, but accepted their decisions and only bent the rules slightly.

Loved his family. All six kids and warm wife, three cats, two dogs, and hamster. Home was like a madhouse. He came to work in the prison for some light relief.

He was a huge, rosy-cheeked man with dark eyes, twinkling deep from his rotund cheeks, like two currants in a bun. He had a huge belly laugh. The inmates loved him. It was they who had initially referred to him as Doll. It had started off as Wallace the laughing policeman, as he was prone to bouts of eye-watering hysteria. Then shortened to Wal the Doll – and soon, just Doll.

He had taken an almost fatherly shine to Jude.

Poor kid, not long out of nappies and in the clink.

He seemed to Doll to be a decent lad, certainly not like most of the lads inside. Cheeky yes, probably a bit of a naughty lad in his day, but not a killer, certainly not the type of killer – 'cold blooded, money-grabbing, no family loyalty' – that he'd been sent down as. A real shame if he was, but Doll would have dropped off his perch had his instincts proved him wrong.

But prison rules dictated that prisoners with a guilty verdict were just that – no argument, no way, ever. Unless a new verdict, for some reason, was given.

All Doll could see was a young lad, pining for the daughter for whom he had a deep and true love and missing his parents; one dead, one so long-gone from him there seemed little hope of reconciliation. A kid with a good set of morals, trustworthy and respectful, whatever his past may – or may not – have been.

And few understood the love of a family like Doll. He was an orphan at nine, in and out of foster care, on the receiving end of some horrific – and some amazing – care.

He had met his wife; a solid, dependable, smiley girl when they were both fostered together under the care of a beautiful, warm, foster carer; who advised them against their relationship – but cried tears of joy from below the brim of an enormously over-the-top hat, at their wedding. He had been head over heels since day one, wanting to make a happy, secure life for the pair of them, come what may – truly 'for richer for poorer, in sickness and in health'. It was his main focus in life and there was nothing more important to him than his wife and children.

He was certain that this was what he could see too, in Jude.

Jude repaid his kindness to him with constant piss-taking about his size, calling him 'The Tank'; but also baring his soul to him as if he was a replacement father.

And so it seemed absolutely right that this was the man, carefully chosen, to escort Jude on his rehabilitative excursions into the outside world.

They had emerged into the sunlight together with Jude, at first, clutching Doll's arm with the excited anticipation of an overgrown schoolboy.

After Doll had dragged him around the town for an hour, the heavens opened and they ran for cover, laughing like drains.

They sat in a café putting the world to rights, laughing about the passers-by.

Fashions had changed out of all recognition since Jude had gone in. No longer did young women seem to dress as he was used to... a sea of incredibly tight jeans with a liberal explosion of 'camel hoof', worn with ballet shoes, had taken over the combat and tight vest combo he was used to. And young blokes were now swamped in someone else's trousers – someone much bigger – so that pants were exposed in a comedy fashion.

And a baseball cap.

And a hood. What was the point of that? One or the other, surely?

They spoke with the strange patois of fake Jamaican – Ja*fake*an – mixed with Peckham, both black and white and some in-between.

Jude felt like a fish out of water.

So much had changed, in so little time.

He was now unused to the mad rush of life, the frantic pace of all around him. Life in prison was ordered and sedate. This was like a strange chaos.

No wonder Arthur had got himself put away again. After more than twenty years inside, the outside world must have seemed like landing on another planet.

But a part of Jude was enjoying it.

Despite the distance between the small town they were now in and London, Jude still watched every face, searched every posture for something familiar. He wondered what his mother would look like now: probably just the same as she had, always. He remembered, bitterly, the shorn hair of their last meeting;

wondered if it had now grown, once more, to its former glory; wondered if she had met someone else, remarried, made a new life and totally left behind her past.

But more than that, he searched the face of every small child, female and blond-haired, which might be his beautiful daughter – the daughter whose face he remembered in infinite detail, every imperfection perfect to him. The daughter that now he may pass in the street and not even recognise; who, more than that, would not know him – or if she did, would have her memory of him defiled with lies.

It was time to go.

But Doll didn't want to.

He'd had a great time with this young, piss-taking, wide-eyed, son-of-a-bitch. It was his good heart... reminded him of his oldest son.

"So what are you going to do when you get out, mate? You need to start planning now. We need to find you a work placement and all that."

"God knows!" said Jude. "No, really, God knows. I need to find my daughter, make everything all right, make her remember who I am."

"Steady on." Doll hoiked a bit of chip out from behind a back molar, finding a lump of decaying pork from the Sunday roast with it and wrinkling his nose with displeasure at the smell. "That ex-cow of yours won't take kindly to that, mate. That'll take a lot of persuasion: Social Services, visits for an hour, supervised in a contact centre – and all of that malarkey. And that's if you can find them. Not meaning to put a downer on things, but that's how it is. You've got to be realistic, mate. You've been done for murder, son."

"I've got to find her." Jude said. "I will find her." He stabbed, angrily at the tabletop with his fork, chin stubborn and eyes dark.

Doll shook his head. *Fat chance, poor lad. Better let bygones be bygones, if he had any bloody sense. He'd already done the time.*

They eventually left, already late, still trying to avoid stair-rods of rain that had not let up since they'd escaped it on their entrance to the greasy spoon.

As they crossed the busy road – Doll in front, leading the way – a motorcycle overtook a bus on the inside lane, reckless with bolshy, outta-my-way, courier hurry. Jude saw him first and grabbed Doll, wrenching at his huge arm instinctively, trying to pull him back like a child.

But Doll weighed a ton and was an immovable object. He was hit with the full force of both bike and rider and smashed to the floor like a rag doll, where he was clipped by a passing taxi as he lay; the sound of the rush of air being squeezed from his lungs by the impact hanging in the air like an exclamation mark.

Jude ran over to him, cradling the huge man's head in his arms, flashes of his dying dad coming back like red-hot pokers burning into his brain.

He couldn't witness this again.

Escape was the furthest thing from his mind.

Doll's eyes were open, looking at him.

His leg was bent.

Twice.

And not at the knee.

His pelvis was flattened.

And his chest appeared to flail, in and out with each breath, on one side. He looked panic-stricken, terrified as a bison brought down by a pride of lions, awaiting the next onslaught of pain.

"CHRIST!" shouted Jude. "HELP! SOMEONE! HELP!"
Onlookers appeared, gawping.

The rider of the motorcycle appeared, limping and shaking, unable to speak. And then turned away and tried to get back on his smashed bike. The cab driver came running, traumatised and shaking, tears welling in his eyes, mobile clutched in a hand that was shaking too much to dial.

"HEELLPP! SOMEBODY CALL AN AMBULANCE!" shouted Jude, tears in his eyes, disbelieving, wanting to make it all better.

"You're a good boy," whispered Doll. He shut his eyes.

"OPEN YOUR EYES, YOU FUCKER! OPEN THEM! TALK TO ME! TALK TO ME!" Jude was screaming at him now, almost angry with him. "DON'T YOU DARE FUCKING DIE, YOU BASTARD. I'VE BEEN HERE BEFORE! DON'T DO THIS TO ME!" Teeth gritted, he was punching Doll's arm, grinding his knuckles in his hand, doing anything he could to keep him conscious.

"Stop it. I hurt enough already." The eyes opened and then shut again.

And the distant wail of sirens finally arrived, ambulance men cutting through the crowd, a sudden hush.

Doll was now drifting into unconsciousness and Jude, stuttering as he tried to describe what had happened, was on his feet. Standing over the paramedics as they worked, desperate for this man to make it, he was embalmed with a familiar sensation of fear and utter uselessness.

"His name's Doll," he said, in a voice strangulated with tears.

Doll's wallet was out, his personal effects grabbed – and he was in the ambulance.

The police were there. To help the ambulance through the crowded streets.

Thank the fucking lord. They had to get him to hospital, quick, quick, quick, please let him be OK.

In a flurry of what's-yer-name-son, Jude gave his name and his former address, not thinking.

He tried to get into the ambulance with Doll, but was not allowed.

"Go home, son. Ring the hospital to find out how he is, or make your own way there."

And the ambulance was gone.

Go home?

Where was home?

He knew he should make his way back to the prison.

But he could not.

Chapter 44

"We need fish and chips!" said Mabel, as she stood swaying, clutching the edge of the sink in a desperate attempt to maintain the upright position. "A celebration for the fact that you've given up that revolting 'thing' you called a flat and finally had the good sense to see me out 'til I pop my clogs."

Sadie chuckled, limped over to the old woman and held her in a huge and loving embrace from behind.

"I... I really don't know how to thank you, Mabel," she said. "It's been so long since anybody – and I mean anybody – has treated me like a human being. You have been so very, very kind."

"Oh, stop all the self-flagellation! I can't be doing with listening to that pile of old claptrap any longer. Not kind. Just normal. And pretty lonely, I must say, before you arrived. And if you want to know how you may thank me, you could start by itching that little bit between my shoulder blades. Lower. Higher. Left a bit. Down a bit. Up a bit. Right. Left. Right. Left. Right. Down. Hee hee."

"You're taking the piss now, aren't you?"

"Oh yes. It's my way of a little sport! There, it's nice to see a smile on your face. It's nice having you around. Anyway, I needed someone to cut my toenails. And you'll just have to do."

Mabel's toenails had long since ceased to grow much in length. Instead, they grew in height, resembling two rows of scaly, brown, crusty horns – the feet of a troll. And her shaking hands and lack of grip had meant that her options had been to either leave the talons to continue growing, until she could barely walk and they tapped alarmingly on the tiled floor in her kitchen – or to risk a vile 'degloving' injury; which generally involved cutting off the end of her own toe with the industrial nail clippers she was compelled to use and bleeding profusely.

It was becoming increasingly difficult for her to squeeze her hooves into anything even resembling shoes. Heels were becoming a thing of the past – although she still rammed them on for special occasions, which she now partook in a wheelchair.

Her Parkinson's was becoming more of a problem by the month. But her resolve and gritty determination stayed second to none.

Her falls were, by now, a weekly event and her body was crenellated with a map of the world, whose oceans were formed with a myriad of bruises.

Sadie, ignoring her own pain – hip and knee in daily agony and spine grating like gravel as she moved – tended to Mabel's every need, tenderly.

She meant every, solitary word of thanks that she uttered.
To her, Mabel was an angel... a particularly gnarled and past-the-sell-by-date version of an angel, but an angel all the same.

Sadie had given up on the human race years ago. But now, her spirit, broken beyond belief, was gradually mending, waking up, being renewed.

She felt a sense of purpose, felt she had a place in the world where she could finally be happy, do some good, be worth something.

She could smile.
She hadn't even thought about a fix.

She had a growing pride that meant the thought of selling her body filled her with horror.

But with that, came a burgeoning shame of what her life, prior to Mabel, had become.

It was best not to think about it.

Cherry was happier than she had been in a long time. The burden of Joe's bad moods had weighed more heavily on her shoulders than she had given them credit for. She had often felt, in their relationship, that she was dragging a cart with no wheels up a steep hill to an uncertain end.

She had let the cart go.

Along with her feelings of humiliation.

And now, she was climbing to the top alone... alone, but happy.

She and Cath had joined an online dating agency.

Neither had dared go for a date yet, but many, many fantastic evenings were being spent perusing the sites, looking at the details of many, many weird men.

Not weird and wonderful.

Just weird.

There was no point in looking at anyone normal. That ruined the fun.

They were particularly enthralled with reading about the ones that were more like Martians than men. Which involved typing in the most bizarre personal details in their own particulars. Like enjoying taxidermy and making glove puppets, Wild West-themed evenings and cross-dressing in libraries.

"Jesus... look at this one! Never married, no kids, lives with Mother. I wonder why!"

"Aaaaargh!! It's the chest rug – trimmed *and* brushed. I'd love to have a go at that with a load of wax. Back, sack and crack… he'd bleed to death!"

"We could stick him in front of the telly, as a rug."

"And what about this one! He's stuck something down the front of his shorts. A French stick… WLTM sexy, discreet lady with wads of cash, to share love and laughs. But can only get out on Monday nights when his wife thinks he's playing badminton."

"Oh, I might give him a ring. I need a laugh. And with that thing down his Y-fronts, he's the man for the job!"

"Oh, stop. It's better suited to shagging a horse."

"Hence the cowboy hat."

"Oh, wow… Cherry. I've found the one for you. Gold Rolex, with diamonds. (So, so wrong.) A grotesquely overweight, psychotic, tasteless, middle-aged, wealthy type in a flowing, silk, Versace robe. Gary Glitter looky-likey, with a penchant for bossy types with no sense of smell, who enjoy wearing jodhpurs every Wednesday. That's a prerequisite. He's right up your street. Better than your last one, anyway!"

"Shut up!"

"OK… huge, buck, rabbit teeth in a shade of yellow-with-brown-nicotine-ends and weasel eyes, a nervous disposition and genital warts. Straight hair and curly teeth. Bed-wetter. Likes sniffing bike seats. Teaches."

"Right. You're for it now. I am entering a revised description of you! Two eyes – that look in different directions. Drooping boobs, which by night are tucked into bed-socks and by day are hoisted up by some miraculous triumph of modern-day engineering that almost makes them resemble two, tightly-packed, water-filled, comedy balloons. Hair. Ginger. Round the sides in proliferation, but none on top. WLTM large ape with hair. All down his back, but none on his head. And a dole cheque and bad credit. And a prison record. Who only eats cheese and onion crisps washed down with garlic juice."

For some bizarre reason, neither of them was enjoying much success.

Cath and Cherry had introduced Mabel and Sadie to the delights of the World Wide Web. And Mabel had been so excited about having hoards of young men at her very wavering and knobbly fingertips – instead of having to wait for their particulars to arrive by snail mail – that she had got the pair of them to arrange for the instalment of a very high-tech, wafer-thin, state-of-the-art computer with a gigantic screen and broadband; so she could peruse at her leisure.

Not that she was getting any action, these days... her increasing incontinence and the arrival, to her dismay, of a leg-bag to control it, had meant that this was now out of the question. She had tried, but there had been a rather terrifying encounter, with an old gentleman with particularly poor eyesight and an obvious lack of fingertip sensation. She liked them that way... it meant that the usual vision of Mabel was blurred into oblivion.

But he had squeezed on the bag, thinking that he was feeling an unexpectedly voluptuous and youthful breast. And then it had burst. Everywhere. It had given new meaning to the term, 'water bed'. Obviously he had not returned her calls.

But Mabel was having a glorious time lying to various unsuspecting victims via the comfort of her armchair and awaiting their replies, with the eager anticipation of a chimp before a tea party.

"So, who else wants fish and chips?"

Mabel was tottering dangerously in the doorway of her newly installed computer room, peering at Cherry and Cath. "Sadie's up for it."

"Oh yes."

"Yes please, Mabel. Actually, I might have a sausage. And keep your cash. This one's on me," said Cath, getting up. "Here, Mabe, sit down here and get an eyeful of this prime piece of rumpy-pumpy... we've found a gorilla masquerading as your hopeful date."

She escorted Mabel, who was taking a million fairy steps in their general direction; wheeled Zimmer high in the air, making no contact with the ground whatsoever.

"Jesus, Mabe, you're lethal with that thing. You're supposed to lean on it, not carry it about. You're going to have someone's eye out."

They had all eaten out of the wrappers. Mabel had broken most of her plates anyway.

Traditional fish and chips.

In proper newspaper.

From a very posh chippie.

Sadie was gathering up the debris of the meal afterwards and chatting vividly, as was her wont with a bellyful, when she suddenly stopped in her tracks.

She was looking at the screwed up, chip-fat-sodden newspaper in her hands.

"Oh no!" she said and then looked up with the expression of one who has just seen a ghost.

She sank into the nearest chair and sat, without expression, face a blank, the colour blanched from her cheeks.

"What is it?"

"Nothing. Nothing. I'm just feeling a bit... sick. I've eaten too much. I need to go and lie down."

And with that, she left the room.

"What the fuck was all that about?"

"Dunno. She was just clearing up the mess and then had a funny turn. Not that it's easy to tell when she's having a funny turn." Cath had turned back to the computer and was typing away, distractedly. "Probably her hormones. What's left of them. Or a rush of chip fat coursing through her arteries and blocking up her brain. Sure she'll survive."

Mabel was not convinced.

When they had all gone, Mabel had made a huge and deliberate racket in the hall, by smashing an old walking stick – from more stable times – around in the umbrella holder as violently as she could.

Sadie, as expected, had come running.

She was still pale, her face still furrowed with worry and doubt and foreboding etched into her lines.

"Oh Mabel, you naughty woman! You absolute bugger! I thought you'd fallen."

"No dear. But you and I need to have a chat. If you're to live with all my weaknesses and old lady foibles, not to mention the frequent sight of the crack of my backside – which believe me, I do NOT want to share with you – I need to know what is bothering you. I have taken you into my home in the spirit of complete trust and honesty. And that is the least that I expect back from you. God knows that's the least you owe me. Apart from wiping up my nether regions, of course. And I know you well enough, by now, to recognise that something has happened. Something that is nothing to do with chip fat. And besides that, I'm a nosy, old baggage and I want to know what is going on."

"Oh Mabel," Sadie said, head in hands. "Oh, I so need to tell someone. But what will you think of me?" There was a long, long silence. "I will, Mabel. But not just yet."

Chapter 45

It was not all it was cracked up to be, this freedom malarkey.

Oh Jesus, what was he supposed to do?

They'd be looking for him by now.

Every day he left it meant the repercussions of his involuntary escape would be worse.

He was now too frightened to hand himself in, even if he wanted to. According to the headlines, he had pushed Doll in front of a motorbike, in order to make his escape. And the sodding motorcyclist wasn't arguing... *why would he? He'd nearly killed someone by not looking where the fuck he was going and was now enjoying minor celebrity and selling his tale to various rags.*

Jude was utterly buggered.

He had spent the last three days walking. To nowhere, in particular. His mind was trying to fashion a plan out of a disaster with no ending and a lack of any remote idea of hope.

Not a good combination.

London seemed the only idea worth pursuing.

At least you could get lost there. God knows, thousands of other people had.

He reached Lewisham on day four.

My God, it had changed. A far cry from what it had been all those years before. Even the school kids waiting at the bus stops were petrifying.

There were the yellow signs bearing details of assault all around, like advertising boards. They positively bragged about what a bad place it was to be.

You wouldn't want to land here from outer space. Or on a sightseeing tour from Japan. It would be like being out-of-your-face, drunk on moon-juice and being offered a violence chaser.

But the anonymity was comforting. Nobody gave a toss, obviously.

And this had been one of his many, old stomping-grounds in times past, when truanting from school; on the days when he could hop on the back of the 36 and hop off again before he was caught by the conductor.

He felt like a fish out of water.

Loampit Vale.

Not far to Peckham, now.

He was not sure why Peckham called him, so loudly.

Except every bone in his body cried out for something familiar, something he knew – something safe.

Not that the Peckham estate had ever been what you would describe as safe.

God, how he wanted to see Connie – just see her once more, just to see how she had grown, see what she had become.

But he didn't even know if she was still alive.

He would have given anything to see her now, even for a second. Even if it meant going back inside, serving the rest of his time.

But now, it seemed, the rest of his time would involve a few more years than previously expected. He had racked up a new offence.

A bit like the first crime.

Without doing a thing.

He was cursed!

Perhaps, in a former life, he had been somebody exceptionally hideous. Crippen? The Ripper? Hitler?

And now he was paying the price for actions past.

It was the only explanation.

Days of avoiding being spotted quickly turned into weeks. Fresh food was a long-distant memory. His daily feast consisted of any remains he could rescue, from anywhere, or anything he could beg for. But he preferred to retrieve it from refuse than to ask for help. Sleeping rough, trying to be anonymous, never making eye contact with anybody – he needed to stay unnoticed, avoid being identified.

He had a change of clothes, stolen from a bag left outside a charity shop. Trousers, too short with a broken fly, an old suit jacket with fermenting pockets and a torn shoulder and gigantic, purple trainers he had whipped from a charity shoe-bin outside a shop; he looked like the average down-and-out that roamed the local streets. He fitted in quite nicely. Certainly wasn't attracting any attention.

Folks around here didn't even have the time to glance at you, unless they too were aimlessly wandering the streets. And then they simply didn't care. Unless you begged for money – then you were liable to receive scorn at best, or a good hiding. He smelt like the armpit of a skunk. Worse.

His newly-grown beard was matted, filthy.

How Bohemian.

His mother would have really enjoyed this change of image.

Would have fitted in very nicely with her positive and loving perception of him.

He wondered, sadly, where she was.

Gaunt and tired, he spent his time waiting outside every last school in the surrounding area – one per day, at end of school, just hoping for a glimpse of anybody who could be Connie.

He had seen no-one who could possibly resemble her, however much he tried to read into their faces, their hair, how she might be. There was no sign of Sam, either.

Perhaps they had moved – started afresh, elsewhere. Perhaps she had reinvented herself as a human and some poor bastard had been taken in by it and was acting as husband, Daddy, lover.

His entire day revolved around planning which school to seek out next, while at the same time remaining undiscovered. But in over six weeks there was no sign at all.

He was truly at the end of his tether.

He needed to wash. Bluebottles had started to home in on him, like heat-seeking missiles. The odd stray dog was showing more than an uncommon interest in his crutch.

Ruskin Park had a children's paddling pool, free and open to the public.

He waited patiently for most of the afternoon, for all the children and the mothers to leave. He had to be careful. But he also had to get clean. He was itching all over and crusts of thick skin were hanging now, like debris, from his withering limbs. His only option was to run into the shallow water when the perfect moment presented itself, roll about for a second or two, fully clothed and run out, to drip dry. That may at least remove some of the stench – on clothes and body simultaneously. Or at least aid the itching, temporarily.

At least it was sunny.

He sat on a bench, in the gated off area with the duck pond, carefully observing the kids and mums with his peripheral vision. He knew better than to openly watch. There was something about a non-fragrant vagrant that attracted the wrong

282

sort of attention: a lingering suspicion in the faces of young mothers and old ladies. And yet all the paedos he'd met inside were the most ordinary, non-conspicuous-looking individuals possible.

Public perception was a strange thing.

Your average paedophile wanted to blend in and attract children. Tramps' clothes were not their uniform of choice.

But still, mothers of children looked at him with suspicion if he so much as glanced at their kids.

The afternoon was fading into evening and the courting couples and mums and toddlers were, one by one, peeling away from the pond, as they succumbed to the dropping temperature – leaving only one or two remaining.

Passers-by arrived in waves, using the park as a commuter route to and from King's College Hospital. An air ambulance landed, the rush of air flattening the grass and its rhythmic noise compressing the atmosphere around it. A squall of activity smashed the peace and quiet.

He would have to plan his launch into the paddling pool at the other end of the park carefully.

It looked like it was going to be a long wait.

He looked away from the paddling pool again and his eyes swivelled back to the duck pond.

Through one of the willows, trailing its drooping foliage into the murky sludge of water below, he suddenly became aware of someone sitting alone, feeding the ducks. He could see only part of her face, dappled with flashes of fading sun reflected back by the water.

His heart nearly stopped.
He was unsure.
It couldn't be.

She looked older. Much older. Her hair was long. She was thin, *oh, so very, painfully thin.* But after all this time, she was still unmistakeable; a face he had known so very well – every pore of it, every flaw. But she was a little distance away and he was still filled with uncertainty. *Perhaps he was just seeing what he wanted to see: perhaps his mind was playing tricks on him, in some sick and twisted way?* But then, a mannerism – nothing more than a familiar twitch that was only hers, a slight, nervous toss of the head, with a familiar finger rubbing at her nose – and he felt his heart in his mouth.

There was no doubt.

He had waited for this moment, for every second, of every day, of every year that he had been put away, a prisoner in both a jail and his own misery. He had waited, filled with love and hate and rage and injustice.

Oh, how he had longed for this.

This moment.

And now it was finally here.

Every muscle and sinew of his was ready; ready to leap into action, seize the moment, not let it pass, not waste it.

But he would have to wait. Think carefully, not react, not blow it, not approach – she would raise the alarm, the police would be called, he would have found her only to be taken away again immediately. And in doing that, lose all hope.

So he waited.

And watched.

And then he followed.

Chapter 46

"I don't know what to believe," said Cath. "I feel sorry for Sadie. But this sounds like bullshit, to me. Reeks of it. Stinks, in fact. I don't believe anybody's past can be that bad. Sounds like complete fantasy. I'm beginning to think that we've lumbered Mabel with an utter fruitcake. I think she's just milking the old sympathy vote, to keep Mabel putting a roof over her head. What do you think?"

"I have to say, I find it difficult to believe anybody, these days," said Cherry, wearily. "I'm not the best judge of character, let's face it."

"Do you think we should talk to Mabel?"

"Probably. But Sadie may, of course, be telling the truth. And then what? We're responsible for Mabel not wanting her around any more? She may go back on the game."

"If she ever was on the game."

"Well, she was obviously telling the truth about Joe." A look of sadness cast a momentary shadow over Cherry's face. She regained her composure. "The thing is, Mabel loves having her around. She's good for Mabel, whatever the truth is. And Mabel needs her. She's getting worse. I think we should just leave it as it is, for now."

They were at the salon. Cherry was sweeping up. Hair met her broom in all the colours of the rainbow, congealed on the horsehair fringe that dragged it over the floor.

"Do you think I could sell this as a new, avant-garde line in hair extensions?" she said.

"I think not. How bloody long do I have to sit here and wait for you? I'm bored."

Cherry picked up a lump of matted hair and mashed it into her friend's face, while she sat engrossed in Catherine Zeta Jones' staggering weight loss.

"Eeuurgh! You dirty cow!" Cath rose to her feet, tossing Zeta Jones to the floor, her brows proclaiming annoyance. She turned away and brushed off the hair, a look of disgust on her face. Their eyes met in the mirror.

Cherry picked up a hairbrush from a nearby trolley and started brandishing it like Zorro. She stood with a swivel chair in front of her, by way of a defence, like a bullfighter preparing for battle. She giggled at her friend's humour failure.

"I'm gonna make you pay for that!" Cath had turned to face her once more, feeling foolish at her momentary sombreness.

"Go on then!"

Cath snatched a disinfectant-drenched mop out of a nearby bucket and came at her, sliding onto her arse, legs akimbo, screeching like a banshee, "YYEEEEEAAARRRGGGHHHH!"

Cherry jumped on top of her, as she lay, winded, on the floor and rammed her knees on her upper arms, pinning them to the floor, before grabbing her wrists and yanking her arms up and down, shouting, "PETROL PUMPS!" and crying with laughter.

Cath was squirming and struggling and kicking. Her face was vermillion with effort. Cherry's knees were hurting her arms and her laughter was beginning to make Cath's anger rise again.

"Gerrofff meeeee!" Cath's ire-tinged shouts only made Cherry worse.

"PLEASE," said Cherry, gleefully.

"Gerrofff meeee pleeeaase!"

"NO!"

"I'll kiss you!"

Cherry relaxed her grip for a second. She stopped laughing.

Cath felt childishly victorious. She was overtaken by a sudden, malicious sense of puerile power. She summoned a reserve of energy she didn't know existed and turned the tables, flattening a horrified Cherry on the floor – who then started crawling off towards the swivel trolley with all the rollers and clips in, which then crashed to the ground as Cath yanked her backwards by the legs. Combs, rinses, grips, slides and tongs scattered all over the floor with an ear-wrenching screech and Cherry lunged at them – ammunition to hurl at her assailant; who was by now descending upon her, with a pair of clippers whirring furiously in her paw and ready to chomp on her hair.

There was a violent knock at the window. Cherry's heart missed a beat.

Oh fuck. It's the boss. I'm going to be sacked.

They both stopped what they were doing, Cherry scrabbling frenziedly to her feet, with her face set into a top-lip-trembling, brow-sweating, cheek-twitching, eye-popping look of terror and remorse.

It was Fiona.

Thank the bloody lord!

She was done up to the nines, Queen of the ghetto.

Cherry's pulse began to quieten to within normal, human limits. She unlocked the salon door.

"Fi… what brings you in this direction?"

"I've done it!" She grabbed Cherry around the waist and started to swing her round in circles.

"You've done what, you maniac?"

"I've done it! I've paid the deposit! I've bought a flat! For cash! Well, most of it, anyway."

"Oh." Cherry looked crestfallen.

Fiona noticed her saddened expression and grabbed her cheeks, squeezing them like an ageing relative encountering a familiar child for the first time in years, with a 'haven't you grown'.

"So, you and I is moving!"

"What do you mean?"

"What do you think? Are you a bit slow? You're moving into my new flat. In four weeks' time. I've already given in our notice."

"But where are we going? What if I don't want to? And what about your men...?"

"There won't be any men! Don't you understand? I don't need to do it no more. I'm sorted. I can go back to college. But I do need you to help me pay the old monthlies. So you can rent with me... and before you say it, same cash daahlin', same cash. And it's in posh parts." Fi clicked her fingers together, Rasta stylee. "You and I is moving to the 'Bello itself. Carnival action, we is a-coming."

Cath was by now sitting in a hairdressing chair, swivelling it with her feet, back and forth, idly. They were so engrossed with each other, Cherry and Fiona, that she was by now bored. And more than slightly jealous that her oldest and best friend was being made such a fuss of. She had put a perming cap on her head and made an enormous moustache out of hair clippings, which she had adhered to her top lip with some hair gel.

After an unending round of tedious jubilation, Cherry and Fiona simultaneously remembered that she was actually present in the room; and condescended to include her.

"Congratulations," said Cath, a little too brightly.

Cherry shot her a wary glance.

Mess cleared, salon clean and in order, they all decided that the only way to celebrate properly was to go to one of Fiona's now former places of work – the Strip Club – and for her to sample life as a paying customer as opposed to an employee.

They had just reached the door of the club – Cath and Cherry in jeans and old sweats and lurking in the shadows in case their attire prevented their entry; Fiona in a white fur jacket, skin-tight jeans and an Afro of extreme proportions (and all over the bouncer like a rash) – when Cherry's phone rattled in her pocket.

"Hang on a mo, ladies," she said, "It's Mabel."

"Oh, ignore!" said Cath, from the shadows, itching to get inside in case an opportunity for a bit of romance – or at least a fumble with someone with more money than sense and a belly full of cheap champagne – was wasted. She hadn't had a sniff of action for aeons.

"No Cath, you selfish cow. It'll only take a minute! She never chats for long. And she gets lonely. Let me humour her for a minute and then we're in, OK?"

They waited, bored, while she fumbled around, pressing the wrong buttons in her attempt to answer.

"Mabe. Mabe? Mabel, is that you? Mabel. MABEL, CAN YOU HEAR ME? Mabe, hold your horses, we're there, we're on our way! DON'T MOVE!" She snapped the phone shut. "Call a cab!"

"Oh fuck off, Cherry!" said Fiona. "This is my moment to lord it up! And anyway, Sadie's there. Can't she help?"

"Don't do this to us. This might be my lucky night! Or at least an opportunity for a good dance! It's been ages since we've all had a night out. And what's up with her, anyway?" – Cath.

"Don't know, not sure, but something's not right. She can't get her words out. I can't bloody leave her and just hope for the best, can I? You two bastards don't seem to give a monkey's, but I certainly do. See you ladies later." Cherry was madly flagging down a black cab, which was swerving over two lanes of traffic towards them. "Have a lovely evening!" she added furiously as she got in, not knowing quite whether her fury was with them – or with Mabel for ruining her night of celebration.

And with that, she disappeared.

Chapter 47

Jude was feeling more afraid as time went past.

It wasn't going to happen.

Day after day, outside the same café – waiting, waiting, waiting, waiting.

Same time, same place.

He couldn't afford to go inside.

The owner was by now looking at him very strangely.

He tried to keep his face away from all eyes, but things were steadily getting more risky every day that he stood there.

If he was recognised now, it was all over.

But he had to be there, in case she came.

She had to come. Even if it was just out of curiosity.

But the more time went on, the more unlikely it seemed.

He couldn't carry on living like this, hiding, begging, and scrounging – in constant fear that someone would recognise him from the news, from the papers. He was caught in a strange limbo with no path out, no road to follow, no-one to talk to. He felt as if he was going insane.

And, it seemed, the only way forward now would be to find Sam, to somehow clear his name.

And for Doll to be OK.

And from the news reports, both of these seemed highly unlikely.

Chapter 48

Doll had been on life support for weeks.

His family kept a steady vigil.

They were not a religious family and yet, now, prayers had become a daily part of their lives, bargains were being struck. *If I give up smoking, he'll be all right. If I give up my sweeties he'll be all right. If I give up my girlfriend, he'll be all right. If I tidy my bedroom every day, he'll be all right. If I don't step on the cracks in the pavement, if I get an A for my English homework, if the next car that passes is yellow, no – blue, no – red, if I give him my best teddy...*

Hours rolled into days rolled into weeks.

He had needed hours of surgery.

The newspapers had had a field day. It had been headline news for weeks now and his family had to fight, daily, through a sea of clamouring reporters, just to get to see him.

'Prison warden's life hangs in the balance.'
'Prisoner still on run while warden lies dying.'
'Cristian crucifies prison warden.'
'Throw the Cristian to the lions!'
'Prisoner makes Hollywood style escape.'
'Hey, Jude. Make it better – hand yourself in.'

Doll was in traction, his pelvis and leg impaled with shining, steel pins like something out of a horror film – no longer ventilated, but being hauled around, unconscious still. He was like an enormous piece of unresponsive meat, as they fought to keep his lungs clear, move his limbs, prevent blood clots, stop the infection that had nearly killed him on top of his multitudinous injuries. He had now been off the ventilator for days. He had been breathing independently, but there had been no sign of response so far, except for the slightest rise in his heart rate as a response to pain. But it had been looking good, no longer life and death, just a question of waiting; his brain scans showing bruising only, nothing serious. He was out of danger.

Finally, when the infection had cleared, he had awoken, groggily, his mind wandering in a bleary, incoherent way, as if he was fighting his way out of some confusing dream.

Or was he still in one?

The lights above him were piercing through his half-closed lids and he couldn't move. He seemed to be in an unfamiliar place with noise around him; faraway voices murmuring, peals of female laughter resonating from somewhere close.

Where the bloody hell was he?

Light streamed into his brain, scorching his retinae, pain searing through his head. He swiftly shut his eyes again and lay, listening, trying to fight back ripples of nauseating fear.

He had no recollection of events. His mind was desperately back-pedalling, clutching at past events in order to make sense of it all, but failing in its attempts.

Nothing.

The last thing he remembered was being in the prison, at work.

He recalled an assortment of incredibly strange dreams, in which he had been gagged and bound by his grandmother – dead for thirty years – because he had tried to run his granddad over with a sit-on plastic tractor. Which had then mutated into him being a trapeze artist, hanging upside-down over the tigers' cage, while his family looked on, clapping. He had soared like a bird over cliff-tops, unable to land and glided over the surface of the sea, just skimming the tops of waves as they peaked, but unable to sink into the water – or pull himself out. He had gone to the end of a long and shining tunnel, pulled by some immeasurable, magnetic force, dragging him against his will, faster and faster all the time. And when he had got to the end, expecting to see someone there, there had been no-one. So he had had to make his own way back, pulling all the time against the drag, the compelling field that tried to stop his change of direction. And then the puissance had unleashed, freeing him and he had gone into free-fall, spiralling down into an abyss with no end, spinning like a sycamore seed, but never managing to reach the ground. He had seen his birth-mother ahead of him, on a long woodland path, brambles catching on his clothes, preventing him from catching her, being able to see her face, to finally see what she looked like, know the woman who had given him away. And he had heard his family, calling him, from somewhere he did not know; voices a singsong of muddled words, sentences that made no sense.

It had not been altogether unpleasant – more interesting.

He summoned all his residual strength to actually open his eyes.

And now, he was here, in this unknown room, surrounded by curtains, enormous pins spliced into his bones, a strange assortment of strings emanating from his body and attached to weights, dangling alarmingly over a Heath Robinson contraption of pulleys from the end of the bed to which he seemed to be shackled.

And there was an alarming amount of pain.

What the fuck was going on?

One leg, two… one arm, two… thank God for that. The rest of it didn't look so hot.

And there was a tiny girl, sitting playing with a doll; a doll he knew well. Relief and love washed through his body and his spirits began to soar.

It was his youngest daughter.

He was back.

"Hello, poppet. How are you?" *It was definitely his own voice, not a dream.* "Where are we? Where is Mummy?"

"She's talking to the nuss."

"What happened to Daddy?"

"You got squashed. It was a bad man what dunnit."

"What bad man?"

"The bad one."

"And what did he do?" *Had he been mugged? Attacked at work? Set upon in some alley on the way home?*

"He pushed you over. It's bad to do that. He should've had a smack. My Mummy wants to tell him off."

"Where is Mummy?"

"I told you. She's talking to the nuss. 'Bout your poo hole. You need a zpeshal pill in it."

He winced.

"How long have I been here, my sweetie – where's everyone else?"

"They're at school. You've bin here forEVER!"

His little child didn't appear to be in the least bit surprised that his eyes were open and that he was talking to her, after all this time. It had never crossed her mind that the scenario could be any different.

"You ditn't buy me a birfday present."

"Daddy's sorry." He let out a small chuckle and immediately stifled it. The pain was excruciating. "What month is it, sweetie?"

"It's Fursday. I muzn't touch your weights," she added, as if it was the most normal thing in the world. "Because they're holding your legs on."

There were footsteps drawing near.

The nurse appeared through the curtains, whipping them back, armed with a vast suppository that looked more suitable to the gaping orifice of an elephant's behind.

"MRS WALLACE!" she shouted. "SOMEONE'S AWAKE!"

Doll's wife rushed into the cubicle and grasped his head in a tidal wave of kisses.

"You stupid, bloody, bad, bad, bad, stupid man!" she said, exploding with relief. "You've had us all worried sick!"

Chapter 49

Sadie had been peeling potatoes, in the kitchen, for the evening's supper, with Mabel.

As she opened the stinking mouth of the bin with her elbow, hands full of coiled and muddy scrapings, she saw an envelope.

It was clearly marked with a name.

In a hand that she knew only too well.

The world went black; she was spinning, thoughts darting through her brain, her synapses firing at a million miles an hour.

She thought she was going to have a stroke.

There was a strange buzzing in her ears and her sight had blurred and she couldn't catch her breath. And she reeled around, bending over the sink, releasing jets of vomit until there was nothing left but bile.

She needed a chair.

What was she going to do?

She sat, trying to clear her mind, to focus, to unscramble her thoughts.

She didn't want this.

She didn't want it.

"MABEL!"

Mabel tottered in, walking sideways and lunging from one piece of furniture to another, like a crab – a puzzled look on her face.

"Mabel! The letter!"

"What do you mean?"

"I don't understand. Why's this here? The letter…" She held it out, unopened, towards Mabel, who sat heavily in another chair.

"But I put that in the bin, dear. It's been in the hall in my pile of junk for days. I thought it was delivered to the wrong address. Who's Robyn?"

"I… Oh God, Mabel. I need you to read it for me. Would you?"

"Well open it then, dear."

"I can't. I can't!"

"Well, I can't, dear! It's time for my pills. I'm an hour late already and getting shakier by the second. I'm stiffer than a lead pipe! You open it and then give it here, if you can't read it."

Sadie's hands were shaking and fumbling and she began to open the envelope.

"Mabel… I can't do it…"

"Oh, Sadie. Stop being so melodramatic! It's a blooming envelope! What on God's clean earth is wrong with you?"

Sadie plucked the dirty, folded note from within the torn brown paper and opened it.

My dear Mum.

There was no mistake. There was no doubt. It was him.

And with that, Sadie let out an enormous, guttural wail, dropped the letter, disappeared into the bathroom and locked the door.

Chapter 50

My dear Mum.

Please, please read this letter. Don't just throw it away. Just give me a chance. Please read it.

There are things I need to tell you, that I need you to listen to.

I have tried so many times to contact you. But all my letters were returned. You wouldn't come to see me.

I didn't do it Mum. Whatever they said, however it looked.

I understand your reasons for not believing. I know what I was and what I put you through. But I loved that man from the bottom of my heart, as I loved you. As I love you still.

I found him there, Mum. He was still trying to talk. He told me to look after you, to tell you how much he loved you. I told you that a million times. But I couldn't look after you because no-one would listen. And now I've let him down.

And now I am out of prison and it's all worse, so much worse. They think I tried to kill the prison warden Mum, but I didn't. It was an accident – the bike hit and they took him away and left me there.

And I was too frightened to go back.

Please, please, Mum, you have to help me.

If there is anything left in your heart, any grain of love for your son, please help me.

I need to find Sam. I don't want anything for me. I just want to know how my daughter is. My darling Connie. And to know that Sam isn't harming her. Please, please just let me know how she is, that she's OK.

If you meet me just once, and let me know, I'll hand myself in straight away.

Just once Mum. Just for five minutes. Just so I can know. And see you one final time. And then I will stay out of your life forever.

I won't come near where you live, just so you know I mean what I say. It's up to you. I will be outside the caff at 143 Old Kent Road at 10 a.m., every day until you come.

Your loving son,
Jude.

Chapter 51

Cath took a deep breath. She was enraged.

"YOU'LL HAVE TO COME OUT NOW, SADIE! AND EXPLAIN WHAT THE FUCK IS GOING ON! YOU'RE WORRYING MABEL TO DEATH. SHE'S STIFF AS A FUCKING BOARD AND NEEDS HER PILLS. YOU'RE GOING TO FUCKING KILL HER AT THIS RATE! AND IF YOU DON'T UNLOCK IT NOW, I'M GOING TO BREAK DOWN THE SODDING DOOR."

After Sadie had vanished into the bathroom, the offending letter thrown to the floor, Mabel had been knocking on the bathroom door and calling Sadie endlessly, to no answer. And then, as time had gone on – and her medication had started to wear off even more, her symptoms had started to get way, way out of control.

She had dialled Cherry's number with a hand curled into a claw, rigid and hunched, her chin set like concrete.

She hadn't known what else to do.

She had been unable to get out the words in the phone call, unable to even explain that she needed help.

But, thank God, Cherry had known something serious was up.

And, thank God, Cherry had got a spare key.

Mabel had then slid to the floor slowly, no longer able to sustain her own body weight and too stiff to save herself. She had lain there, sprawled for what seemed like an absolute eternity, listening to the muffled sound of weeping from behind the locked door and hoping against all hope that Cherry would come. There was no way she could even make a sound, now. Her LinkLine pendulum was in the kitchen and she was unable to dial any more numbers. She had totally lost control of her body.

The offending letter was an inch away from her nose.

Cath and Fi had got half way into the club and, both feeling guilty, decided to chase Cherry up the road in their own cab.

They could hardly go and have a great night out while Cherry was left sorting out whatever was wrong with Mabel, could they? Not the best example of friendship. And there'd be other nights.

They had arrived at Mabel's to find her in a state of utter rigidity, lying sidelong on the floor outside the bathroom door, her body stuck in the shape of a chair: legs bent at right angles. Her eyes looked petrified, like a startled rabbit. She was staring, expressionless, at them; eyes wide with terror.

She was in trouble.

Cherry had been unable to haul her to her feet on her own, despite nearly giving herself a rupture by trying and had propped her against the wall until she could get help – but Mabel was unable to stay sitting, was continually sliding sideways, so Cherry had been forced to leave her on the floor, her head on a cushion hurriedly fetched from the sitting room while she searched.

She was ripping through the contents of the kitchen drawers, spilling papers and nick-nacks all over the floor.

"What's going on?"

Cherry had whirled round, crazed like a wild animal.

She threw the letter at Cath, who started to read it, blankly. "What…?"

"Forget that for now. Got to find Mabe some pills. That stupid cow Sadie has locked herself in the bathroom and won't come out. Mabe has seized completely. She's got lockjaw or something. I'm trying to find any old bottles of spare tablets she may have. For Christ's sake stop standing there and give me a hand. Look for anything with 'Mado-something or other written on it! Look in her handbag!"

Cath tipped the guts of Mabel's trusty, old bag onto the floor. "Mado. Mado. Mado. MADOPAR! Is this it?"

"YES! That's it!"

"It's empty."

"Oh God!" Cherry's voice was now tearful, desperate. Cath and Fiona looked at each other, not knowing what to do. "Bloody help me, before we have to ring an ambulance or something!" Cherry resumed her quest for medication in the dresser – the other drawers yielding no joy.

Cath and Fiona turned their attention to Sadie, behind the bathroom door.

Cath, temper rising, started shouting and screaming at her, kicking against the door, trying to break the lock.

"I AM GOING TO WRING YOUR BLOODY NECK, SADIE! IN FACT, I AM GOING TO RING THE POLICE!"

"For Christ's sake, Sadie!" Cherry had joined them now, her search for pills fruitless. "Mabel needs her fucking drugs! Stop being so selfish. She needs them now!"

Fiona was crouched down beside the old lady; stroking her face, mad Afro wilting with perspiration. "God, we've got to do something. Give me the bloody phone."

303

"SADIE, I FUCKING HATE YOU!"

"Cath, that's not helping. Get the phone."

"Sadie, please!" Cherry's lips were curled in anger and she tugged at her hair as she tried to keep her voice soft, unthreatening, coaxing, although she was shaking with fury.

Sadie, in her state, had not considered Mabel.

She had been lost in her own private hell, hands over her ears to block out the world, wallowing in despair and self-pity. The crescendo of voices and fraught activity from beyond the safety of the door finally penetrated through her terror. She was suddenly struck by what her actions might be causing for the old lady who had taken her in without question. Reality hit home and she returned to the present, with a resounding thump.

At the sound of the lock being pulled back, Cath forced her way into the room, fist raised, ready to punch.

Sadie was sitting on the floor in a heap.

Her eyes had swollen until she could barely open them and her hair was wild, where she had been clutching it. Lumps of it lay on the floor beside her and her scalp was bleeding.

Cath lowered her fist, shocked.

They had all seen her upset many times now. But not like this.

Nothing like this.

Cherry pushed past them both to the cabinet and got out Mabel's medication, returning to Mabel at a run, in order to stuff it into Mabel's mouth by prising it open with both hands, like a vet with a particularly stubborn dog; and then tipping in a few drops of water in an attempt to swill it down. The old lady was barely able to swallow.

"God, we're going to have to call an ambulance." Cherry was embracing Mabel, rocking her gently, and holding the water to her lips.

"You stupid, stupid… can you now see what you've done?" Cath spat, starting to dial with a shaking hand.

Mabel began to grunt. She had managed to get her pills down. She knew it was now only a matter of time before they would start to take effect.

She was looking at the phone in Cath's hand and making strange faces.

"What is it, Mabel?"

"MMMGGHHH."

"Do you want me to ring an ambulance?"

"Mmmgghh." Mabel's head moved a fraction in a 'no'.

"You sure?"

"MMWWGGHHH!" A definite 'no'. She began to look calmer and her eyes swivelled toward Sadie.

"What the fuck is going on, Sadie?" Cherry was feeling the blood drain back into her own face as waves of relief washed through her – it seemed that Mabel was a fraction better.

Sadie had resumed her snivelling and her face was clamped between her knees. Mabel's eyes were filling with a bit of her old sparkle and she was watching the proceedings with interest.

"Explain, Sadie. Just explain. Just try us… what on earth can be so very bad?" asked Fiona, softer. "Come on, Mabe is going to be fine. Aren't you, Mabel."

"No thanks to her!"

"Come on, Cath. Not helpful." Fiona shot her a glance.

Fiona knelt beside Sadie and put her arms around her.

"Come on, Sadie. Come and sit down. There's no point in staying in here."

Sadie rose, with her help and followed her, as she was led, by the hand into the dining room, like a naughty child getting over a strop.

There was silence.

Cath helped Cherry pick up Mabel. It took all of their combined strength – her body remained rigid and chair-shaped – to lift her from the floor and haul her into the sitting room and into her recliner. They snatched cushions from every available sofa and propped them all around her to keep her from slumping to the side and when she was quite comfortable, she twinkled at them, wryly.

And then all eyes turned to Sadie.

Cath was waving the letter. "Who is 'Robyn'?"

They were all looking at her, their faces searching for answers, not understanding the events.

"And who the hell is Jude?" she added.

There was a long silence. Sadie was wringing her hands. Finally, she spoke.

"I am Robyn."

"OK. Explain."

"I am Robyn," she repeated. "I *was* Robyn. Oh God." She searched for the right words. "Sadie was who I became. After it all happened." – head in hands, long breath out.

"After what happened?"

"Sorry, you lost me. Who's Sadie, then?"

"Me."

"So, you're both?"

"Yes."

"And this Jude bloke? The one that wrote the letter?"

"And Jude... Jude was my son."

"Was? Sounds like he's still very much here. And you said you didn't have any children. And that your husband had been killed in a car crash. No more lies, Sadie. No more lies."

"Come on Sadie, spill."

"Let the poor dear speak." – faltering, barely a whisper, but a small voice of calm in the mayhem. It was Mabel, who was slowly regaining control of her errant and faulty bodily parts.

"I'm Robyn. Jude was my son," she repeated, almost in disbelief.

She stood up and began to pace.

The words began to tumble out, faster, faster, faster – years of torment, years of lies and shame and loss and sadness spilling out in a melodic rush.

"My name is Robyn. My husband was a good, good man. A man of the cloth. The most beautiful man. He never hurt a fly. And we had so many plans. Plans to grow old together, to have an allotment, to go on a plane, to bring a child into the world. He was my best friend. And we had only just begun. We had years ahead. And I never said all I wanted to say to him and there's no going back. And I still love him and miss him and need him. And the pain is too much to bear. And it is with me all the time, everywhere I go, whatever I do, every day I wake up and I know yet again that I will never, ever see him again, hold him, laugh with him. Ever. He used to brush my hair."

She was crying again now, as she walked around and around the room, repeating the same pattern of steps on the carpet, oblivious that they were still there, listening. Oblivious to them all, talking to herself now, wounding herself with the words, the words she had only spoken in her mind, never spoken to a single soul, the thoughts and self-recriminations she could never bear to share with anybody. She unburdened herself of her secrets.

And it was all coming back, flooding, unstopped, into her brain; she was reliving the horror as if it was happening now, as if the past was the present and she was still in it, still in the moment, feeling the emotions that she had felt when she had found them, her beloved husband and son. Pandora's box had been opened.

And she explained about her grandchild, the only thing she had left – now lost to her. And her descent into drug addiction. And how she had left the hostel because she needed drugs more then she needed life. And about him: being taken in, abused, sold into prostitution, shot. And she talked and talked and talked and talked until she was spent.

And she told them all. Every last detail. And she felt years of 'Sadie' fading away.

And they sat, concussed with information, too shocked for words, all of them knowing that this was the truth.

And at the end, as she sank to her knees, they all rose, went over to her, held her, held her tightly, *held her like he had done, oh, so many, many times.*

And she felt the waves of relief sweep through her soul.
She was no longer alone. And she was Robyn once more. Stripped of pretence. Stripped of lies. Naked.
Naked and very, very frightened.

"Are you sure?" said Cath to her, eventually – softly, kindly.

"Sure?" Robyn was almost angry now. "Sure? *Sure?* Sure it all happened?" She was incredulous.

"No. Sure it was him? Your son. Who did it."

Robyn, *the vicar's widow, the murderer's mother* was looking at the floor now. Her face looked like it had collapsed in some way and her eyes were empty.

"No," she said, quietly. *"I'm not sure. I'm not sure at all. And that's why I hate myself."*

Chapter 52

She had to go and see him.
But there were two things she had to do first.

The next morning, Robyn went to the hospital.
It wasn't hard to find him.
It had been all over the news for weeks. And these days, the news left no detail untouched. His wife had been on the news too, appealing to the public.
So she knew his name. Knew whom to ask for.
And they wouldn't be looking out for an old woman.

She walked onto the ward with chocolates and flowers, limping in her usual way.

He watched her come in with a look of interest. *It was boring sitting there all day. The entrance of other people's visitors was always a nice diversion.*
He was a big mound of a chap, the sheets virtually sitting on top of his frame, rather than enveloping him.

He seemed rather surprised when she stopped at his bed.
"Can I talk to you?" she said, sitting down.
"Yes." – eyebrows raised, a faint curious smile.
He looked a nice man.

"I am Jude's mother," she said, "Robyn. Call the police if you need. It's about time. I've neglected my responsibilities for a very long time."

"There is no need," he said. "I've spoken to them. Your son is a good boy."

Robyn threw her arms around his thick, walrus-like neck and squeezed him.

"Thank you," she whispered and looked up into his kind face.

And suddenly she was sure. Finally. Sure. Sure that she had been wrong. Sure that she was even more terrible than she had ever previously imagined. Sure that she needed to make amends, gather the strength she needed to put this all right. Sure that she had let him down – let them both down. Sure that she would never let them down again.

She knew what she needed to do.

And she couldn't go and see him before she had done it.

She was filled with a life force she had never felt in all her days. She felt invincible. She was an unstoppable missile on a certain course. She was finally awake.

"Go and find your son," he said.

The nurse appeared with the lunch menu as Robyn got up to go.

"This is my friend Robyn," Doll said, to the nurse, as Robyn started to make her exit.

"And when you find him, make sure you tell him to come and see me!"

But Robyn was already halfway down the ward.

Chapter 53

NEWSFLASH

THERE HAVE BEEN SEVERAL SUSPECTED SIGHTINGS OF JUDE CRISTIAN IN THE SOUTH EAST LONDON AREA. POLICE HAVE BEEN GIVEN A NUMBER OF LEADS AND ARE FOLLOWING UP ENQUIRIES. IF YOU SEE THIS MAN, RING IMMEDIATELY ON THIS HOTLINE: 0207 777 777. THERE IS A REWARD FOR ANY INFORMATION LEADING TO THIS MAN'S ARREST. ALL CALLS WILL BE TAKEN IN THE STRICTEST OF CONFIDENCE.

Chapter 54

It had been years since she had been here.

Nothing had changed.

Even the net curtains were the same grey as before.

She knocked, hesitantly. But there was no answer.

Robyn crossed the road, looking up for any sign of life.

Upstairs, a curtain twitched, a watching face jumped away from her glance.

She crossed back to the grubby door and knocked again.

Still nothing. And then she heard the muted tone of faraway steps, getting closer. Robyn's heart leapt with anticipation.

The footsteps stopped on the other side of the door of the communal entrance and a thin, reedy voice asked, "Is it you?"

"I don't know. I don't know whom you are expecting. It's Robyn. Can you open the door, please?"

The door opened, just a crack and the completely unfamiliar face of a middle-aged woman peered around it.

"It is you, isn't it? You used to knock. Years ago. For the little girl."

"Yes."

"You'd better come in. Is she all right?"

"That's what I've come to find out."

The door opened wide and Robyn went in.

"Where is she?"

"I don't know. What are you? Her Gran?"

"Yes."

"Did you know?"

"Know what?"

"Come upstairs."

Robyn followed the woman, who hauled herself up the stairs – hands squeaking on the banisters – to the flat above. They went into a neat, but sparse kitchen, with a red, Formica sixties' table and matching, vinyl-cushioned seats. The wallpaper had never been changed, but everything was spotless, smelled of the choking fragrance of plug-in air freshener and was the result of daily elbow grease. It was rather beautiful – a testament to a different era.

A cup of milky, sugarless tea arrived, in a beautiful bone china cup, which wobbled with a tinkling tone on its saucer.

"She left. The little girl downstairs. After Social Services were called. They came a load of times. I don't know where she lives now."

"Social Services?"

"You know, because of the beatings and that. We did call the police a few times ourselves and all that. But we had to be careful. In case her mum knew it was us who'd told on 'er. She was a scary so-and-so. Nasty piece of work. Would've come upstairs and given me hell again. We learnt to avoid her. Did drugs, I think. Something, anyway. Not right in the head, that one. Didn't you know? We always thought you might come and take the little girl away. We saw you come a few times. Not that we were prying or anything."

Robyn was aghast with horror.

"Beatings?" she whispered.

"Oh yes. All the time. Poor little girl. She was a little darlin', too. We did all we could. But no-one came."

"Oh, my God."

And suddenly Robyn was overcome with the enormity of how she had let them down.

So engrossed in her misery, she had let them *all* down. Connie. Jude. *And him. Her poor, sweet husband.*

He had married a better woman than that.

She had failed. More than she had ever known.

And Jude. Her poor Jude. She had turned her back on her own flesh and blood, wasted years, deserted him in his hour of need, just as the bible described; a traitor, her belief not strong enough. She was the Judas, not him – not her son. And so many lives had been ruined.

The woman read quite clearly the shock of the hard, brutal facts on Robyn's face and her crisp and judgemental demeanour softened.

"I know what school she goes to though. If that's any help?"

Chapter 55

"Get in!"

Oh fuck. It was all over. They'd caught up with him.
They hadn't even thought he was worth a Panda.

Jude had been waiting in his habitual morning spot, outside
the cafe. He couldn't go in. The proprietor would not allow it.
He had drained the last drops of lukewarm, milky coffee, bought
with begged-for coins and his heart had sunk, as it did every day.
When she didn't come. He couldn't sit there any longer: the cold
had reached his bones. He had to move.

He had checked left and right, before moving towards the
kerb to cross.

The huge, gleaming, unmarked, black car with blacked-out
windows had pulled up a few doors away, several minutes ago.
Jude had instinctively noted it. A large man in a smart suit had
got out and leant against it, smoking, looking at an A-Z. Jude
had relaxed.

Now it was right on top of him, blocking his way.
Adrenalin rushed through Jude's veins. As the door jerked open,
Jude's heart rate instantaneously trebled, after an initial lurch
that travelled from his chest to somewhere deep within his
bowels.

Maybe there was still chance to run.

But he felt mysteriously paralysed.

His legs were leaden.

The game was up.

"GET IN!" – the authoritative voice of the man he had seen.

Plain clothes. Shit.

Jude did as he was told, with his arms raised above his head, anticipating the request to do so.

He was also anticipating far worse.

You heard about it all the time, inside; countless tales. Any old excuse to lay into a lag.

He found himself physically crossing his fingers, hoping that superstition might help. His top lip was beaded with perspiration.

"AND GET DOWN!"

What had happened to 'Let me read you your rights.'?

His mind a jumble from the last request – and too bewildered to do what the man said – instead of 'getting down', he looked round, flinching in anticipation of a potential blow.

And then he saw her.

In the back.

Just as she was when he'd seen her in the park.

His mother.

She looked old. Frail. Nervous.

"Mum." He hardly dared say her name.

"You heard the man, Jude; for God's sake get down!"

Jude did as he was told.

A blanket was thrown over his head.

Chapter 56

"Get down!"

There was the slam of a door. Hushed voices were just audible: a buzz above the sound of birds singing sweetly, nearby children squabbling, a football being kicked against a garage door. The crisp crunch of feet, on gravel.

"GET DOWN, I SAID! They'll see!"

Cath, Cherry and Mabel were at Mabel's window, jostling for position.

Mabel's butler had pulled into the drive and was in the process of walking around to Robyn's door, politely, to let her out.

The footsteps changed in tone from one set, to three. There was the 'blip-blip' of central locking and the brisk crunching moved towards the front door.

All Mabel's curtains had been drawn. As the sound of gravel was replaced by shoes on Edwardian tiles and the scrape of leather on a doormat, they all resumed their agreed positions in the drawing room, feigning innocent reading and knitting and watching of TV. Even though Cath couldn't knit, Mabel couldn't see the television and Cherry was reading a map of Slovenia. Upside down.

They heard the sound of the key turned in the lock, coats being hung on the stand.

"Meet my son," said Robyn.

He had not been what they expected from the pictures on the *News At Ten*.

"Hi," he said, flushing. "I'm so sorry to put you all out. And I know I stink," he added, looking straight at Cath whose hand was clamped over her face. She averted her gaze, instantly and blushed. And went back to her non-knitting.

Fiona had been back at the flat she shared with Cherry, her mobile phone stuck to her hand, like glue. She had been instructed to call the police if she hadn't heard from Cherry within the hour.

She'd never met a murderer before.

Not to her knowledge, anyway. Might have shagged one, inadvertently – it wasn't as if they'd have announced it. And come to think of it, that Nigel bloke was always decidedly dubious; eyes of a madman, teeny-tiny, podgy legs that didn't touch the floor when he used to sit on the side of her bed, screeching his insanely repulsive requests, in his high-pitched, loser voice. Obviously bullied at school and out to wreak his revenge on womankind for his lifetime of rejection. But only able to get one near him, if he paid.

She shuddered.

As soon as she had received the OK, she had smashed Cherry's piggy bank and removed its contents to scrape together the cab fare, to avoid wasting any more time.

Cherry would understand.

She wondered why on earth Cherry had a selection of buttons in there and wondered if the cabbie would accept them as legal tender.

Jude reappeared from a long bath, with Robyn, who was smiling and holding his hand.

He had shaved.

He was rather gorgeous, in a slightly effeminate way. A bit skinny. Great smile! Gorgeous eyes. Big chin. Shame he was a bit of a 'ginga'. Although the freckles were a nice addition.

He held her hand too, with a vice like grip, like a child, nervous, still, unthreatening and unsure of himself.

"Is it OK if I sit down?" he said. "I'm pretty tired."

He sat and faced them all.

"Mum has just told me what you've done for her," he said. "Thank you."

Simple. Sweet. Grateful.

"And now I just want to know what happens next. I'll go without a fuss. Like I said in my letter. But someone needs to find Connie for me. What do you all want me to do?"

"Turn the TV on," said Cath, ever practical. "Let's see if you're on!"

They scoured all of Mabel's many channels, but there was nothing, not even a mention.

"Looks like we're OK, for now." Cherry could barely mask the disappointment in her voice.

Suddenly, they were all in it together.

"Don't you look like your Mum," she added.

Chapter 57

Life had to go on.

Yes, there was sudden and overwhelming excitement.

They all felt that they were part of a Douglas Coupland novel.

But there were livings to be earned, hospital appointments to attend, documentaries to be filmed, university courses to continue.

Pubes to be coiffed.

Life had to go on.

The last two weeks, they had all spent together – out of working hours – hatching ridiculous, impossible, implausible, unattainable plans.

None of them made any sense.

They were all at a loss.

Jude had remained humble throughout, indebted to these women; inspired, but not full of hope, his prayers not quite answered.

He was doomed.

He just knew it.

His only way out was to prove that he was innocent of his father's murder.

But how?

He was now living full time at Mabel's.

The woman was a one-man-band-aid.

The friendship between Cherry and Cath was as strong and resolute as it had been, way back, at the beginning, before adult life began.

And the friendship between Jude and his mother was as strong and resolute as it should have been, way back, before life ended.

One night, as Mabel had been tucked away, resplendent in incontinence pads, hairnet, support tights and leg-bag – attached to the rail at the side of the bed that prevented her from inadvertently rolling out and escaping its confines, in the dead of night – and Robyn was snoring like a steam train in a faraway room, Cherry (the only one still up) went and knocked tentatively at Jude's door.

"Who is it?"

"Cherry."

"I thought you'd gone home." There were sounds of him making himself decent and shuffling to the door.

"What's up?"

"Nothing, really."

The door opened. And she went in.

He sat back on the bed, back against the wall and knees drawn up against his chest, like a little boy, waiting patiently for her to speak. But nothing was forthcoming. After an embarrassed silence, not knowing what else to say, he asked,

"How are you?"

"OK."

"Jolly good."

He waited for a bit more. After what seemed an eternity, Cherry finally spoke.

"What has your Mum told you? About me and her."

"That she met you. And you've all helped her. I didn't ask too much. She's a very private lady. And we've got so much to catch up on. There's never the moment."

"Oh."

'Oh.' Suddenly this sounded ominous.

"OK, Cherry. What gives?"

"I don't know that you realise what she's been through."

"Oh, Christ." There was a sharp intake of breath. "I'm not going to like this, am I?"

"No. Not much."

For the next hour, Cherry described her own life with Joe, Spencer. David. Satan. How she'd met Robyn – Sadie as she'd called herself then. And, in full, about what Jude's mother had become, after she had left the hostel with nowhere to go and been taken in by Joe. *Him*, the vile, atrocity of a man who had been supplying Robyn with drugs while she was still there, in the hostel; preying on her, a defenceless and heartbroken, old woman. And then slowly and steadily, piece by piece, destroying the few remnants of her spirit that had remained.

After she had explained, they were quiet, for a long, long time.

"Why did you tell me?" His head was in his hands. He looked as if he was going to cry. "Perhaps Mum didn't want me to know. Until she was ready to tell me. Oh, fuck."

He was struggling to get his head around it all. *It was all so, so much worse than he'd ever even imagined. And it was all because of him.*

Jude's brain was imploding.

He rose to his feet and started to pad, in circles, on the carpet; retracing the same steps on the pattern again and again, just as his mother had done, so many times. The visions that he tried so hard to banish in order to stay sane came to the fore of his brain, quashing all other thought. His head hurt. The lump in his throat had grown and grown until he could barely breathe, barely swallow. He thought of his loving, gentle father, torturing himself with memories. And of his dignified mother, whose strong morals and kindness had been the backbone of the family, however impossible Jude had made it for her. *How proud his father had always been of his beloved wife, 'his love'.*

"Oh no, no, no, no, no, no, no…" He was turned now against the wall, elbows and forehead on the floral wallpaper, hands linked behind his head, rocking. The tears he had been restraining could no longer be held back and he sobbed like a small child.

Cherry turned towards him, in the darkness, alarmed; reached out and put her arms around him. She held him until his shoulder-shaking subsided, tightly, tightly – not knowing what else to do.

"Sorry," she said. "I'm so sorry."

"She mustn't know you told me." Jude's sobbing had finally abated. He turned and looked at Cherry; noticed her own anguish. "But I'm glad you did."

He enveloped her in his arms, pulling her face onto his chest, encircling it gently with the crook of his elbow, ruffling her hair. And there they stood.

It was too late for her to go home.

Chapter 58

Robyn fought her way up the gravel drive, with bags of shopping cutting into her hands, so that her fingers were clawed and set into position. She rummaged for keys with her hands still fixed, painfully – fingers purple – and let herself in.

The house was quiet.

She went from room to room, tiptoeing so as not to wake Mabel. She eventually found Mabe asleep, in a deck chair in the garden: mouth open, legs akimbo, swatting at a persistent bluebottle with an automatic hand.

She unpacked the bulging bags, dropping the eggs on the floor and smashing all but one. And then turned to reach for the cloth and knocked the teapot off the side, smashing that too.

The cacophony set off a series of snorts from the garden, as Mabel regained consciousness and sat bolt upright in her chair, her hat over her eyes, thinking it was dark.

"Oh flippedy fuckadeedoodaa!" Mabel had tried to get up, but her leg-bag was still firmly attached to the side of her deck chair and was now pulling at her groin, impeding her progress. Robyn rushed out to help her disentangle.

"Where's Jude?" she asked.

"Oh, him," said Mabel, dismissively. "We had a lovely lunchtime putting the world to rights. And then he made me some marvellous grub and hauled me out here. To sleep off the

325

old vino. He's rather gorgeous, I do think. If I was ten years younger… "

"So, is he inside?"

"No. He said he needed a bit of fresh air. I think he was secretly scared that, left to our own devices, he might just fall for me. So he went for a little walk."

"Oh dear. Oh, no. When?"

"About two."

"It's now six."

Robyn started to pace the room, picking her fingers until they were red raw.

By nine, she was at her wits' end. By eleven, she was apoplectic with angst. She had flicked through every TV channel, scouring the news.

There was nothing.

Chapter 59

Jude got in a little after midnight.

He'd had some thinking to do.

Darkness was his only time of safety. Apart from that, he was a total prisoner in the house. Freedom was little better than it had been confined in prison.

As he unlocked the front door, the downstairs of the house lit up, like a Christmas-light-bonanza at a shopping precinct. He stayed still; alarmed, stuck, unmoving while his eyes and brain adjusted.

"Where have you been?" Robyn's voice: a loud, harsh, angry whisper.

They were both suddenly transported back to Jude's past misdemeanours, the crimes of his youth and Robyn's desperate attempts to keep him under control.

"I was worried sick. You have no idea what it feels like to be worried sick about your ch…"

"Oh, you can stop right there, Mum. I've been to see Connie," he said. "So, yes. I do know what it's like, thank you."

"You did what? Are you completely insane?"

"Don't worry. I didn't charge into the school at pick-up time wearing a banner. No-one will have seen me. She certainly didn't! I just had to see her. Nothing else. I just needed to see that she was… all right."

"And? "

"I saw her. She's not all right. She's so frail and small, Mum – so lonely looking. She came out alone, no friends, no-one to pick her up, nothing. She's too little to be walking home on her own…"

"I know. Her old neighbour said."

"What do I do? Someone's got to do something."

"I don't know, Jude. But you can't do that again. Ever. It's too risky. We need to think of a different way. It needs to be me who does something. But it's likely to be a long and drawn out process. The whole Social Services shebang. And it most certainly cannot be you! They're highly unlikely to take your word for anything."

Neither of them was ready for sleep.

Robyn bustled quietly in the kitchen, boiling the kettle, while Jude perched on the work-surface, toes curled over the edge of the huge butcher's block for balance, watching her. He was reminded of years ago, in a different kitchen, as she would do the same thing – having shouted at him for returning late, for 'keeping her up, through worry'. Her actions were interspersed with tutting and head shaking.

"What is it, Mum? Is it way past my bedtime?"

"What?" She turned to face him, sharply.

He smiled at her. "I've missed you."

She turned back to her tea-making, without comment.

"I've missed you, Mum."

Robyn stopped what she was doing; stayed still – her back to him.

"Mum?"

She resumed the adding of milk. Jude cleared his throat, suddenly uncomfortable.

"I've missed you too," she said, finally, in a voice he didn't recognise. "Jude, I…"

"Come here." Jude slid down and went to his mother, caught her face between his hands, bent and kissed her forehead. Just as she had done to him as a child, so many times.

"Love you, Mum."

It was all she needed to hear.

Chapter 60

Jude had arrived at the school way before the children were kicked out to go back to their various lives: some full of privilege, some full of divorce, some full of nothing, some full of pain. Human nature in every way, shape and form manifested itself at those gates, in miniature.

He hadn't been sure what to look for. The hair should be unmistakeable; a wild, blond Afro of fuzz – hairs contorted in multiples as the follicles twisted them at the point of exit. Teeth like grains of rice, poking though a gummy grin. Fat arms.

But that was then.

She would be big, now.

The hair darker?

The plump arms stretched into the slender arms of youth.

The little teeth replaced by adult versions.

Her teeth.

When he thought of her, he remembered tiny, neat, gappy rows of whiter-than-white pegs, beautiful and perfect.

Oh God, how he missed those toddler teeth.

He would never see them again.

Jude looked into every face, trying to gauge who was of what age. He hadn't been around children for so long that he was unable to tell.

Oh God!

He was never going to recognise her.
She may be having a day off, sick.
Detention – if she was anything like him.
Anything.

The tidal wave of children spewing forth from the doors – laughing, sulking, pulling hair, tripping friends, waving at parents, swearing, talking about who they were going to shag – was now slowing to a trickle.

Jude had squinted in the sunlight. He was not blessed with the best vision in the world. But any closer and he would draw attention.

As it was, he looked odd – still sitting in the bus shelter opposite, although four or five buses had passed without him embarking on one.

And then, without warning, there she was, right beside him.
Tiny. Fragile. Miserable. Huge, pale blue eyes, set in a sea of freckles, skin pale as alabaster. His father's eyes. His father's freckles. Absolutely unmistakeable. How could he have doubted that he would know her? The ginger gene shone through, loud and clear. A tone of skin, like he had... ready to burn to a frazzle should it be touched by sunlight for a matter of seconds. But she was blond, like her mother.

She was so translucent, she was almost green. No make-up on her. She looked way too young to be at the school. Her overriding expression of fear made her seem younger than anyone else there.

He had turned away from her then – away from her beautiful, familiar eyes, terrified that she'd recognise him, that the game would be up, she'd make some sign, some tiny act of recognition and then his cover would be blown; his whole world would come tumbling down once more.

She got on the bus.

Shit, he had no fare.

Shit. Shit. Shit. This couldn't be it? A glimpse, a few seconds to see her – and then gone again?

He started to walk to the front end of the bus, in desperation.

Where was it going?

And then, thirty seconds later, Jude became aware of a sudden commotion – the raising of voices – as she was kicked off again.

"Not you again! No fare, no ride. You know the score. Get off the bus. I've told you before!"

She had stumbled off. Close to tears. It was about to rain.

He was almost glad.

Jude would have done anything, anything in the world at that moment, to sweep her into his arms and press his face into the softness and musky smell of her sweet, sweet neck; to tell her he'd look after her, he'd make it OK. She was limping.

No. Not now. Hold back. Don't fuck it all up now. Think of something. Something else. Touch her. Don't touch her. Keep your distance. Don't be seen. Follow.

Follow. To where she lives. Just to check she's OK. That's all you wanted, after all. But now, it seems that's not enough, not nearly enough.

And you've been walking for fucking miles now. And she's limping. And it's raining and raining and nobody is here to pick her up and nobody cares. Does she have to do this day after day after day? Where is her fucking mother? And she's stopped. At a maisonette you don't know in a filthy, godforsaken block crammed with hell, where nobody gives a fuck, on the corner of

Depression Street and South Shit Road. And she's going in, letting herself in with the key hanging like a noose around her neck and she's all alone: no-one and nothing there for her. And your heart bleeds and your soul aches; aches for a little girl who's yours – was yours; is now lost to you – and you don't know if there's any hope of getting her back and you love her so much and you're holding out your arms now like a ridiculous fool and you hurt deep in your chest and you would do anything for that small person, that part of you... and she's gone.

Gone.

And all you want to do is see her again and again and again. Like it was supposed to be. Like it was right from the start. Just you and her. Before it was all ruined.

Before you were left with nothing.

And no-one.

****

The next eight hours had been lost to Jude. Alone with his thoughts, he cried and cried and cried.

Chapter 61

NEWSFLASH

THERE HAS BEEN NEW INFORMATION REGARDING JUDE CRISTIAN, THE ESCAPEE OF BLANTYRE HOUSE OPEN PRISON. THERE HAVE BEEN SEVERAL SIGHTINGS OF A MAN MATCHING HIS DESCRIPTION IN THE VICINITY OF SE14. THE POLICE ARE STEPPING UP THEIR SEARCH IN RESPONSE TO THESE SIGHTINGS. THE PUBLIC ARE REQUESTED TO REPORT ANYTHING SUSPICIOUS, WITHOUT HESITATION. ALL CALLS ARE STRICTLY CONFIDENTIAL AND THERE IS A REWARD FOR ANY INFORMATION LEADING TO HIS ARREST.

THE PUBLIC ARE URGED NOT TO APPROACH THIS MAN, WHO MAY BE ARMED AND IS HIGHLY DANGEROUS.

Chapter 62

Jude lay in the bath.

The water was now tepid.

If he could hold his breath for a minute under water, it would all be all right; there'd be a way, a way to save his daughter, clear his name, prove his innocence, be free.

51... 52... 53... he was fighting to hold his breath now: lungs straining deep within his chest, mouth clenched to not allow anything in or out, eyes open, seeing the blur of the ceiling above, its cracked plaster moving as the water vibrated, writhing now as he fought his desperate urge to breathe, his overwhelming need of oxygen, bargaining with himself every second. 56... 57... and he was up, head breaking through the water's surface, gasping for air.

A minute. Sixty seconds. One bloody minute. That's all he needed.

It would be a sign, like walking clockwise, not stepping on the cracks, passing that lamppost before the next car, putting the same number of teaspoons in each side of the cutlery drawer.

He tried again.

49, 50, 51, 52, 53... and up again, fighting to regain his breath.

Jesus, this time it was worse, his time was less; he had to try again, had to do it, had to prove himself, for his daughter's sake, for his mother's sake. He had to do it.

Again and again he tried, his mind now fixated with the idea, more and more frantic with each consecutive failure; upset now – angry, hating himself, failing, failing, failing, failing.

It was no good.
It was all over.
And suddenly, the wet running down his face from his eyes to his lips tasted of salt.

Chapter 63

Fiona was with Cherry when the news was repeated.

They were surrounded by packing boxes and had been reduced to two plates, two mugs, Fiona's television and a teaspoon. The rest was all packed in crate upon crate, stacked in precariously teetering towers, ready for their moving date in a week. Fiona liked to be organised and had been so excited about the new place that she'd got everything sorted way too soon. But she didn't care. It was a fresh start – a new life, a future. And she couldn't wait.

They had been taking a well-earned breather when Jude's familiar face had popped onto the TV screen.

"Oh my God, Fiona. They're going to get him. What do we do?"

"I don't know! What can we do? Like, nothing? It's going to happen, Cherry darlin'."

"But he can't be at Mabel's when it happens. She'll die of bloody fright! She's an old lady – too old for all this. It's not fair."

"And the option is?"

"Here?"

"Are you out of your tiny, white mind?"

"Yes. Maybe. So what's new? It's my fault in the first place. If it wasn't for me dating that utter arsewipe-drug-dealer-con-merchant boyfriend of mine, we'd have never met Robyn, she'd have never ended up living with Mabel – and all this would have been someone else's bloody problem."

"Jeeeeeesus, Cherry. It's not your fault though, is it, girl? Just the bad hand of fate – a lousy hand of cards. But us taking him in implicates all of us when he's caught. My past is bad enough already. I just can't have anything to do with this, Cherry, honey. My luck is running out... I've just started uni again. They're not going to love it if we get caught hiding a crim. And then we'll be all over the paper too. And all my shit is going to come tumbling down like a house of cards. Former punters'll sell their stories for cash. I'll get a record. And then my law degree is well and truly fucked." She sucked her teeth. "You know I love ya, Cherry – and I'd do anything for ya. But this is too much."

Cherry was looking dejected, despairing, and desolate.

"So how do we help Mabel?"

"Cherry! NO!"

"Just for a week. Just here. 'Til we move. No longer. For Mabel's sake. Pleeease. Just so he's out of her house and out of her hair – and we can talk to Robyn and tell her to sort something else out for her and Jude. She's not stupid; she knows this is putting Mabel at risk. And after all Mabel's done for her, the least Robyn can do is to move out of there with her son – and find somewhere of her own to hide him. He's her problem, not Mabel's."

"And not yours, Cherry darlin'. Is he?" Fiona looked into her friend's eyes. Cherry hadn't replied. "Oh Jesus, Cherry! Will you never learn? What's wrong with you? Set up a dogs' home! Work for a charity! Build an orphanage! Stop wasting that mushy heart on men with problems. OK. He comes here. But it is NOTHING to do with me. I repeat, NOTHING. If you get caught, you're on yer own. AND HE'S NOT COMING TO MY NEW PLACE. Understand? My new place is for a new start. With nothing illegal. And we've only got a week to go."

Jude moved in that night.

Chapter 64

"Cherry, I can't."

"What do you mean, 'I can't'?"

"I've got a date."

There was a pause. "A date. What do you mean?"

"The thing you do when you're terminally single. Like us."

"But I need you there."

"Cherry, stop. I'm not going to fall for that one. You're not going to make me feel guilty."

"Oh, OK. Don't worry then. Enjoy your date." The narkiness was not even remotely disguised.

"Stop sounding disapproving! You're not my mother."

It was amazing how their roles seemed to have reversed.

Cath was becoming quite stroppy in her old age.

And no longer at Cherry's beck and call. Cherry was not enjoying this lack of compliance.

Things would have to change.

"Who's your date, anyway? You haven't mentioned it before."

"Jane."

There was no response down the line: just a sharp intake of breath, just audible above the crackle and hiss of the ageing, Bakelite handset. Cath wished she could see Cherry's face.

"Cherry…" she added, reproachfully. "His name is John."

There was a gush of exhaled air indicating relief. Followed by a worried, "Not that John?"

"Of course! No – of course NOT, you bloomin' idiot. Another one. But do you know the best thing? My old John is working for this John. It's his boss. Revenge is mine. Hope he's there with his wife. It's a works do… and I can't wait to see him squirm. New John knows about old John, so no embarrassment for me. But old John doesn't know about new John! It's the battle of the Johns! Do you like my toilet humour?" There was copious giggling down the line.

"But it'll be our last day here."

"Well, thank God for that. Your place is a shit-hole. You need to throw a match in, as you leave. It's the only way to clean it up. Oh, and by the way, how's things going with thingy?" Cath said, in a whisper.

"Not good," – whispering back. "And why are we whispering? Anyway, you must have seen the news. 'Thingy' has got to hand himself in. There's no other option. Fi won't entertain him being in the new flat. And he can't go back to Mabel's. We're all screwed."

"Speak for yourself. I'm not harbouring a fugitive. You're screwed all on your own. See ya!"

The line clicked dead.

Chapter 65

"Turn up the volume!"

Cherry's hands dug into the top of her client's hair, like an eagle swooping down onto its unsuspecting prey. She had stepped forward onto the woman's foot. She remained, crushing the woman's toes, with a vice-like grip on her scalp as she carried on screeching, in utter, utter horror.

"I SAID TURN THE BLOODY THING UP! IT'S AN EMERGENCY! EVERYONE SHUT UP! SHUUUTT UUUPP! I NEED TO HEAR!"

She was frozen, looking at the silent picture on the plasma screen on the salon wall. There was no sound coming from the screen at all. The only sound in the salon was the gentle clicking of scissors, the nondescript warbling of this week's repeating CD played on loop and the usual, inane drivel from stylists and customers – about holidays and hairdos and the best place for Botox.

The plasma screen covered half the far wall of the salon. Usually MTV showed incessant videos of all the latest hits, but today it was on daytime TV for a change. Cherry had been working away on a head of hair, half an eye on Jeremy Kyle's brows – furrowed in aggression, as he squared up to a flea-bitten odd-bod, with multiple piercings interspersed with custard-topped boils; who was sitting next to a gigantic girl whose wobbling, walrus thighs were straining against the Lycra of some white, cellulite-enhancing leggings. A camel hoof at crotch level nestled alluringly under a fleshy pudding of a stomach. Her crying eyes were almost lost within the blueberry doughnut of her face. Cherry was riveted. Especially when the pudding rose, livid, to her pig's trotter feet (having to prise herself out of the chair to do so) and wobbled towards 'pierced man' like a vibrating jelly: fists raised at the end of arms more like over-stuffed piping bags, ready to strike. Cherry, merrily brandishing an enormous brush, nearly had her client's ear off.

The change of image on the screen was highly unexpected.

It was the news. *Obviously something important to have warranted ruining this moment of TV genius.*

What's more, it was footage of a house.

A very familiar house.

It was Mabel's house.

And there were police. There were police swarming all over Mabel's front garden.

Nobody turned up the sound. They all just looked at Cherry, agog. Her mouth was gaping open and a huge vein was pulsating in each temple. She looked like someone possessed.

It took only a few seconds, still in silence, for Cherry to assimilate the information.

"SHITFUCKBOLLOCKS! SORRY! SEE YOU LATER! SORRRREEEEEYYY!" she shouted, removing her heel from her client's foot; leaving the brush still suspended in her hair and dropping the dryer on the floor, where it smashed. She ran through the salon, grabbed her bag from the coat stand and made a run for it – faster than a greyhound at the opening of the traps.

Her client, of course, complained.

Chapter 66

Cherry arrived at Mabel's as the police were still hammering on the door and shouting with loudhailers. Unfamiliar people were swarming all over the enormous front garden, wrecking Mabel's carefully manicured beds. The azaleas were being brutalised underfoot.

There was a woman with an enormous, fuzzy microphone, tossing back her carefully brushed-and-stiff-with-lacquer, auburn barnet and straightening her tweed suit and far-too-low-cut, silky blouse, preparing to say her piece, live on air.

And there were several camera crews.

One from the BBC.

Cherry ran up the drive, legs wobbling like a newborn foal on its first encounter with the joys of walking, screeching, "MAAABBEELLL!" at the top of her voice, before being rugby tackled to the ground by an overenthusiastic copper. "GET THE FUCK OFF ME!" she shouted. "I'LL DO YOU FOR ASSAULT!"

She scrabbled furiously to her feet.

"I was trying to keep you out of danger!" he said, stumbling backwards to get away from her.

Quite a crowd had gathered.

"WHAT THE HELL IS GOING ON HERE?" shrieked Cherry. "THERE ARE TWO OLD LADIES IN THERE! ONE

WITH PARKINSON'S AND ONE WITH BAD HIPS AND A HEART CONDITION!" – She was always one for a bit of poetic license – "THEY MUST BE TERRIFIED! THIS IS ELDER ABUSE!"

The Chief of Police – dragged in from his holiday and not best pleased with his lot in life before Cherry had even made an appearance – came over to see what the commotion was about. He was carrying a loudhailer. "Move, young lady, before I have you arrested for breach of…"

"OH, YOU CAN SHUT UP AS WELL! GIVE THAT THING HERE!" she hollered, wrenching it out of his hands. "Just let me talk to them through that trumpet thing," she added. "Then they'll come out. They certainly won't with you lot scaring the fucking hell out of them! But what the hell are they supposed to have done?"

"They are suspected of harbouring a fugitive."

"OH. DON'T. MAKE. ME. LAUGH!" She felt bold as brass now, happy in the knowledge that Jude was safely ensconced on the other side of London. "And what sick fucker told you that?"

The Chief of Police murmured something about language and nodded in the direction of the neighbour, who flushed a shade of vermillion and started to slope off.

"YOU? YOU?" yelled Cherry with renewed vigour. "YOU WHO STARES AT MY TITS WITH BINOCULARS WHEN I'M IN THE GARDEN IN MY BIKINI? DO YOU THINK I HAVEN'T SEEN YOU? IN FACT, WE'VE ALL SEEN YOU, HAVEN'T WE?" she added, nodding to all the other neighbours – who then started nodding in agreement although they'd never seen any such thing.

"PICKING ON TWO DEFENCELESS, OLD LADIES! YOU'RE A DISGRACE TO HUMANITY!"

The neighbour had started to move off rapidly now, horrified by how events had turned. He had somehow ended up as the focus of the entire camera crew. He could see his impending promotion at work hanging by a thread.

"THAT'S RIGHT, RUN AWAY!"

The rest of the neighbours were now all turned to look at him, murmuring to each other. The old adage about sticking mud was ringing in his ears.

Cherry raised the loud hailer once more. She was on a roll now. There was no stopping her.

"MABEL. YOU CAN COME OUT NOW. THE OLD PERVERT'S GONE. THERE'S NO NEED TO BE FRIGHTENED ANY MORE. THESE NICE OFFICERS ARE HERE TO PROTECT YOU FROM HIM. BUT YOU NEED TO EXPLAIN TO THE NICE POLICEMAN EXACTLY WHAT YOU'VE BEEN UP TO WITH YOUR YOUNG MEN!" She stopped shouting and turned to the cameras. "And then the nice policemen can go inside and have a look around. COME ON MABEL! OPEN UP!"

The door opened.

And Mabel emerged.

In a marabou boa and silk opera jacket. And a peach coloured, gigantic wig that would have housed an entire family of blackbirds and put Amy Winehouse to shame. And lipstick applied at least a foot over her lip-line and sinking into the surrounding lines, making her mouth resemble the anus of a cow. And long, white gloves. One of which was over a brow, like Gloria Swanson.

But there was no skirt. Or, in fact, any form of underwear.

But there was a Wellington boot.

In fact, her muff was fully on display. As was her leg-bag. Which happened to be at bursting point, its contents the colour of stewed tea. It was swaying, gently, in rhythm with her shakes.

And when Cherry peered closely, it appeared that Mabel had powdered her pubic hair.

"You can take me now, officer," said Mabel, feigning a theatrical swoon. "I won't put up a fight. Be gentle with me. It's been a long day. Is this about the humiliating matter of the small ham I inadvertently stole from Harrods' Food Hall, last year? I'm very sorry to have put you out. I did mean to return it. It was lodged in the wheel of my wheelchair as I left – and I simply didn't realise it was there until my chauffeur informed me of my faux pas. You merely had to ask. And aren't you young!" She held out her wrists to be cuffed, turned her eyes heavenwards and let out an enormous sigh. "I feel so very, very ashamed."

Three hours later, after a perfunctory house search by the police, which revealed nothing – and long after the cameras and news crews had vanished – Cherry was sitting at Mabel's, recovering.

"Well done, dear. Wasn't that fun! I am waiting for the first offers of television interviews to come in. I do enjoy that Jonathan Ross. I find him a most cheeky, young, whippersnapper and I think, judging by his wife's appearance, that I may be just up his street. And you, Cherry! You should have gone to RADA. You are obviously wasted in the salon."

"And what about you? Have you no shame? What's with the grand display of your 'great downstairs'? And on national television. You're unbelievable!"

"I was more worried about the possibility of Jude having left an item of clothing here, in error. But all was well. I don't suppose he had any spare garments to leave. I did have to double my medication to manage it though, dear. Heaven help me tomorrow morning. But so satisfying. It was quite like old times."

"How like old times, you nutcase?"

"I did tell you I was in films, dear. Don't you ever believe anything I say?"

Chapter 67

Cherry called in sick the next day.

They quite understood.

They'd all been watching television.

Her excuse about the conjunctivitis hadn't quite made the grade, however. She needn't really have bothered.

She did not dare go home on the day it all happened, in case by some freak act of God, she was followed.

She needn't have worried.

No-one was interested. The police had written the whole thing off as a nutter's hoax and had gone back to trying to apprehend fifteen-year-old, acne-ridden hoodies, with infinitely microscopic specs of hash in their pockets.

She did hope, with a small scrap of remorse, that the neighbour did not decide to hang himself as a consequence of her outrageous allegations.

And then half hoped that he would, so she would never have to clap eyes on him again.

She eventually headed a convoluted route back home the next morning, still feeling twitchy and changing buses three times when there was no need.

As she hiked up the stairs, Fiona burst out of her bedroom, jumping up and down. All her Rasta mates were in there as well. They were all gathered round the television in the midst of packing-crate-bedlam, sitting all over the floor. Cherry wondered, briefly, how a house-leaving party was going to be at all possible in the mayhem of their possessions.

The air was so thick with spliff that she could barely see to put one foot in front of the other.

"We've all been watching you! We're watching the re-runs!"

They were all clapping.

Cherry almost felt embarrassed, but was way too chuffed with her newly-found celebrity to let that bother her. She did a little bow and said, "I'd like to thank my fans…"

And then, out of the gloom, appeared Jude.

She had forgotten about him in the excitement. *He had caught her being a complete prat.* Embarrassment finally conquered infamy.

He looked quite gorgeous.

"You were magnificent," he said. "But how's Mum?"

Chapter 68

Jude wrote the two letters on Mickey Mouse children's notepaper that he had found in a pile of rubbish to be chucked and sealed them carefully in two envelopes.

He left them on top of the packing boxes.

And then decided that wasn't conspicuous enough, so put them on the floor in the entrance of Cherry's room. *She'd have to be blind not to see them.*

****

Cherry had gone out to New Look. The new Agyness Deyn-style collection had just come in and she was using this day of illegal sick leave to go and kit herself out for the evening's party.

She had decided that she deserved a reward.

And, as it was the last day that Jude would see her for the foreseeable future before he went into hiding once more, she thought that she could use it as a last-ditch effort for him to notice how special she was.

Worth a blooming try, anyway. Even if he was a convicted felon.

Jude was still all over the news, whenever he turned on the television.

There was no other option. He knew what he had to do.

His only option was to find Sam.

And to get her to confess.

And to see his lovely little girl. Just one hug. Just to tell her how much he loved her, to give her something positive to remember him by.

At least he was off the hook – if the news was to be believed – as far as attempting to murder Doll was concerned. In the last few hours, reports had gone from him being a 'dangerous menace to society', to somebody who only needed to 'step forward and hand himself in to be not penalised for his escape'.

Time for it to all end, peacefully.

The big man, Doll was behind the change in Jude's criminal status. In the past few weeks, he had been forcibly sheltered from the news, to 'aid his recovery'. He had been sneaking a peek at his neighbour's portable TV when war had broken out in Mabel's garden. Horrified about what he was witnessing on the news – and realising from the vision of armed police exactly how much trouble Jude was in – he had appeared on television himself, from the hospital – and made his own appeal to say that Jude was not responsible for his injuries.

After weeks of floundering in a state of concussion-induced amnesia, his memory had returned, bit by bit – and although he could not quite remember the exact moment the bike had hit, he pretended that he did. *He'd always had a soft spot for Jude.*

And of course, as soon as he'd done this, several witnesses had emerged, all saying the same thing. *That Jude had stayed with Doll until the ambulance had arrived and even then tried everything in his power to go with him to the hospital.*

351

Even the ambulance driver had stepped forward and said the same. Although why on earth they'd all waited this long to cough up the information was beyond him.

Bloody sheep, the lot of 'em.

Doll couldn't really be sure that this change in the portrayal of events was the truth. But he preferred to believe that it was.

It was the driver of the motorbike who was now in deep lumber.

*Served him right...*his tale of what happened had mutated and exaggerated every time he'd said anything. And he'd got himself a large, double-page spread about how he'd been 'face to face with a killer and survived'. What was now on his face was not so much an egg, but an entire omelette cooked up in a pan the size of a UFO.

Tosser.

But Jude, of course, in spite of it all, had still not handed himself in.

That afternoon, knowing he would not return, Jude left the flat.

Chapter 69

It was Cherry on the phone.

"He's gone, Robyn!"

"What? What do you mean? Gone where?"

"To see Connie."

"WHAT? How do you know?"

"There's a letter…"

"And what else does it say? What is he going to do?"

"I don't know, Robyn. It doesn't say!"

"WELL WHAT *DOES* IT SAY?"

"Just that he's going to do the right thing. And to see Connie."

"And why didn't you stop him?" shrieked Robyn, "You were supposed to be looking after him!"

Cherry looked down at the new garments on her bed. Robyn was right.

If she'd been with him, she could have maybe stopped him, changed his mind. She should have been there.

She felt absolutely bloody terrible.

"I'm sorry I wasn't there," she said, a waver in her voice. "I popped out. Not for long. He wasn't here when I got back. It wasn't for long! He left me the note. And one for you."

"POPPED OUT? YOU POPPED OUT! AND WHAT DO YOU MEAN 'ONE FOR ME'? WELL, WHAT THE HELL

DOES *THAT* SAY? WHAT DOES IT SAY?" Robyn was shouting angrily at her now, desperation mounting in her voice.

"I don't know! I haven't opened it!"

"WELL, BLOODY OPEN IT THEN, YOU STUPID GIRL! READ IT!"

Cherry's hands were shaking as she tore open the ridiculous, cartoon envelope – whose comedy design was doing nothing to lighten the mood of the moment. She felt a complete and utter fool.

"It says he is just going to see Connie... to wait till 3.45pm... and to then call the police and tell them to go to Sam's house. Where he will be. And it gives Sam's address."

"Then that's what we must do."

Robyn suddenly felt clearer. Alert. Her head was buzzing. *He was going to see Connie. Probably get her from school and take her home. And then what?*

Her brain spun with possibilities, memories, doubt, guilt, fear. She wanted to be there, at Sam's house, to support him. But she knew that was not what he was asking of her.

And she was not strong enough. Not strong enough to see him being led away again. Her beloved son.

She remembered his words when she had asked, "What was prison like?"

"As you hear. As you'd expect. Except much worse. Always waiting for the sharpened blade of smuggled cutlery to hit you between the shoulder blades in the yard if you get on the wrong side of the wrong person, or to feel a large groin at your backside in the showers, or a hand on your shoulder as they find a wrap on you that someone's pushed in your pocket while you weren't looking. They put murderers among murderers."

And she felt very, very afraid.

Robyn dropped to her knees and started to pray; praying for her son, hoping against all hope that He would be listening, despite all her years refusing to acknowledge Him – despite her sin, despite all that she had become. She begged for forgiveness. And she begged for mercy: begged Him, forehead pressed on the floor, eyes screwed shut, pleading. Pleading, to a greater power, that her beloved son would not be taken away before he had the chance to tell his little girl how much he loved her.

The letter said that was all he really wanted to be able to do.

Robyn knew what she had to do. There was no doubt.
She would not let him down again.

Chapter 70

Connie had had a relatively uneventful day at school.

Nobody had picked on her today.
She wondered if it was because, when she was changing for gymn first thing in the morning, they had all seen it?

She had been making feeble excuses of feeling sick, for the last week, to get out of PE. She had, in truth, been too sore to take part. But the teacher had lost his patience with her catalogue of different excuses and made her get changed.

In front of them all.

And they had all changed already; so they all stood and gawped, taking the piss, as she had started to undress.

And then they had all seen it.
And they'd all stopped being horrid to her.
And they'd all been quite nice to her, for the rest of the day.

The bruise was, in fact, the clear and unmistakeable imprint of a multitude of boot marks, laid down on the same place over her back.

Connie couldn't see all of it – only the outer edge, which was marbled purple and black and green. But from the back, it spread over her spine and covered all of her left side.

The children had all stepped back, nudging each other and beginning to ask questions – until the teacher, who was struggling to hold back his own tears at the sight of it, ordered them outside. He felt physically sick.

The previous school had warned him about this – they'd all been warned to keep a close eye. But nobody said it was this bad. And somehow, over the last while, they'd all forgotten about her.

****

Sam had given Connie a really good hiding over the previous weekend.

Connie'd really done it this time, the little whore. She deserved every second of her punishment. She was like a millstone round her neck, with her whining and whingeing and needy ways.

Sam had been getting ready to go on a date with one of her numerous boyfriends.

There had been a break-in at their maisonette a week before… nothing taken, just a brick through the window, the writing of SLAG in huge letters on the sitting room wall, in aerosol.

The police hadn't been involved.

Sam would have had too much clearing up to do.

And anyway, she wasn't a slag.

Just because that old cow's husband preferred her to his wife, it was hardly her fault, was it? The stupid bitch should have looked after herself a bit better, instead of letting herself go. Looked after him a bit better. Then he wouldn't have had to look for it elsewhere.

It had happened at night, the break-in.

Connie had been frightened out of her wits.

Sam typically wasn't in. And Connie had hidden at the sound of breaking glass, the men's voices coming through the door, while they stamped about. Listened, shaking with terror, as they climbed the dark stairs, with their cruel voices; then the sound of harsh footsteps in her room – right by her bed, the place where she was alone and frightened even before people had smashed through the door. She lay, terrified out of her wits, under her bed, alone in the dark, not daring to breathe, hearing the laughter downstairs as they went back down to smash things. *I want my Mummy. Please Mummy, come home. Please, somebody hear. Please, somebody, don't let the bad men find me.*

So when, a week later, Sam had slung on her jacket and begun to apply lipstick – thick like jam on her mean mouth – Connie, for the first time ever, had asked her mum to stay in.

"Please, Mummy. Pleeeease." She was crying. She was only eleven.

"Selfish, little bitch. Do you think anyone else would want you? Do you? You think I should stay in? Do you? SELFISH."– A kick to the ribs sent Connie crashing to the floor in pain.

"LITTLE." – a kick to the ribs. Connie lay with her back to Sam, waiting for the blows, eyes shut, praying for it to be over soon.

"SON." – a kick to the ribs.

"OF." – a kick to the ribs.

"A" – a kick to the ribs.

"BITCH!"

Connie had crawled on her hands and knees to her usual place – her place on the stairs, where her mind could wander to the things that made it all better – as Sam had left the house.

****

As Connie left school that day, having promised her teacher that the bruising was from when she fell down the stairs because she was being silly, she did notice the man at the bus stop who had been there the other day.

She thought she knew his face.

Perhaps he was on the telly.

She began the long walk home.

Chapter 71

Jude stayed back, his heart beating wildly, fighting for his own breath.

There she was! His daughter. His precious, beautiful little scrap. His life force.

He had to be careful.

She had started the long walk home, light reflecting from her fuzz of unruly hair, like the halo of an angel; knee socks scruffily at half-mast, shirt un-tucked, her books in an old carrier bag. He waited 'til she was virtually out of sight to begin his own journey after her. She had already looked back two or three times at him, as he watched her.

He didn't want to fuck it up now.

But he could hang back this time. He knew how to get there.

****

When Connie reached her battered, front door, she knew immediately, instinctively, that something was wrong.

It was not shut.

It was ajar, just a little bit. And it wasn't time for Mummy to be home yet – it was that little patch of time she had each day when she felt safe, was on her own with her own thoughts; when no-one would shout at her. But today, someone was in there? Was it Mummy?

She couldn't go in. Already the tendrils of fear were winding around her heart, strangling her breath in her throat. She stood in the doorway, one tentative hand against the gnarled wood, peering into the gloom, ready to run.

"Mummy," she called, worried. "Mummy. Are you there?"

There was no answer.

She stepped back a few steps and very quietly threw her bag of sweets in the Sulo bin, making sure the lid did not bang shut and give the game away. She knew she wasn't allowed them: that their presence would cause her hours of abuse at her mother's hands. She knew she shouldn't have stopped at the shop to get them.

But the man in the sweetie shop did let her have some, on Fridays. Even though she hadn't got any money. He used to live above them in the last flat, before they moved.

And he would wait outside the door of the shop, on Fridays, when she came out of school. And ask her how she was. He was very nice.

She called out again, her voice reedy and vibrating with fear, "Is anyone there?" There was nothing. She was too scared to go in.

She went back down the concrete path and up the adjacent path, knocked on the neighbours' door. But there was no answer.

And then to the other neighbours. Still no answer.

Her heart was now beating wildly. She had no-one to go to. She had no-one to ring. She was scared that someone was in her home, waiting. She just could not go in.

She didn't know what to do.

"Connie?" She reeled round at the voice behind her, face set in alarm; half happy to hear a human voice, but terrified it was one of the bad men from the other day, come back to hurt her, to use her to make her mum pay.

It was the man from the bus stop with the kind face. The one she sort of knew. He was standing in the gate.

"Connie," he said again.

"Yes."

"Are you all right?"

"No. I think someone's in my house." She started to cry.

"Let's go and have a look shall we?" He held out his hand. It was a very big hand. She was petrified.

"I don't want to go in. In case the bad men have come back. Are you one of the bad men? Are you going to hurt me? Please don't, I haven't done anything."

Jude, hearing these words, felt sick. *What the hell sort of life was his beautiful daughter being forced to live?*

He hesitated outside the gate, still – not wanting to get any closer, not wanting her to be any more frightened.

"No, Connie. I'm not a bad man. I'm not going to hurt you. I want to help you. I'll go and have a look inside. And then if it's all OK, I'll come and tell you. And if you want, I'll stand in the doorway until you feel safe in there. Would you like me to do that?"

"Thank you."

It was 3.30pm.

Jude gagged as he went in.

Bluebottles buzzed around carrier bags, strewn on the floor, that were overflowing with refuse. The place stank. The carpet was sticky with filth.

When his eyes adjusted to the dimness of the room – curtains closed and hanging from gaffer tape at the windows – an anger started to rise from deep within his guts.

The word SLAG was written in three-feet-high aerosol on the peeling wall. The kitchen sink overflowed with old takeaway containers. The sofa's guts were hanging onto the gore-spattered floor. The wrecked table was scattered with the unhidden remnants of heroin abuse. There was nothing else there. And there was no sign of anyone.

He went upstairs.

Two bedrooms presented themselves at the top of the filthy stairs, wallpaper brown with grime. A bathroom with a smashed toilet seat and crumbling tiles sneered at him in the dim light.

He went into the bedrooms.

One was quite decent. Double bed, fairy lights, lilac walls.

The other had a single bed and nothing else.

Not even a light.

The single sheet was brown with dirt. There was no pillow. There were no other bedclothes. A child's book of bedtime stories lay neatly by it, the only piece of evidence that the place had even had a sniff of a child within its walls.

There was old blood, smeared all up one wall.

He began to shake.

He poked his head back outside the front door, squinting into the rush of outside light that hit his eyes before his pupils had quite had time to constrict. Connie was still there, waiting patiently.

"It's OK, Connie. There's no-one there."

"Are you sure?" She was hesitant, not sure to trust him. His hand was outstretched towards her again. *He looked nice. He seemed gentle, like the teachers at school, like the man from the sweetie shop.*

She took it.

When they were inside, as her eyes adjusted to the gloom and she had had a cursory glance around, she said suddenly with a voice tinged with near hysteria, "Oh no! The television's gone.

What am I going to do? Oh no! Oh no! Mummy's going to be cross!"

She looked at him. "Mummy's going to be cross. What am I going to do?" she said, again, her voice sounding tearful and fraught with worry. "Do you know my Mummy?" she added, her face searching his.

"Oh Connie."

The man started to cry. He just stood there in front of her, looking at her, big tears rising from his eyeballs and starting to stream all over his cheeks.

She didn't know why.

Or what to do.

The grief of so many years was rising, rising to the surface. He tried to keep it down. He tried to keep on top of it.

Not now, not now, he had to stay in control!

But his sweet, little angel did not even know who he was.

No memories of their times; the loving, her seeking him out at five o'clock in the morning, eggy bread, soldiers, sneaked fish and chips on their own, bath-time blowing bubbles, going eeurgh if she caught sight of his willy if he was naked, on the slide at the park, running to him when Mummy was cross, squeezing Grandpa's cheeks, each one making a different sound, covering Daddy's face with her sweet, wet, baby's kisses. All those memories of their times.

All gone.

"Connie," he said, his voice hoarse with the sorrow he was trying to force back down into his stomach, the deep place within, where he had kept it for so long, locked in its box, where he wouldn't have to face it. "Don't you remember me?"

She was confused now.

She did remember.
But she didn't know what.
She knew he was a nice man.
But she didn't know why.

"Connie. It's Daddy."

"Daddy." The word fell from her lips, with ease unfamiliar to her. Her face changed expression rapidly, her lips twitching like someone in a dream. She started to remember things she had not thought of for years – a rush of images and information, a maelstrom of events: things pushed out in order to survive. *Good things.*

And bad things.

She held out her arms to him, remembering something nice, and warm, in a garden somewhere, somewhere sunny, and laughing with lots of people there being nice to each other, someone giving her legs 'horse-bites' between pinched fingers. *She remembered feeling happy.*

He took her in his arms, squeezing her tighter, tighter, kissing her hair, smelling her, kissing her tears, wiping her nose on his shirt, looking deep into her face, drinking it all in, every detail, her freckles, her beautiful, pale, haunted eyes, squeezing her again and again, wanting this to last forever, for this to never end, feeling the joy in his heart expand and expand until he was bursting with it, until it was too much for him to bear and he hugged her even tighter, almost wanting to envelop her, blend with her.

And then she winced. The wince of pain.

And he looked down to his arm, hugging so tightly and saw her shirt pulled up. And under it, a multicoloured, lurid sea of battered flesh.

He pulled away, as if he had been electrocuted.

"Connie," he whispered – knowing, already, the answer. "How…?"

She hid his face in his chest and began to cry.

She let the tears wash the tension out of her body, muscles wound tightly as a coiled spring. She let emotion rise up within her chest, spilling out of her unrestrained, no longer stifled and held back and locked in. She relaxed into his arms and sank into his chest and let herself wail, the sound coming from her spewing into the air, tainting it with grief; sorrow exploding from her with the relief of finally having someone to tell, someone she knew, someone she knew would listen to her, protect her. She remembered.

"When is she back?" he said. His voice was hard, controlled. And deathly, deathly quiet.

"I don't know," she whispered. "I'm frightened."

It was 3.50pm.

Chapter 72

It was 3.50pm.

Robyn had rung the police. On the dot of 3.45 p.m. As he had asked.

She had been put through to the special phone line.

Along with many others.

Finally when she got through, after being placed on hold what seemed a million times, she spoke to a faceless voice who simply would not understand what Robyn was trying to convey. It wasn't the woman's fault... they were having hundreds of calls a day about sightings. Mostly fiction.

"You don't understand," Robyn said. "I'm his mother. I know where he is."

"You're the third person claiming to be his mother this week," the woman said. "Hang on a minute, I'll get somebody."

There was silence.

There was no time for this. No time to hang around. She couldn't fail her son again.

Robyn turned to Cherry, who had arrived, red-faced and ashamed, an hour before – and sat clutching her hand.

"What do I do? They're not listening to me!"

Cherry was silent, trying to understand what was going on from Robyn's side of the conversation and the squeaky words she could snatch on the other end, as she leaned towards the phone, pressed with white knuckles to Robyn's ear.

"Hello. Hello?"

The phone line was clicking as she was transferred to another, faceless voice.

"Hello, how can I help?"

"Hello! I am the mother of Jude Cristian. You have to help me – it's an emergency. There's no time for all this being passed to and fro."

"Can I take your name and address, please?"

"Robyn Cristian. You don't need my address, you need to send someone to this one straight away; 43…"

"Sorry, I need your address and date of birth."

In desperation, Robyn hung up.

'999' she dialled.

Chapter 73

He scooped her up into his arms.

"She won't hurt you again," he said. "Daddy won't let her."

And then a voice came, from the doorway. A voice that made him feel sick to the core.

"You. YOU. GET OUT! CONNIE, COME HERE. NOW!"

The little girl squirmed free from her father in habitual acquiescence, took a step towards Sam and then stopped; bewildered, blinking, looked around at Jude, frightened.

"GET OUT OF MY HOUSE." Her face was older, harder, harsher; ravaged by time and her addiction and set into a cold, cold expression of hate.

Sam stepped towards him and grabbed Connie roughly by the arm, tearing her away from him, *his little girl, his beautiful little girl.*

Connie flinched the practised flinch of someone to whom it is second nature: cowering away from her mother, face screwed up, in anticipation of the blow.

And Jude lost it.

In Jude's eyes, he saw his father bleeding to death, as he pleaded for him to live. He saw the chisel, so deep in his father's heart. He saw the fear in his father's eyes as his life ebbed away and his spirit lifted from his mortal body. He saw his mother's face; heard her screams as she saw them both. Saw pictures of his mother doing things – things that made him feel sick, things that degraded her and went against everything she believed in because her life was ripped apart, destroyed – pictures he had made in his mind, from the stories he'd been told. And he saw his daughter's face as he was led away and his daughter's face as she was told she would never see him again – and his daughter's face now: full of fear, waiting for the blows. And he saw the bruises on her small body.

And he saw his father's face, blurred, transparent, right there in front of him, unmistakable; the face he missed so much.

And he saw Sam.

And he saw the devil.

And he saw red.

Blood red.

A voice that was not his rose from his chest to fill the room; and he walked towards Sam without thinking and without emotion, wanting to crush her, for her to be gone, to extinguish her evil like wet fingers putting out a flame. And there was a loud rush in his ears like a horrific choir, deafening him. And still he walked towards Sam as if he was removed from his own body.

And Sam ran into the kitchen and was there again before him, with a knife – *a knife that she would plunge into his chest, as she had done to his father.*

In front of his child, his beloved child.

"Connie run…" His voice again, but Connie did not move.

"CONNIE! RUN! DADDY SAYS RUN!!"

But still she remained, not moving: a little girl staring, watching, long-distant memories visibly crossing her pale face; all her years of horror enveloping her and tying her there like a pair of invisible handcuffs.

And Sam was there, right in front of his face, so close he could feel her breath on his mouth and her twisted features were malignant with poison. And his hands were sliced through like butter as he reached towards her to try to stop the blade from entering his stomach: he was bleeding, vivid red and he could see his own tendons, white sinews shining through his open palms and he looked surprised and then the knife flashed again, in his cheek and the pain burned his face. *And his daughter was still there and she was looking at it all. And his dead father's face was behind his child and she was two again and his father was smiling and saying something he couldn't understand and had his arms wrapped around the little girl, holding her, keeping her safe as he nodded; but where was his dog collar?* And Jude blinked, amazed and disbelieving, transported away from the present for a second as he wondered what his father was doing there and then realised he could not be; that this was an illusion. And then Jude snapped back into the present and his hands were around the neck of his little girl's mother, his nemesis, his ex-wife and he was squeezing hard, her flesh tensing and flexing like an eel beneath his fingers, slippery with blood.

Tighter, tighter, tighter he held the pulsating throat and he was only there in body: his mind was emotion-free, still, unyielding, concrete, watching dispassionately, removed from the scene of horror unfolding around him and inside him and because of him – and her eyes were staring and incredulous and she was making strange, sucking noises and turning blue-grey-dull and she looked afraid and then blank and there was water coming away from her all over his shoes as she still stabbed, with ever-weakening effort at his arms, anywhere, anywhere she could reach and her legs were going now: buckling and twitching and jerking – but his rage would not let him stop and his ruined hands were still strong and powerful around her throat and he stayed solid and cut himself off from the pain that burnt within them as he held, held, held. And he saw his father's face begin to gradually fade and then disappear and his daughter's face with her eyes panic-tight-shut.

And Sam's eyes were growing cloudy and her expression was fixed and her jerking legs began to relax, until there was nothing.

And he dropped her.
Sam lay on the floor.
She did not move.
It was all over.

******

When the police got there, Jude was sitting on the hard patch of concrete outside the house.

Connie was on his knee.

She did not cry.

As she hadn't cried the first time. The first time she had seen a death.

The death of her grandfather.

And she remembered.

She remembered it all.

And she had the words to say all the things that she had been unable to say the first time.

Because she was so small.

So small and so terribly, terribly frightened.

And her Daddy hadn't been there any more to help her.

Help her when Mummy got cross.

And Mummy had been all that was left.

So she had to be good.

And then she had made it all go away. By not thinking about it any more. And pretending it wasn't there. And

372

pretending to talk to Daddy and Grandma in her head, because she couldn't remember their faces. But she could remember Grandpa. She knew Grandpa's face as well as she knew her own, because Grandpa came at night, when she was all alone. Grandpa came all the time. And Grandpa talked to her and hugged her every day that things were horrible and told her one day it would all be all right. And it was the only thing that made her able to face the next day. Grandpa always made it all better.

And he was right.
Today, it was all going to be all right.
But where was Grandpa this time?
He was gone.

The nice policeman came over.
She knew policemen were nice.
Miss Appleton told her that at school.
They helped you.
You only had to tell them the truth.

"It wasn't Daddy's fault," she said. "My Mummy tells fibs. My Mummy hurt my Grandpa. I saw. And she was trying to kill Daddy."

And as Jude looked into her eyes and knew finally, for sure, that his daughter knew him, remembered him, knew what was in his heart, he didn't care what happened to him any more.

Chapter 74

The court took ten minutes only to reach the verdict.

Guilty.

Unanimous decision.

No question about it.

It was manslaughter, they said. On the grounds of diminished responsibility.

They felt sorry for him.

But there was no getting away from it.

And he'd seemed like such a changed boy.

You never could tell.

3 years.

No bail.

He was 6 months past his twenty-eighth birthday.

Chapter 75

It was his mother.

She looked regal.

She held her beautiful, aged head high.

"Hello," he said

"Hello, Jude."

"I'm sorry."

"You have nothing, absolutely nothing to feel sorry about," she said. "I love you more than life itself. And I am proud, Jude. More proud than I will ever have the words to describe. I can be proud of the man that my son has become. You are very, very like your father."

"My father wasn't a murderer."

"No, my love. But he would have done anything for his family. And that takes a strong, brave and fearless man. A man to be proud of. A man like you. I must go, now. I need to get Connie from school. I will see you tomorrow. With her. She's done you some drawings. And it looks like you have another visitor..." She left, smiling.

Cherry sat down in her place.

And kissed him full on the lips.

And suddenly, in spite of everything, life was finally looking up.

Chapter 76

Requiescat In Pace

Today is one of those first glimpses of summer that happens in April, when you've forgotten how happy it makes you for absolutely no reason, but suddenly it's there and warm and lovely and you're smiling and up for anything and all's well with the world.

Well, all's hell with the world actually. But you can forget that – because despite it all, it is bearable once more. In fact, the rays of light are breaking through the cloud, your brain is clear and you are prepared for the future. You can forget that – despite the silver scar of the words **'igneus in abyssus'** *cut into your arm. Your scar means* **'burning in hell'***. But you are no longer sure to whom you referred – or what it meant – when you cut these words into your flesh, all those years ago.*

You feel reborn.

An elegant and proud woman took her granddaughter to a beautiful graveyard. Her grey hair was in a perfect, French pleat. She was carefully made up, carefully scented, her body smoothed with an expensive and particular cream. She was clothed in a beautiful, new dress, bought especially for the occasion. It had taken her a great deal of time to pick out the dress; a dress she knew he would have loved, been proud of her in, as he always was.

After a little time searching, limping between the headstones with purpose, she found the grave she was looking for.

She hadn't been for years.

Not since her first visit, when she knew that he was not there, that the ground contained his body, but not his soul. He had not been there. And she had needed him to be.

But this time, she could feel him, all around her, in the grass and the sunlight and the stone and the flowers and the breeze that caressed her cheeks, as he once did.

She knelt beside the grave, untended for years and placed there a bible, a small bunch of lilies and a child's drawing.

"Hello, you. Hello, my love," she said, to the small, white marble headstone inscribed simply with the word 'LOVE'. "I'm sorry it's been so long. I miss you. I really, really miss you. You were everything to me. Where were you?"

"Grandpa's not in there, silly!" said the little girl, smiling.

The woman, a vicar's widow, looked up, surprised, at the beautiful, blond, curly-headed girl standing next to her, gathered her thoughts and chuckled.

"Of course, you're right; silly Grandma! He's not in there, is he? He's in heaven."

"No, he's not, Grandma. Not yet. He hasn't gone, yet. There's Grandpa. He's over there!"

And Connie turned away from her and skipped towards him, waving.

"Hello, you," whispered Robyn.

And then, the heavens opened.